shelter me

Also by Alex McAulay

Oblivion Road
Bad Girls
Lost Summer

Available from MTV Books

shelter me

alex mcaulay

Pocket Books   MTV Books

New York   London   Toronto   Sydney

Pocket Books
A Division of Simon & Schuster, Inc.
1230 Avenue of the Americas
New York, NY 10020

First MTV Books/Pocket Books trade paperback edition January 2009

POCKET and colophon are registered trademarks of Simon & Schuster, Inc.

For information about special discounts for bulk purchases,
please contact Simon & Schuster Special Sales at
1-800-456-6798 or business@simonandschuster.com

Designed by Carla Jayne Little

Manufactured in the United States of America

10 9 8 7 6 5 4 3 2 1

Library of Congress Cataloging-in-Publication Data

McAulay, Alex.
  Shelter me / Alex McAulay.
    p.   cm.
  Summary: Fifteen-year-old Maggie leaves London during the 1941 German
blitz to stay in Wales at what is thought to be a secluded boarding
school, but when it turns out not to be as safe as it was supposed to be, she
and three other girls flee and begin a harrowing journey back to London.
  [1. Coming of age—Fiction. 2. Survival—Fiction. 3. World War,
1939-1945—England—Fiction. 4. Great Britain—History—1936–1945—Fiction.]
I. Title.
  PZ7.M12873Sh 2009
  [Fic]—dc22   2008025690

ISBN-13: 978-1-4165-4583-5
ISBN-10:   1-4165-4583-2

For Lisa

Acknowledgments

This book would have been impossible without the support of my friend and superagent David Dunton, and my brilliant editor, Megan McKeever, who encouraged me every step of the way. Huge thanks also to Erica Feldon, Lauren McKenna, Louise Burke, and everyone at Pocket Books, as well as: Regina Starace, Jane Elias, Nikki Van De Car, Ryan Outlaw, Pamela Cooper, Bobby and Sarah McCain, Manish Kalvakota, Matt O'Keefe, Leah Stewart, my mom and dad, and my parents-in-law.

In addition, I'm grateful for the research assistance of my resident UCLA librarian and beautiful wife, Elizabeth McAulay. I'm also indebted to the reminiscences of my parents, both of whom lived through World War II as young children in England and Wales. Anyone wishing to read real-life accounts of survival and exile during the war might enjoy the following sources, which I found invaluable in writing this book: *The Longest Night* by Gavin Mortimer, *Parachutes and Petticoats* by Leigh Verrill-Rhys and Deirdre Beddoe, and *Fleet Street Blitzkrieg Diary* by Gordon Robbins.

shelter me

Descent into Hell, 1941

The day the bombs fell on Maggie Leigh and tore her life apart, she was out shopping for fabric with her aunt Joan. Maggie usually didn't spend too much time with her aunt, because the family considered her a bad influence.

"Joan is a lost cause," Maggie's mom had told her more than once. At first, Maggie wasn't sure what she meant by this cryptic statement, because her mother wouldn't elaborate. She'd just say with a resigned sigh, "Your aunt's morals have been compromised—I'll explain when you're older." But from overhearing hushed conversations between her mom and other relatives late at night, Maggie learned that her aunt had gotten involved in a secret relationship with a married Indian officer.

Maggie's aunt had left Britain five years ago to work at a civil service office in Bombay, an Indian city that according to Maggie's mom was "godless," and therefore suited Aunt Joan much better than London did. Maggie's mother was extremely conservative and religious, and had tried to raise Maggie the same way, although the indoctrination hadn't fully taken. Maggie imagined she took after her scandalous, travel-loving aunt much more than she did her strict mom. Her aunt always talked to her like she was full-grown, and not just fifteen. Maggie could ask Aunt Joan questions she'd never dare ask her own mother, and her aunt would usually give her pretty honest answers.

Aunt Joan's illicit romance with the Indian officer was seen as tawdry and immoral by some, but to Maggie, the whole thing sounded like a great adventure. She tried to picture the Indian man, his features coalescing in a vague way out of clichéd images from the Rudyard Kipling stories she'd been forced to read at school. She wondered if he had a beard like coiled black wool, and maybe a turban or a sash to go with it. India seemed like a world she couldn't start to understand, a mystical place where the rules of daily life were suspended. Maggie had never left the British Isles in her entire life and found it hard to imagine exotic places like India actually existed.

The fateful day that Maggie got caught in the blitz of German bombs, her aunt had picked her up from her house, and they'd taken a taxicab to the fabric district near Oxford Street. Maggie was excited, because since the outbreak of World War II nineteen months ago, her mom didn't let her go many places anymore, except for school and the local market. Maggie still remembered hearing the prime minister's shocking declaration of war as she huddled next to the wireless radio. "We shall be fighting against evil things," he had said. She hadn't realized his words would bring an end to many of the childhood freedoms she took for granted.

The war also marked the beginning of many other nasty new experiences, such as cowering during air raids and learning how to put on gas masks. War rationing also meant that luxuries like certain foods and items of clothing were in short supply. However, Maggie's mom had always been frugal before the war, so this element of wartime Britain was no great change. Maggie's dad had left the family three years earlier; he'd been a part-time coal trimmer, and a full-time alcoholic. No one had any idea where he was, and in his absence Maggie and her mother frequently had to scrimp and save out of necessity. But Aunt Joan was an oasis of relief from all that. She made good wages in India and wasn't afraid to spend her money whenever she returned to visit London.

In the back of the taxi on the way to the fabric store, Maggie noticed that her aunt's palms were decorated with strange red designs: tattooed lines and patterns in concentric circles. Her aunt saw her looking at the markings, and she held up one hand for Maggie to scrutinize. "It's not permanent. It's henna, see? Only lasts a few weeks."

"Henna?" Maggie asked, peering closer. The color of the ink nearly matched her aunt's hair.

"It's a decorative tattoo they do in India. Don't you think it's neat?"

Maggie couldn't decide. "Sort of," she said, because she didn't want to sound critical, although truthfully she wouldn't have wanted that mess all over her own hands. She glanced down at them unconsciously where they lay, small and white in her lap. To her, they still looked like a little girl's hands, with short, stubby fingers.

Her aunt laughed. "It's okay if you don't like the henna tattoos. I thought your mother was going to faint when she saw them. You'd think we were fifty years apart, not five. She's like a decrepit old biddy in that chair . . ." Aunt Joan was referring to the fact that Maggie's mom had been confined to a wheelchair for the past two years, due to premature arthritis in her joints.

"Mum doesn't take to new things very well," Maggie pointed out. "She's old-fashioned."

Her aunt smiled. "Your mum takes after our mother—your grandmother—in that way. I was always the black sheep of the bunch, always breaking the rules . . . always getting punished." She glanced down at her hennaed hands, flexing them. "I got these done by a lady on Dinsbury Lane. She didn't do a half-bad job for the price." She looked out the window and saw they were close to their destination. "Driver, stop here," she called out, and the cab came to an abrupt halt in front of a row of stores.

The driver didn't say anything, and Maggie thought he looked unhappy, slumped behind his well-worn steering wheel. Because of the curfews, and the blackouts at night—which meant that cars couldn't turn on their headlamps—most people used the underground trains to navigate London these days, so there wasn't much use for taxis. Many of the streetlamps and traffic signals had been taken down or permanently disabled.

Maggie slid out of the cab while her aunt paid, the soles of her black boots landing on the cobblestones as her eyes scanned the wide street. It was an upscale neighborhood, and Maggie instantly felt out of place. She saw two girls her own age at the other end of the road, both in fancy black dresses, with colored ribbons done up in their hair. She suddenly felt self-conscious about the way she was dressed, which was in a cheap gray skirt and a brown sweater-blouse, so she looked away from the girls. She caught one of their voices and could tell from the accent that they were posh, and probably lived somewhere in this rich neighborhood. Maggie and her mom lived in the lower-middle-class district of Hudsworth Green, which couldn't compare.

Maggie knew these girls would probably hate her if they realized where she was from, because class warfare remained intense, even during a real war. As the taxi slunk off down the street, Aunt Joan walked over and put her arm around Maggie's shoulders, distracting her. "Come this way, dear. I'll show you why the British empire can't hold a candle to India when it comes to cotton and silk."

When Maggie and her aunt entered the fabric store, which had an indecipherable name written in Sanskrit symbols, the shopgirl behind the counter greeted Aunt Joan warmly. Maggie noticed the air in here was thicker than outside, thicker even than a London pea-soup smog, and it held the sweet tang of oriental incense. The smell was strong enough that she could taste it, like cinnamon, oranges, and pepper tickling the back of her throat. She fought the urge to sneeze, afraid it might make her seem unsophisticated in a place like this.

As she looked around, she realized the store contained a blizzard of fabrics, all kinds of shapes and colors and textures. They were piled in bales against the walls, hanging from the ceiling, and wrapped around large wooden slats, like giant rolls of Christmas paper. Fabric was even draped over several lamps, muting their glow but casting warm, colorful patterns across the walls.

Maggie's aunt moved around the store, swiftly assessing the different fabrics based on their colors and textures. Maggie followed, unsure what her aunt's standards were but certain that she had some definitive ones. Her aunt picked out a swatch of fabric from a pile on a table and turned around. She held it up to Maggie's chest and said, "This blue silk matches your eyes. We could make a sari out of this. Turn you into a real maharaja's bride." Her aunt made a funny fish face, and Maggie couldn't help laughing, even though she was also flushing faintly with embarrassment. The idea of herself as a bride seemed a million years away.

"Auntie, please," Maggie said, looking around to see if anyone else in the store had heard. But there was no one else except the shopgirl, counting receipts. "I'd like to go to India one day, to see what it's like," Maggie said, trying to change the subject. "It sounds so different from here. It sounds fun."

"If you want to go there, you probably will. Desire can provide excellent motivation. Remind me to stop by the bookseller on the way home, and I'll buy you a real book about India. I can't imagine your mum buys you too many books, does she?"

"The only book she ever gave me was the Bible."

Her aunt laughed. "Why am I not surprised? Now come on, I want to talk to the stock girl. I need to ask if she—"

Her aunt suddenly broke off midsentence, her mouth still open.

"You okay?" Maggie asked.

"Listen, do you hear that sound?" Aunt Joan's voice had dropped several octaves into a husky whisper of fear. She reached out a hand and grabbed Maggie's arm. "Tell me I'm imagining things."

Maggie cocked her head to one side and followed her aunt's gaze through the front windows of the shop. It took her a moment to realize that faintly, in the distance, she could hear an unmistakable whine that had become all too familiar in the past several months.

"Oh no," Maggie whispered. It was the rising and falling sound of an air-raid siren, the kind that signified great danger. Usually when she heard this sound, she and her mother were already on their way into the Anderson bomb shelter at home. But here in this store, on this cobblestone street in an unfamiliar part of London, she and her aunt were trapped.

Then, under the noise of the sirens, Maggie heard the rolling thrum of an airplane engine. From the loud, harsh sound of it, it was a German plane, and it was getting closer. Maggie knew from the increasing pitch and intensity of the engines that they only had a few moments before the plane passed overhead, and there was a very good chance it would be distributing some bombs along the way. The sirens almost always gave much greater warning. This German plane must have sneaked in unnoticed, or turned in some unusual direction, Maggie thought.

"Where to go, where to go," her aunt was muttering in a

sudden panic. From the corner of her eye, Maggie saw the shopgirl crouching underneath one of the oak tables. She met the girl's eyes and saw her own fear reflected back in them. Maggie and her aunt crouched down too, between racks of orange cotton.

"Is there a shelter out back?" Aunt Joan yelled to the girl.

The girl mutely shook her head, too scared to speak.

"It's getting louder!" Maggie said, focusing on the drone of the engines. It was easy to tell the German planes from the British ones, because she'd had so much practice.

"If it drops any bombs, they won't hit us here," her aunt declared loudly, with forced cheer. "The plane will pass overhead. They always do. They go to the other parts of town, to the East End."

What Aunt Joan was saying was true—that the Germans usually bombed the poorest parts of London in a misguided attempt to cause an uprising of the poor against the rich—but this demented Nazi logic couldn't always be counted on. Occasionally, a German plane got lost, or went rogue, and then anything could happen.

It's not a good sign that this plane is out in the daytime, Maggie thought. Usually they only came out at night, in sneak attacks, like cowards. Either the Germans were getting bolder, or maybe this pilot was suicidal, because in the daylight over London he'd make an easy target for the RAF.

As Maggie listened to the plane, she thought she detected an additional noise, almost inaudible against the sound of the engines. It was a thin whistle, like a teakettle left too long on the stove. She knew in that moment her aunt had been wrong, and her worst gut fears had been right. It was the sound of a German bomb cutting its way through the air, from the belly of the aircraft down to British soil.

Maggie's aunt realized what was happening too, and she grabbed on to Maggie, trying to shield her with her own body. Maggie tucked her head under her aunt's chest, feeling her aunt's pounding heartbeat. The whistling grew louder and then cut out completely, only seconds from impact.

Maggie couldn't believe this was actually happening to her, although she'd known it was possible that one day it would. And now that the day had found her, she felt completely unprepared. Her teachers at school had drilled everyone on what to do if something like this occurred, but in the panic of the moment, all their best advice went straight out of her head.

As the instant before impact came, she was surprised to feel a final burst not of fear but of unhinged excitement. The emotion shocked her, and it was coupled with the knowledge that she was going to be okay, that she would somehow be protected. Her aunt's words swam around in her mind, merging with the remnants of half-forgotten prayers, forming a holy invocation: *It won't hit here. It'll pass overhead. Dear God. They always do.*

For a fraction of a second, Maggie thought that maybe the bomb had been a dud, or that perhaps some kind of divine grace had rescued her. But then Maggie's entire world exploded, like the ground was being wrenched apart underneath her feet.

The bomb hit and detonated with the force of a tidal wave. The front windows of the store shattered inward, showering Maggie's hair with glass and toppling her backward. She felt a blast of burning air, and gasped as the strength of the explosion pinned her to the floor and compressed her lungs. Then the air darkened with clouds of gray smoke and suddenly she couldn't breathe.

Oh God, she thought, panic rising as she fought for air, feeling her eyes and nose burning. All the excitement was gone, and only terror and shock remained. The store was completely filled with acrid smoke now, and it felt like she was deep underwater. Coughing and gasping, she groped around for her aunt, or for anything familiar. All her hands found were reams of tattered cloth, now sharp with broken glass and bits of shrapnel. Her hearing was muffled from the roar of the blast, but she could faintly hear her aunt's voice saying "Quick! Quick!" She turned toward the sound and felt fingers pulling at the sleeve of her blouse. She realized her aunt was right next to her in the smoke, and had been all along. "We have to get out of here!"

Still dazed, Maggie tried to brush glass from her hair as she forced smoky air into her lungs. True fear was with her now, and she felt her legs shaking like she'd just biked twenty miles. Supported by her aunt, Maggie staggered outside, blinking against the light and trying to get dust out of her stinging eyes. The shopgirl had made her way outside too, her face blank with dead eyes.

Maggie glanced back at the store. One of the doors had blown off its hinges, and the other one was askew, hanging by a splintered piece of wood. The warning siren continued wailing its unearthly cry, and more and more sirens joined in from neighboring streets. Maggie's right hand hurt, and she saw that a piece of glass had sliced it along the back, so finely that the wound looked like a paper cut. Yet it was deep, and blood was oozing out its edges. She looked over at her aunt, who had an abrasion on her cheek and a cut on her forehead. Her hair was white with fallen plaster.

"Wow," her aunt said. "That was something, wasn't it?" She sounded like she was in shock too. "Look up there." A hundred yards to their left, a crater had magically appeared in the street. It was about ten yards in diameter and had swallowed a car and part of a building. Maggie realized it was the center of the bomb blast. All along the sides of the street, the windows had been blown out, and there was rubble everywhere. Maggie knew that if the bomb had landed just a little closer to the fabric store, she and her aunt might have been killed. She felt both sick and giddy at the realization that her own life was so fragile and could end so quickly. She also realized the plane had only dropped one bomb for some reason. She didn't know why, but she was grateful for that twist of fate. *Things could have been much worse*.

Maggie saw that not everyone was so lucky. She looked in the other direction down the street and noticed a man on fire. He was spinning and writhing on the cobblestones like a dancer who'd lost his mind. He was wearing a gray flannel suit, and the suit was engulfed in flames, the fabric annealing to his melting skin. He wasn't screaming: he was completely silent, engaged in his solitary battle with the fire. Damaged people were warily emerging from shops, clutching their heads and injured limbs, but no one moved to help him. Perhaps they were too preoccupied with their private pain, or scared of getting burned themselves. The more the man swatted at the flames, the more they burst and flared, bubbling his skin. The fire was burning his clothes and his hair completely away. *He'll be naked soon*, Maggie thought. *Like a baby.*

Maggie suddenly felt a rough hand over her eyes, jerking her head sideways.

"Don't look!" her aunt commanded. It sounded like Aunt Joan's moment of shock had passed, and she was back in control of herself. Still, her voice was tight with jagged emotion, a mix of fear and relief. "We can't help him. An ambulance will get here soon and take him to the burn ward at St. Bartholomew's." Maggie wasn't foolish enough to ask her aunt if the man would be okay; she knew he'd probably die from his burns.

The two of them started walking hastily down the street in the other direction, Maggie propelled forward by her aunt. She wanted to turn and look back at the man, but she was too afraid. She thought she heard the sound of people rushing to help him at long last and extinguish the blaze, but perhaps it was just her imagination. Her aunt kept her arm tightly around Maggie's shoulders, holding on to her. "We can only help ourselves. More bombs might be on the way. Who knows what those bloody Krauts are up to? I can't let you get hurt more than you already are—what would your mother say?"

"Who cares?" Maggie asked, her tongue feeling large and dry in her mouth. "It's not your fault the Germans want to kill us." Her mouth was gritty, like sand had got inside it, and she wiped her lips on the sleeve of her blouse. A little stain of blood came off. "Are we going home now?"

"No. We're going to the closest tube station," her aunt said, walking as briskly as her shoes would allow. "We'll wait there until we're sure the raid is over and the all-clear has sounded."

Maggie nodded, and then winced, because her neck hurt. The tube made sense to her. The teachers had told them in school to run to the closest underground train station if they were ever outside when bombs fell, she remembered that now. Most of the underground stations were deep enough that they acted like massive concrete bomb shelters.

"There's one at Hawk's Cross," her aunt said. "It's not far, and I know the way." The sirens continued to wail. Other people had started walking and running in the same direction. Not enough to form a crowd or a mob, but enough that Maggie and her aunt had become part of a steady stream of traffic. No one was making much noise; they were all as well-behaved and orderly as possible. Behind them were the sounds of fire engines arriving at the epicenter of the blast. Nervous, Maggie looked up but didn't see any planes in the sky, at least for now. She wondered where the RAF were, and when they would shoot down the German.

Maggie's thoughts returned to her mom, who was back at home waiting for them, oblivious to the danger they were in. She knew it was doubtful that anything had happened near her own home, but the safety of her mom was becoming a pressing thought as her own shock wore off.

Her aunt picked up the pace and Maggie struggled to keep even with her. Her hearing had come back, but now carried with it a ringing sound that nearly matched the pitch of the sirens. Her senses all felt heightened by the traumatic experience, and her skin was tender and raw.

Maggie's aunt was still gripping her around the shoulders, as though afraid Maggie might suddenly bolt, or someone might snatch her.

"John Gielgud comes down here," her aunt started babbling as they approached the opening to the underground station. "The stage actor. Have you heard of him? He's famous."

"No." Maggie knew her aunt was just talking to try to keep them both calm.

"I read about it in the *Times* last month. Actors come down to the underground and perform shows for the crowds during blackouts. They recite monologues from Shakespeare."

"Why? That seems weird." Maggie's voice sounded shaky and thin to her own ears.

"It's their way of helping. They're doing their part for the king. Not every man can be a soldier, I suppose."

Maggie and her aunt reached the station entrance, and Maggie saw the narrow steps leading down at a perilous angle into the semidarkness. She was conscious there were people behind her, and she got nervous she might slip and fall, but no one was pushing or trying to move quickly. Again, she was struck by the orderliness of the whole endeavor.

Maggie and her aunt began descending the brick steps,

and Maggie's eyes struggled to adjust to the dim light. The air in the stairway was damp and stale, and old cigarette smoke intermingled with the unmistakable tang of human urine. The main station lights were turned off, so they had to make their way by yellow emergency lights on the walls that barely emitted a faint glow.

Maggie's hands grasped the wooden railings as they continued downward. She could see the station platform way below them, crowded with refugees from the current blast, and also from previous German assaults. So many families had lost their homes in the war that some were temporarily living in certain underground stations, on thin army cots supplied by the government. This didn't stop the trains from running, so that every few minutes an unearthly din shattered the air and disrupted everything. To Maggie, the idea of living in a tunnel sounded like a total nightmare.

She finally reached the platform with her aunt, and they merged with the crowd. Maggie was relieved to be off the stairs, but still unnerved; she kept running her hands through her hair and finding tiny bits of glass that pricked her fingers. Even a long, hot bath wouldn't remove all the remnants of the blast.

Maggie saw her aunt scan the refugees, looking alternately horrified and saddened at the beaten-down parade of humanity. Then Aunt Joan unexpectedly took something out of her pocket and held it up to her eyes.

"What's that?" Maggie asked, puzzled. It was an object no larger than a pebble, but it appeared to be intricately carved out of dark wood.

"Ganesh," Maggie's aunt said. "An Indian god. He's a good-luck charm." She pressed the item into Maggie's hand. "Here, feel it."

Maggie did as she was told, trying to avoid getting jostled by a family heading past them, deeper into the station and the waiting mob. "It's warm." She peered at the charm in the dim light. "It looks like an elephant?"

"Yes, that's right. The Hindus worship animals, just like your mother venerates Jesus and the Virgin Mary. You can keep it if you want. It's supposed to protect its owner from harm, understand?"

"Sure." Maggie didn't really know what to do with the little Ganesh, so she stuck it in her pocket with her uninjured hand. *I'll take any luck I can get,* she told herself.

A man brushed past, inexplicably selling newspapers and bags of potato crisps. Churchill was on the front of *The London Times* again, his silhouette inked there in smudgy black newsprint. Another man was passing around bottles of Lucozade. It was like a whole new city had set up shop down there in the dark, driven beneath ground by the unforgiving Germans. Maggie thought about an H. G. Wells book she'd read in school called *The Time Machine*. In it, one race of people forced another conquered race called the Morlocks to live underground in squalor and pain. Maggie thought to herself that if the Germans won and took England, it would be a Morlock world from then on for her, and for everyone else who wasn't a vicious, mindless Nazi. It was not a comforting thought.

Just then, there was a loud rumbling above them, and from all around, as though another bomb had struck the earth above. Maggie knew that here, a hundred feet or more beneath the earth's surface, they were almost certainly safe, but it was still nerve-racking and made her worry even more about her mom back home. Bits of brick and mortar from the high ceiling of the tunnel fell down, shaken loose by the impact, and the crowds of people grew even quieter. Maggie felt the muscles of her neck and jaw tensing up.

Her aunt noticed her fear and tried to reassure her. "We're safe, Maggie. Don't worry any more than you need to."

But the words were practically drowned out by another, louder sound, a droning, rippling noise like a peal of thunder. This time more chunks of debris fell down, and the crowds were not so silent. People began to murmur and complain, and shift uneasily on their feet. Maggie glanced up at the tiled ceiling. She was starting to get the feeling that they weren't so safe here after all. The rumbling continued, getting louder, seemingly endless.

"Move back!" a voice suddenly yelled. "Move back! All of you, dammit!" The crowds tried to comply as Maggie searched for the owner of the voice. She finally saw it belonged to a young policeman, his wide face flushed and sweaty as he passed under one of the emergency lights. He was moving up the tracks with an electric torch.

"What's going on?" someone yelled from the crowd, over the din of whatever destruction was occurring above their heads.

"Move back, I said!" the policeman yelled again, as though those were the only words he could say. Another policeman appeared up the tracks, pointing a flashlight directly into people's faces, eliciting angry cries.

Maggie looked back in the direction of the stairs that had brought her to this place. She couldn't see the sky, only darkness black as pitch. More people were running down the long flight of steps into the tunnel. Some had blood on their faces and clothes and were clearly injured, while others just looked terrified. Maggie's eyes lit upon one woman who was clutching a small child in her arms, cradling him in a red blanket as she negotiated the steep stairway. Maggie couldn't tell if the child was dead or asleep.

She had a sick feeling in the pit of her stomach. A man in the crowd, perhaps a crazy person, or someone who'd just been underground for too long, began to fling abuse and curses at the police. Another man in the crowd started to argue with him, and they got into a shoving match.

"I hope it's not another September seventh," Maggie's aunt murmured to her. "If so, we might be here for a while." September seventh of the previous year had been the very first day that German Luftwaffes had flown over London, dropping their payloads of fire and destruction. That attack had lasted all day and night, and was still one of the deadliest on record.

Over the concussive din of the bombs, Maggie dared to ask her aunt, "So is this tunnel really safe?"

Her aunt looked back at her with wide eyes and said, "Of course, dear." People were still screaming at the policemen, and the police were screaming back, fear turning into rage. In the dim light and noise, everything was becoming frightening. The people looked possessed and scary to Maggie, no longer everyday Londoners.

"Should we stay down here?!" Maggie yelled to her aunt, trying to be heard over the increasingly loud crowds. She knew it was a stupid question, because where else could they go? They'd have to remain in the tunnels until the raid was over, no matter what. Her aunt didn't even hear her, but stared up at the curved roof above the train tracks, which now seemed to be shaking slightly. For some reason Maggie thought of all those pretty, priceless fabrics in the Indian store. They were ruined now, burned and shredded, impossible to repair.

Aunt Joan was just about to speak when a noise louder than anything they'd heard so far came roiling down the tunnel toward them. It was nearly as loud as the initial bomb blast itself, and it enveloped Maggie with a physical force. It was a rumbling, groaning, crushing sound, like a building being imploded by a thousand charges. Brick, plaster, and earth started to rain down on everyone's heads, pelting the crowd like hail. It took Maggie a fraction of a second to realize that the roof of the underground station was going to cave in on them, and that they were about to be buried alive.

Maggie's aunt understood at the same instant Maggie did, and instead of trying to shield her this time, she pushed Maggie as hard as she could in the direction of the stairs and screamed, "Run!" Maggie didn't hear the word, she just saw her aunt's lips move and knew what she was saying.

Maggie didn't hesitate. Assuming that her aunt was

right behind her, she dashed through the surging crowds toward the staircase, which was the sole avenue of escape from the platform. Many people reacted more slowly, a decision that might have cost them their lives. As Maggie tore through the crowd, people just stood there, gaping upward as though they couldn't believe what was about to happen to them. Others got confused and hopped down off the platform onto the rails, as though they could seek shelter from the pending collapse there.

Maggie looked back behind her only once, after she'd reached the stairs and hauled herself partway up. The staircase rails were shaking like an earthquake was happening, and it was hard to hold on. To Maggie's horror, her aunt wasn't behind her at all but was still back in the crowd, unable to fight her way through. Maggie's vision was seared with a horrific image that looked like it came out of a Hieronymus Bosch painting of hell she'd once seen in the National Gallery. The roof of the tunnel was slowly caving in on the people way down in the blackness, many of whom were now, finally, surging up the stairs behind her. Yet the people were stumbling and falling down, creating a nearly impassable barricade of human flesh. Men were crawling over the heads of women and children, clawing their way upward to the faint light.

Someone slammed into Maggie and spun her sideways, knocking the wind out of her. For a sickening moment she thought she might fall down into the morass of churning bodies, but instead she got pressed against the cold stone wall of the tunnel, her fingers grasping to find purchase. She heard the muffled sound of an explosion and couldn't tell whether it was coming from within the tunnel, or whether it was another German bomb somewhere up above her. Death could come from either direction now. *God help me*, Maggie thought in terror and dismay.

The stairs started shaking even harder, and she broke her momentary paralysis, lunging forward. She ducked under a man's arm and headed desperately toward the gray light that danced above her through the oval opening of the tube, like a cruel mirage.

2

Life During Wartime

Five days later, Maggie and her mother were on their way back from visiting Aunt Joan in London's Greenview Hospital. Maggie was pushing her mother's wheelchair down the narrow streets in brooding silence, still trying to come to terms with what had happened to her and her aunt on that awful day, which seemed like an eternity ago.

Maggie's aunt was still alive, but she'd been badly injured in the partial collapse of the underground tunnel, and left comatose with a fractured skull. The doctors had shaved part of her beautiful red hair, made an incision, and put in a tube to reduce the pressure on her brain. No one knew when Aunt Joan would wake up, or if she'd ever wake up at all. Maggie was afraid that even if she did, she might not be the same person that she was before. One doctor had told them that Aunt Joan might wake up tomorrow with her faculties intact, or she might wake up a year from now, unable to speak or dress or feed herself again.

Maggie blamed herself for not staying down there in

the tunnel with her aunt. What if she'd grabbed her aunt's arm and pulled her along? Instead, she'd just run for her own life, like a coward. She knew there was nothing else she could have done, but she was surprised it hadn't even occurred to her to help her aunt until it was too late. All she'd wanted to do was save her own skin, and the thought made her feel hot and guilty inside.

Maggie wished she could rewind time and go back to before the bomb blast. The cut on her hand was already healing, but she knew it would take far longer to get over the mental trauma. Since the attack, she'd been plagued by intrusive memories, almost like waking nightmares, in which she was back down there in the station, with all those desperate people. Loud noises triggered these flashbacks, and she'd nearly had one at the hospital. She didn't know what was wrong with her, but supposed she should just be thankful she hadn't died in the tunnels, like so many others. The death count was sixty-eight and still rising.

When Maggie had staggered out of the tube station and onto the ruins of Straighley Avenue, she thought for certain that her aunt was dead, crushed in the rubble below. She'd been breathing hard in a panic as policemen and fire engines converged on the scene of destruction and chaos. Behind her, victims were surging from the opening, but not as many people as Maggie had expected. The underground station had been destabilized by the force of the bombs, and had buried most of its inhabitants inside, like a tomb.

Maggie had stumbled away from the opening, too stunned to cry, her clothes marked with mud and ash. A fireman rushed past her into the smoking hole, yelling out incoherent commands. After what Maggie had seen happen in the tunnels, she had no faith that this man would be able to rescue anyone. But other firemen and police quickly followed him; one of them eventually stopped and helped Maggie to the side of the road, where she sat down, trembling, on the curb. Later, after they had loaded Aunt Joan into an ambulance, a member of the Home Guard had given her a ride back to Hudsworth Green in his car.

As Maggie now pushed her mother's wheelchair along the street, her mind came back to the present, and she slipped one hand into her pocket to squeeze the Ganesh statuette. Maggie decided that from now on she would always keep it with her, as close to her as the silver cross that hung around her neck. Perhaps both items were useless, or maybe they would magnify each other's power. *Who knows how such things work?* she mused.

"I told Father Hanley what happened—the entire congregation will pray for Joan this Tuesday night," her mother suddenly said, twisting around to look back at Maggie. "From their mouths to God's ear, your aunt *will* be healed. Faith has miraculous power, I tell you. More than those heathen doctors possess."

Maggie heard the vehemence and certainty in her mother's voice, and she didn't dare dispute this prophecy. It was mostly because she hoped her mom was right, but also because she was slightly afraid of her mom's religious fervor. The more frail her mother got, the more she leaned on the church as a necessary crutch, and began heading toward the realm of total zealotry. So Maggie just nodded in response and said "Yes, Mum," and kept pushing the wheelchair.

Luckily, their semidetached house in Hudsworth Green was close enough to the hospital that they could make the journey without taking the tube. Maggie didn't know if she'd ever work up the courage to go inside another underground station again, and they didn't have the money for a cab.

Maggie's mother fell silent as they traveled, holding on to the arms of her chair. Maggie knew this kind of trip was painful for her mom, that each rattling shake of the wheelchair over uneven cobblestones sent arching pains through her mother's tender joints. She was glad for the silence, though, because it gave her time to think. Her sorrow and guilt over her aunt's condition were constantly there, nagging at the back of her mind. To distract herself, Maggie gazed out at the city before her, thinking how much it had changed since the war began in earnest.

The German bombs had destroyed many buildings, yet the social effect of the bombs had been far greater. As a child, Maggie had never known fear on the streets of her city, fear that her life could end at any moment. But now a pall hung over all the inhabitants of London and its gray, downtrodden landscape. Maggie tried to covertly peer at the grim faces of the passersby, who were mostly older men in suits, and glean their thoughts. *What do these grown-ups think about?* All of them wore dour looks of concentration and worry. There was no levity in this place anymore, only stoic perseverance.

Maggie remembered that on this very street there had

once been young children playing, and mothers sitting on stoops, watching and gabbing as they folded laundry. But all the little boys and girls were gone, sent away in a mass exodus of three hundred thousand children the year before. They now lived and played in remote parts of Wales, Scotland, and Ireland, some even in Australia and other colonies. And many of the mothers had either left with their children or were now working in factories, or were stuck inside their homes preparing for the next onslaught from the skies.

The grocery stores were all depleted too. Everything was rationed now, and even items that should still have been in good supply had dwindled down to nothing. It was impossible to get oranges, bananas, or—worst of all—chocolate bars. Gaping holes had appeared in shelves once stocked to overflowing, and the windows of many greengrocers were covered with sandbags to protect them from blast damage.

Maggie thought her family's relative poverty had been good training for their new life of rations and food shortages. They lived off her mother's small pension, plus a stipend from the church, so money was always tight. Maggie was used to preparing a meal for herself and her mom from nothing more than chicken stock and bread.

"Not so fast!" Maggie's mother snapped, her voice taut with pain. Maggie realized she was getting lost in her thoughts, and the chair was jouncing up and down as she'd inadvertently sped up.

"Sorry," she murmured, slowing her pace.

"Show more care, child," her mother grumbled, and Maggie muttered "Yes, Mum" again.

The pedestrians and the traffic thinned out as Maggie and her mother approached their neighborhood. Here, the winding streets were lined with terraced, working-class homes. It was not a good part of town, necessarily, but not a bad one either—not bad enough to get bombed on a regular basis, at least. Maggie always felt relief when she came back from school, or from an outing with her mom, and saw that their house was still standing.

Maggie pushed her mother along the cracked sidewalk, with the occasional dandelion poking its head through a crevice, and up to the gate of their home. Overhead, the sky had grown darker, and Maggie thought the clouds were about to let loose the fine drizzle that passed for rain in this part of London.

Maggie's mother was silent as Maggie pushed her up the path to the front door. She felt bad about going too fast earlier. "You okay, Mum?" she asked, and her mother nodded in response. Maggie reached out and unlocked the door, opening it so that her mother could wheel herself inside, the chair making violent clacking sounds as it passed over the stoop. Maggie followed, closing and locking the door behind them. She and her mom inhabited the lower level of the house, which included two bedrooms, plus a small kitchen and a tiny sitting area. The loo was a stark, stone outhouse about twenty feet behind the building.

Above them lived an old widow named Mrs. Criley. She was kind, but frequently got confused, and sometimes came wandering downstairs in the middle of the night. Maggie had once found her completely naked in their kitchen, scavenging for food in the waste bin. Maggie had helped guide her back upstairs, all the while feeling sorry for her, but also creeped out. Mrs. Criley couldn't see or hear too well either, which was an asset because Maggie could play the radio as loudly as she wanted without Mrs. Criley complaining.

Living with her mom and Mrs. Criley, Maggie often felt more like a nurse in an old-age pensioners' home than a fifteen-year-old student. It didn't help that most of her friends had been evacuated many months earlier. Maggie had settled into a routine of isolation and solitude, and her favorite library books and radio shows were her constant companions. She also liked going to the local movie theater, although the newsreels of the growing Nazi menace were often too upsetting for her mom, and they'd have to leave early. Due to the war, Maggie's world had shrunk down to just a fraction of what it had once been. Yet for the past months, barely a day had gone by that she hadn't found pleasure in something, or at least had one fleeting moment of happiness. Only her aunt's injuries and the trauma of the underground attack had changed that for her. London seemed more sinister now, and the threat much more real.

That evening, after a dinner of soup and beans scrounged from tins in the back of the cupboard, Maggie sat across from her mother on the couch. They'd hung their blackout curtains as directed by the government, so that from the outside, the house emitted no visible light. Mrs. Criley was already asleep, because she usually went to bed before seven in the evening. Often at this hour, Maggie did schoolwork or read while her mom studied the Bible.

But today something was different, because her mother wanted to talk.

"Maggie, I've been thinking," her mom began, softly and almost tentatively, which was rare for her, because she was usually brusque and demanding.

"About what?" Maggie asked, putting her copy of *Rebecca* facedown in her lap. She looked over at her mom, whose features were smoothed by the soft yellow light of the oil lamp.

"Do you remember your Uncle Harold? And Auntie Mays?"

Maggie nodded. "Barely." They were distant relatives on her mother's side who lived in the south of Wales, in a town called Carmarthen.

"I got a letter from them three weeks ago. I put it out of mind until recently, but they've invited you to shelter at their home during the blitz . . ."

It took Maggie a second to realize what her mother was saying. "You mean leave London? Go and stay with them?"

"The letter expresses great concern for you, and for me." She paused. "I think now it was a mistake to let you stay here. I can survive on my own, with Mrs. Criley to assist with the shopping and the chores. I never imagined the bombings would get so frequent or severe." It sounded like an apology to Maggie, but no apology was necessary. Maggie had wanted to stay too.

"It's okay, Mum," Maggie said. "I'll be fine here." But now that the notion was on the table, it was impossible to disregard. Maggie turned the idea over in her head, probing it from all sides. It was something she'd already given a great deal of thought to during the past months. When the exodus of children had occurred, she had to admit she'd felt envy at their escape. More than that, she'd also felt fear at being left behind, not knowing what would happen to her in the city when the German raids began. But her mother had needed her, so she'd stayed, simple as that. "I don't really want to go anywhere."

"Your wishes are immaterial, Maggie Leigh," her mother continued, sounding quite firm. "We're going to take Uncle Harold up on his offer and send you to board with him. In fact, I've already sent the telegram. A train leaves for Carmarthen in two days, and you're going to be on that train. He's expecting you. You'll enroll in the local school there, and live with your uncle's family for the duration. After what happened in the tube, I can't have you ending up like your aunt. London is no place for children anymore—it has fallen from God's grace."

In the awkward silence that hung between them, Maggie tried to picture Uncle Harold, Aunt Mays, and her cousins, but they were just shadowy faces from the past. She supposed she liked them well enough, but it had been at least eight years since she'd seen any of them. She and her cousins had been little kids the last time they'd been together. There was a good reason for such a long absence: her mother's condition made it hard to travel, especially as far as rural Wales. And her uncle oversaw a coal mine and found it difficult to get away.

Yet now this uncle wanted to provide a safe haven for her. Maggie sorted through her sentiments and finally figured out that she was feeling relief. The feeling was tinged with guilt at leaving her mom behind, but it was relief nonetheless. She felt even more conflicted about leaving Aunt Joan, but that situation was so tragic, it seemed better not to think about it than to face it head-on. Leaving London could provide an escape from her emotions and darker thoughts.

Maggie took a deep breath. "Okay. Fine. I'll go," she said finally, looking into her mother's rheumy blue eyes. "I'll go to Carmarthen."

"Of course you will," her mother replied hastily, as though she'd been expecting more resistance and didn't want to give Maggie time to change her mind. She started rummaging in her pocketbook with her bony fingers and finally extracted a folded brown envelope. She held it out and Maggie took it. "You'll give this to Uncle Harold when you arrive," her mother instructed.

Maggie thought the envelope probably contained money, but it felt very light to her. She was surprised her mom was so organized and had planned everything out already. Yet she didn't feel the urge to fight or complain. She realized that subconsciously, she must have been hoping for something like this all along, at least since the attack on the underground.

"It's a letter," her mother continued. "They'll understand when they read it. Don't open it on the journey, it needs to remain sealed. It's for adults only."

Maggie guessed then that it was probably news about Aunt Joan, and she felt sad. She put the envelope into the side pocket of her skirt.

"Don't lose it," her mother added.

Maggie fought the urge to roll her eyes. "I won't, okay? I'm not a six-year-old." Then she had to remind herself that because of the arthritis, it was a big effort for her mom to grip a pen and write a letter, so she added, "I'll keep it safe. Promise."

Her mother nodded. "We'll talk more about this in the morning. I'm too tired to continue, but I'm glad you see the wisdom of my decision." Maggie wasn't sure there was much more to say, other than to figure out the details of the journey. Her mother rubbed her swollen knees, as though using her pain to change the topic of conversation. "My joints hurt something dreadful. Fetch my hot-water bottle and fill it for me, would you?"

Maggie stood up, still barely believing what she'd just agreed to. It was hard to wrap her mind around the notion that a few days from now, she'd be far away from London. As she moved to the kitchen and prepared to heat some water on the stove, she felt a tingling sensation of excitement and nerves, butterflies in her stomach, as she thought about escaping this dismal place and beginning a new adventure.

3

Dark Passage

The days passed quickly, and Maggie soon found herself waiting to board the Great Western Railway train that would take her to her uncle's home in Carmarthen. She had very little luggage, just one brown suitcase with some everyday clothes and school uniforms inside, and a knapsack with some pilfered library books and toiletries. In the pocket of her jacket was a miniature copy of the Bible that her mother had foisted on her. Maggie had said goodbye to her mom at home, because the journey across town to the station would have been too arduous for her. Their parting had been brief but emotional, with both of them fighting back tears.

"Be good, and don't cause trouble for anyone," her mom had said gruffly. There were no "I love you"s, because overt displays of affection were not her mother's style. Instead, Maggie had leaned down to hug her mom, and her mother had whispered in her ear, "God is great, and He is all-knowing. Don't forget to say your prayers."

Over the lump in her throat, Maggie whispered, "I won't."

Her mother had waited with her at the bus stop until the number 10 came and Maggie clambered on board, awkwardly waving good-bye. From there, Maggie had taken a series of buses to get to the train station, a journey that had taken nearly three hours because so many streets were closed due to debris.

By the time she bought her ticket and got to the station's platform, Maggie was cold, exhausted, and thirsty. She wanted to buy a drink from the vendor, but her mother had given her only a few shillings beyond her bus and train fare. Maggie sighed, checking the clock. She had another forty minutes until her train arrived. The platform was nearly empty, with just a few hard-bitten souls waiting gamely in the cold wind, wearing hats and tightly wrapped scarves.

Maggie sat with her bags on a wide wooden bench, scared but feeling very alive. She wondered what her uncle's family would think about her, and if she'd get along with her cousins. She also wondered how long she'd end up staying with them. *Could be as long as a year, or maybe even longer.*

Maggie tried not to think of her aunt's fate in that dreadful hospital ward, or the struggle her mom would face at home with only crazy Mrs. Criley to help. Maggie dug in her knapsack and took out an apple, and her beloved copy of *Rebecca* with its cracked spine, to distract herself. As she curled up on one end of the bench to read, she told herself to focus on the present, and that the past and the future would sort themselves out.

The time sped by, with her head immersed in the Gothic world of the book, and soon she heard the rumble of the approaching train. She stood up and gathered her bags as the twelve-car train pulled into the station, black and implacable, its pistons churning up and down as it shot plumes of dark smoke into the gray sky. Maggie wanted to plug her ears for a moment, it was so loud, but then with a final hiss, the sound lowered in volume as the train came to a halt. The doors opened, and the conductor appeared with his tall black hat, staring down the length of the platform imperiously.

"All aboard!" he called out over the lingering sound of the engine. "All aboard, I say!"

Maggie headed toward one of the open doorways and climbed up onto the iron step with her knapsack slung over one shoulder, lugging her bag behind her. Soon she was inside the tunnel-like interior of the train. Because of the war, some of the windows were blacked out, and all the normal lights had been replaced by dim blue bulbs, so that it was harder for German bombers to spot the train from the air. Most of the seats and compartments were full; many of the travelers were soldiers in uniform, their eyes haunted from whatever nightmares they had seen. Maggie guessed they were heading west to the military installations Churchill had positioned near the beaches. None of them looked like they'd slept in days; their unhappy eyes slid over her and then disappeared back into vague, dazed stares of insomnia and despair. As she walked down the aisle with her bags, Maggie also noticed there were some fellow refugees on board, including several families with young children.

Maggie put her suitcase in the luggage bin and found a window seat. She wished she had the money to pay for a berth in the sleeper car, but there was no way to afford such an expensive ticket, which cost nearly double the usual fare. She knew she'd have to sleep upright in her seat, not that she minded much. In some ways she doubted that sleep would find her at all, as she was too keyed up to relax.

The engine of the train soon came back to full volume again, and Maggie's journey to Carmarthen began in earnest. As the wheels turned noisily on the track, Maggie gazed back out the window at the station as they passed it. It looked very small from her vantage point on the train, much smaller than when she'd been sitting on the bench. The sky was starting to grow dusky, even though it wasn't very late yet, and the lights in the train allowed Maggie to see a faint blue reflection of herself in the window, her face superimposed over the urban landscape. She wasn't sure she liked what she saw. Her hair looked unkempt and messy, too curly, and she tried to rearrange it in a more pleasing style, but failed.

Maggie looked past her reflection and out into the city. The train was now away from the station and rushing past factories and homes, picking up steam. Maggie knew that if she'd taken this journey just a few years before, she would have seen lights on everywhere, the happy glow of an industrious city. Instead, there was almost total darkness because of the blackout. She knew that behind thick curtains were hidden families and secret lives, but the darkness made it seem like the city was abandoned, like all the inhabitants had suddenly got up and fled. In a way the Germans had already won, Maggie thought, because they'd changed everyday British life irrevocably. Yet she hoped their victory would be short-lived, as she had nothing but faith in the resilience of her own country.

Maggie's reverie was interrupted by the conductor, who was standing over her, asking if she had a ticket. She gave it to him, but he didn't say a word as he took it and punched a hole in the corner. "Thanks," Maggie murmured, but he'd already moved on, heading up the aisle.

The journey to Carmarthen would take around six hours, or so Maggie guessed. She'd probably be arriving before midnight at the station, where her uncle would pick her up and take her to his house. Maggie was already dreaming about how nice it would feel to sink into a comfortable bed after having a hot bath, but those luxuries were still hours away. She rummaged in her knapsack and took out her book again, curling up against the window to read by the fading light in the sky and the strange blue lightbulbs.

The next time she looked up from the pages, the train had drawn out of London and into the bleak countryside. It rolled past slagheaps of coal, and areas that looked like burned wastelands from the smelting factories. It was much darker now, almost night, although Maggie could still see the misshapen silhouettes of trees, standing ivy-choked and blighted against the sky. The land was no longer flat, and rolling hills had started to emerge, as well as the occasional scattered farmhouse. It already looked like a different country to her.

Maggie wondered what her mom was doing now, and how she would be coping with the chore of preparing dinner for herself. She refused to think of her aunt because it was too emotional, and she already felt tender and on edge. She didn't want to have to find the train's WC, go inside, and secretly cry. So she turned back to her book, letting the fantasy of the novel replace the severity of her reality.

A while later, she took out a cheese and pickle sandwich she'd brought from home and unwrapped it, wiping off the pickle. She'd been keeping it safe in her jacket pocket along with her mother's letter to her uncle, and the Ganesh statue. The bread looked blue in the light, but she ate the sandwich anyway, holding it in one hand as she continued to read her book. When she finished eating, she still felt hungry. She balled the wax paper up and shoved it into her knapsack. She hoped there'd be food at her uncle's house, and lots of it. She knew things were tight all over Britain, but nursed the idea that out in the countryside, food might not be as tightly rationed and controlled. *I'd murder someone for a Mars bar,* she thought, her mouth watering at the thought of chocolate.

After a time, Maggie's eyes grew tired from reading, and she put *Rebecca* down across her lap. She shut her eyes and leaned back against the seat, the rhythm of the train thrumming around her on all sides as it continued its inexorable journey west. She figured that she had plenty of time to sleep without worrying about missing her stop, so she tilted her head sideways, resting it against the cold glass of the window.

When her eyes flickered open for a moment, she saw that now they were in the barrens, with no sign of towns or human civilization anywhere, only trees and hills under the light of the moon. She wondered if the Germans would be bombing London tonight, or anywhere else in Britain. The open fields of the country were rarely bombed, at least so far, although Maggie was a little nervous about the lights of the train. Out here, they were the only lighted thing for miles, so they'd be an easy target for a wayward Luftwaffe fighter.

The train stopped several times, pulling into small stations where soldiers disembarked. They slipped out the door into the cold air, their heavy gear slung over their shoulders like it was weightless. Maggie wondered what the life of a soldier was like; she guessed it was pretty brutal at this point. Every day the papers were filled with accounts of more and more young men getting killed in their effort to defend the homeland. Some were as young as sixteen and seventeen, just a bit older than she was. *Will the soldiers on this train still be alive a few months from now?* she wondered, and the thought gave her an extra dose of nerves.

Then, for a long stretch, the train didn't stop at all. Maggie's car was now almost empty, except for an old lady sitting behind her, and a few other passengers. Maggie must have finally fallen asleep, because some time later, she was woken by a change in the noise of the train. She opened her eyes, blinking away sleep, and saw that the train was slowing to a halt. Out the window, she noticed a large sign that read "Carmarthen and Pensam," and with a start, she realized this was her stop. She struggled to get up, irrationally afraid the train might start moving before she had time to disembark.

Maggie lugged her bags onto the platform as the cold wind whipped at her hair, extremely relieved that she'd woken up in the nick of time. *I almost made a total mess of things*, she thought. She looked around, expecting her uncle and his family to be right there, but she saw no one. The train station was pathetic—it was merely a small metal shack with peeling paint and a crooked wooden overhang. It didn't seem like anyone else was getting off at this rural outpost, so Maggie stood alone on the platform, trying to hold the collar of her jacket tight around her neck for warmth. It was much colder here than in London, and the air felt different, thinner and cleaner.

The conductor leaned out one of the doorways and called to her, "Is your party here, young lady?"

Maggie shook her head. "I don't think so."

The conductor frowned. "We've got to go! Got to make haste. Someone's coming for you, right? This isn't the place for a girl all alone at night."

"They're coming," Maggie said, convinced that Uncle Harold would never abandon her in the wilderness. "My uncle and aunt, and my cousins. I'm staying with them in Carmarthen."

The conductor gave her a long look, and then finally said, "Jolly good." His head disappeared back into the train. At about the same moment, Maggie thought she saw a glint of light behind her, reflecting back from the windows. She glanced over her shoulder and saw a vehicle emerging from the road that led to the station's car park. *This must be them*, she thought, relieved that she wasn't going to get stranded.

The conductor poked his head out one last time, perhaps to check on her again, and Maggie waved at him. "They're here!" she yelled over the noise of the train. She pointed at the black sedan that had now come to a stop on the gravel patch behind the station house. "Look!"

The conductor saw and nodded. "Safe journeys, lass!" he called out by way of a good-bye, and his head disappeared from view for the final time.

Maggie gathered her bags and headed toward the waiting car. She didn't want to stay outside in the cold any longer than she had to. She walked past the empty ticket booths toward a short flight of wooden steps that led to the gravel lot. Behind her, she heard the racket of the train as it began to pull away from the station and continue its journey across the hinterlands of Wales.

By the time Maggie reached the car park, the noise of the train was already receding into the distance. Other than the black sedan, everything around her was deserted and quiet. The waiting car's headlamps illuminated narrow swaths of grass and gravel in a peculiar yellow glow.

Maggie was only twenty paces from the vehicle when the door to the driver's side swung open and a figure stepped out. She couldn't see its face too clearly in the darkness, but from its shape she could instantly tell that it was neither her uncle nor her aunt. The person was too short and squat, while both her relatives were tall and thin, and her cousins were too young to drive. She paused in surprise, almost as a reflex, as her stomach lurched.

"Hullo?" she called out. "Who's there?" Maybe they'd sent someone else, she thought. One of their neighbors, perhaps.

"Maggie Leigh?" the figure said to her. Maggie didn't recognize the voice, but thought it was a good sign that this person knew her name. The voice was female, old sounding, and had a distinct Welsh bite of harsh consonants and constricted vowels.

Maggie took a few hesitant steps forward, her feet crunching on the gravel. She was still nervous but figured things were going to be okay. "Yes, that's me," she called out. "Did Uncle Harold and Auntie Mays send you?"

The voice did not respond to the question, and Maggie still couldn't see the person clearly, because the headlamps were in her eyes. Instead, the voice commanded, "Step into the light, girl! I need to see you nice and clear." The voice didn't exactly sound friendly, but it didn't sound nasty or menacing either. Just a bit cold and weird.

"Uh, who are you?" Maggie called out, hoping she didn't sound rude. She was searching her memory to figure out if this was some other distant relative she'd forgotten about—a stray great-aunt or something. She took a step toward the headlamps, revealing herself.

"Yes, yes," Maggie heard the voice say with pleasure. "It's just how I thought. You look exactly like she did, child."

"Like who?" Maggie asked, completely confused. She glanced around at the blackness of the night that surrounded her on either side. Her eyes were struggling to adjust from the glare of the headlamps, and she was having trouble seeing. "What's going on? Where's my uncle?"

"Your uncle?" the voice asked. "I wouldn't know much about him, Maggie Leigh. But I do know about you and your mother."

The headlamps abruptly snapped off, and the bulky figure started approaching her. Maggie stood still, letting the figure cross the distance between them. Some part of her wanted to run, merely from fear of the unknown, but there was no place to go. She hoped there was a good explanation for all of this.

Just before the figure reached her, it held up one hand, and suddenly Maggie and the stranger were bathed in the light of a small oil lantern.

"There we go, child," the stranger said. Maggie now got a full look at the owner of the voice, and was startled to see that the woman was a nun, dressed in full, flowing Catholic robes, a wimple covering her head, and rosary beads around her neck. She looked as old as she sounded, with a face that had as many creases as a crumpled sheet of notebook paper. Her dark eyes were set far back in her head, almost completely hidden by shadows, like a skull.

"Okay, wait— I don't understand," Maggie said, no longer feeling frightened, just perplexed. "I'm trying to get to my uncle's house. Who are you, and how do you know my name?" There was something impossibly surreal about this odd nun out here in the wilderness, clutching her lantern.

"Your mother told me your name," the nun said, staring

at Maggie as though she was trying to memorize her features all at once. "My name is Sister Bramley. I taught your mother at convent school many years ago, when I lived in Shepherd's Bush." She paused to let this curious piece of information sink in. Maggie was starting to get a really bad feeling about where things were headed. She knew her mom had attended a harsh school run by a strict and brutal sect of Catholic nuns; she'd heard stories about it from her aunt, who had gone to a traditional school. "Now I live in Briarley," Sister Bramley continued, "and I teach at a rural convent there called St. Garan's of the Cross. Your mother has sent you to me, to have you board at our school and study with us."

"I think there's been a huge mistake—" Maggie began, but before she could say anything more, the sister suddenly lunged forward and hugged her tightly, banging the lantern against the small of her back. "You're the spitting image of your mother, Maggie Leigh!" she cried, between a whisper and a sob. Her strong accent garbled the sentence so that *You're* became *Yer* and *spitting* was transmogrified into *spettin'*. Maggie's limbs froze in the strong grasp of this woman, her mind reeling.

She tentatively tried to disentangle herself from the nun, sliding her arms out of the embrace to put some space between them. With difficulty, she succeeded. Attempting to sound as certain of herself as possible, Maggie said, "I'm not here to go to your school, Sister Bramley. I'm here to stay with my aunt and uncle in Carmarthen. Briarley's a long way up the coast, isn't it? I'm not supposed to be going there—"

Sister Bramley interrupted again, and now Maggie could detect a note of impatient irritation in her voice. "I know where Briarley is, child! That's what the car is for. To drive you there."

"Look, I need to talk to my uncle," Maggie said, trying to think quickly. There was no way she was getting into a vehicle with this nun and driving up to one of the most creepy, isolated parts of coastal Wales. Briarley was famous for being a cold and desolate place where few people wanted to live. "There's a phone back at the train station, and I have coins for it. I can ring Uncle Harold, and he can come and get me. I'm sorry for the misunderstanding."

"Stop it!" Sister Bramley snapped, grabbing at Maggie's arm. "Enough! There is no misunderstanding." She gripped Maggie firmly, her pincer-like fingernails digging into Maggie's flesh through her jacket.

"Ow!" Maggie exclaimed. "Are you crazy or what?" She tried to break away from the nun, almost falling to the ground, but the woman had latched onto her arm with great vigor.

"Your uncle sold his house two winters ago," Sister Bramley hissed. "The family packed up and sodded off to America! No one lives there now. His house is abandoned to the mice and the flies. Your relatives are all gone!"

Maggie felt like she was going to be sick. "No," she said, as she tried to push Sister Bramley away from her again. "That's not true! My mum told me I'd be staying with them, and she wouldn't lie."

"She said what she had to say in order to get you here." Sister Bramley finally released her, and Maggie stood there shaking. She ran her fingers up inside her sleeve and rubbed the fingernail marks on her forearm. "Truth is like an iceberg, child," Sister Bramley continued. "Only some small fraction is visible on the surface. The real truth is underneath, where you're too young to see. Your mother wanted to send you to Wales for your safety during the war, but also because she detected a lessening of faith in you." Sister Bramley paused for breath. "She phoned me and said you'd come under the sway of her sister, a heathen, who chose India over Britain. I offered to help, as I helped her keep her own faith when she was your age. God's path is a narrow one, like a thread across an abyss. Once you fall, you fall forever! Do you understand me?"

"Not really." All Maggie understood was that she couldn't tell her true feelings to this woman. Maggie had been taught all her life to respect her elders, especially priests and nuns, but she'd learned it was pointless to question their views and policies, even if they were cruel or inconsistent. That was just the way the world was, in the same way it was pointless to rail against Nazi bombs. The Germans would stop their attacks when they got defeated; words alone had no power against them. So Maggie didn't tell Sister Bramley what she really thought: that her own mother had tricked and betrayed her, and that Sister Bramley herself seemed to be crazy or, at best, extremely deluded. She held her tongue and stood there, waiting for whatever calamity would happen next.

"You have a letter on you, I believe," Sister Bramley continued. "Take it out."

Maggie slipped her hand into her jacket pocket and extracted her mother's missive. She held it out to the nun, but the nun shook her head. She was holding the lantern up high, so they were encircled within its warm glow. Maggie was just glad the nun wasn't trying to grab her again.

"The letter's not for me," Sister Bramley said. "It's for you. It always was. Open it now."

Surprised, Maggie tore open the carefully sealed envelope and extracted the piece of paper within, struggling to read her mother's spidery writing in the dim light.

What she read on the page made her heart sink from her chest down into her stomach, as though the ground had dropped out from beneath her. The words confirmed what Sister Bramley had just told her, that the fantasy of safe harbor at her uncle's house had been a ruse to put her in the hands of this strict religious order.

"Dearest Maggie, Your godless aunt has perverted your mind," she read silently from the page, frustrated tears threatening to blur her vision. "I believe the bombing of the Hawk's Cross underground station was a punishment for Joan's lack of faith, and possibly yours as well." *What?!* Maggie thought, outraged. She forced herself to continue reading, partly because she didn't want to stop and have to look back up and see Sister Bramley's face.

The letter proceeded like the rantings of a street preacher in Trafalgar Square. "I know the German bombs will continue until Britain embraces God's will," her mother had written. "The Lord is great, and He is also all-knowing. He knows your sins, and the sins of this nation. You will spend the next three months at St. Garan's on a scholarship, where you will be protected from the Germans, but also from yourself. God will enter your heart and transform your life. I have prayed over this matter, and I know that it is the only choice I can make. You will return home to me safe in body, and correct in spirit . . ."

Maggie's blurry eyes skipped down to the bottom, unable to process any more of the letter. Her mother had signed it "With all my love," a dedication that seemed cruelly ironic to Maggie. She tore the letter in half and tossed the remnants onto the ground, then looked up at Sister Bramley defiantly. To her surprise, she didn't see a look of gloating triumph on the nun's face. Instead, Sister Bramley was gazing at her in a manner that looked vaguely sympathetic.

"I know, child," the nun said. "You're hurt and you're angry. No one wants to be away from their parents, not during wartime. I remember the Great War, and the wars before that. I was once your age, and I know that war injures us all, in places we aren't always aware of."

Maggie wasn't exactly sure what the nun meant, but the kind words and tone were a relief. She rubbed at her eyes. She didn't want to start crying in earnest because she knew if she started, it would be difficult to stop.

"Come with me now," Sister Bramley said. "It's three hours or more to the school by road, and it's already late."

Maggie guessed she didn't have much choice but to follow the nun to the waiting vehicle, because there was nowhere for her to go back to. Her mother didn't want her, Aunt Joan was badly injured, and Uncle Harold's family had apparently moved away. Besides, she didn't have any money to try to get another train ticket back to London. As frightening as the idea of a strict religious school in rural Wales was, it was better than being on her own. She was a war refugee now, in every sense of the word, or at least that's how it felt.

Maggie moved slowly after Sister Bramley toward the car, her hands stuffed in her pockets against the cold. Soon she was sitting inside the freezing vehicle, with the bulky nun at the wheel. Sister Bramley started the engine and began to drive across the gravel lot. They turned out of the car park in silence and onto a narrow dirt road, beginning the long journey to St. Garan's of the Cross.

Maggie felt numb. The food, warmth, and companionship she'd been expecting from her relatives had been snatched away from her. She marveled at the unexpected deviousness of her mother's plan, as much as she felt hurt by it. Maggie wondered whether she could ever fully trust her mom again. *Pretty doubtful*, she thought. She shut her eyes and leaned back against the leather headrest, relieved that Sister Bramley seemed to sense her pain and wasn't pushing for conversation. Maggie was so tired, she just hoped they'd get there soon. But she didn't really know what to expect. So far things weren't going well at all, and there was no sign that they were about to get better.

More than three hours later, Sister Bramley and Maggie finally pulled onto a long cobblestone driveway and up to the gates of the school. They'd turned off the main road long ago and had been driving down small, winding country lanes for a good hour in silence. Maggie saw dim lights through the windows of the car, and realized they were lanterns on poles, swinging in the wind. Their light cast creepy shadows back and forth across the cobblestones and illuminated the pair of tall, wrought-iron gates that swung open with dreamlike grace. Maggie didn't know who had opened them; perhaps the gates were motorized. She glanced over at Sister Bramley, who was looking straight ahead. The car passed through the gates and stopped on the other side, as Sister Bramley turned off the headlamps and brightly declared, "Here we are."

It wasn't until she was out of the car, stretching her aching body, that Maggie realized how massive St. Garan's was. Even in the dark, she could see it was much more than a simple school or chapel like she'd expected, and she had to scan her eyes across it to take in its full dimensions. The place reminded her of one of those desolate and windswept castles from an Edgar Allan Poe story.

The school was comprised of several wings of varying styles of architecture, as if the building had grown organically across the landscape, like a living thing. It was dark and imposing, with walls of gray brick sweeping upward at least five stories above the barren landscape. Nearby, Maggie could hear the sound of roiling surf crashing angrily against rocks, and she realized they must be close to the ocean. Most of coastal Wales consisted of narrow rock beaches and tall sea cliffs, and she guessed that the school was located high above the water. The damp night air carried with it the distinct odor of seaweed and brine.

Sister Bramley had parked on the driveway under a

stone arch that extended outward from the front of the school. Torches burning under the eaves shone down wanly, creating pools of liquid light. On either side of the driveway were overgrown gardens, and a thin fog hung in the air, giving the school a distinctly ominous feeling. The wings of the building grew sideways in both directions, topped with turrets and spires, and dotted with lead-patterned windows. *This place looks medieval*, Maggie thought, with a mix of dismay and awe.

"Get your bags, child," the nun instructed her. "Don't stand there gawking—you'll have plenty of time to explore the place soon enough." Maggie struggled to obey, but she was still transfixed by her new realm.

Here and there, lights burned from within the massive school, and in the gloom Maggie could see several additional buildings nearby, including a large chapel. Behind her, outside the gates of the school, stretched nothing but endless forest. There was no sign of other homes or buildings in the area, and when Maggie peered back down the driveway, she saw that it just curved into the trees, as if nothing beyond the convent even existed.

Maggie followed Sister Bramley across the cobblestones and up a short flight of brick stairs to the massive wooden front doors. To Maggie, the school had the strange air of a large, forgotten mansion. The nun didn't even need to knock on the door; it opened for them as if by magic. Clearly, someone had been waiting for them, expecting them.

Maggie entered the school after Sister Bramley and was surprised to realize it was almost as cold and dark inside as out. She stood, shivering, in the large brick foyer. She saw that everything here was made of brick, the high walls, the floor, and the arched ceiling several stories above them. Dimly lit hallways sprouted outward like tunnels in various directions from the foyer, presumably leading to other sections of the school. There were no decorations save for a huge, gory crucifix hanging on one of the walls, lit from beneath by a row of devotional candles. Maggie felt a fresh chill run through her bones, and not just from the temperature. Right then, another figure in black robes, barely visible in the darkness, unexpectedly swung the front door shut behind them.

Maggie felt a hand on her shoulder and realized it belonged to Sister Bramley.

"This is Maggie Leigh," the nun said, introducing her to the shadowy figure who had closed the door. The figure shuffled closer slowly, until the light from the candles caught the side of her face and allowed Maggie to see her features.

Maggie let out a gasp, and then bit down on her tongue at once to stop from crying out in fear. Sister Bramley's hand tightened on her shoulder, digging into the muscles. But the pain still couldn't distract Maggie from her terror.

"This is our Reverend Mother," Sister Bramley said calmly. "You will call her Mother Superior. She is in charge of the convent and the school." Maggie swallowed hard and forced herself to look at Mother Superior's face again. The cowl of the nun's habit framed a visage that was horribly scarred. The woman's skin looked like it had been burned completely away, and she was missing her lips and most of her nose. Only two nostril holes decorated the center of her face, and her eyes were thin slits, with their lids charred away. Maggie had never seen a burn victim like this, not even in London with all the bombings. Her skin was so ravaged and warped that the woman didn't look entirely human, more like some sort of species of lizard, or an otherworldly creature. Mother Superior locked eyes with Maggie across the darkness, as a pale tongue slipped out and flicked its way around her nonexistent lips, as though Maggie were a morsel she wanted to consume.

"She's pretty," Mother Superior said, almost to herself. Her voice was thin and raspy, as though she'd suffered massive smoke inhalation, and her thick Welsh accent added another harsh dimension to her speech. Maggie tried to do as she'd been taught growing up and ignore the nun's disfigurement. She held out her hand and said, "How do you do?"

She expected Mother Superior to hold out her own hand in response, but no such thing happened. Her hand just hung limply by her side, weighted down by thick silver rings. Maggie saw that one of her eyes was clear as ice, but the other was clouded slightly with a gray-blue cataract. The nun ignored Maggie's friendly gesture completely and turned to Sister Bramley. "Take her to the baths," she said, or rather, commanded. She spoke brusquely to the other nun, as though used to giving orders that were uniformly obeyed. "Prepare her for boarding." She made it sound like Maggie was a dog being prepped for a stay in a kennel.

Sister Bramley just nodded and said, "Yes, Reverend Mother." But then she hesitated. "It's very late, though. Perhaps—"

Mother Superior turned her ruined face toward Sister Bramley and hissed in a shrill, damaged whisper, "She's infested with lice and mites! They always are! Bathe her at once, or she'll spread her diseases to the other girls. We can't suffer another outbreak of lice at St. Garan's. They're being blamed for the cholera in Rhydwyn, you know."

Maggie felt her face start to flush. This was beyond humiliating, because she knew with a hundred percent certainty that she didn't have any lice or mites. That was something only the poorest, most downtrodden people generally suffered from in England, not she. And they were talking about her like she wasn't even there.

"I don't have lice," she said. She was so horrified by the suggestion that she found herself smiling slightly out of nerves and embarrassment. She knew it was a bad habit of hers to sometimes smile when she felt unsure of herself, but she couldn't help it.

Mother Superior took a step toward her. "What did you say, girl?" There was an edge of menace to her voice. Maggie glanced back at Sister Bramley, who seemed fairly weird, but far more appealing than Mother Superior. Yet Sister Bramley was now backing away into the shadows.

"I said, I don't have lice," Maggie repeated louder. "I come from Hudsworth Green in London. I'm not infested with anything. I'm clean."

"Clean?" Mother Superior repeated, her whispery voice dripping with heavy sarcasm. "You think you're clean, do you?"

Maggie nodded, starting to lose her nerve. She didn't want to argue or cause trouble, at least not yet. All she wanted to do tonight was have some food and get to sleep. She'd traveled hundreds of miles from her home, been stabbed in the back by her own mother, and now she had to deal with these nuns. There'd been enough drama in the day already, and she didn't need any more. "Look, I know I don't have lice," she mumbled, "but I'll take a bath if you really want me to."

It wasn't enough for Mother Superior, whose scarred face twisted into a cruel approximation of a smile. "Will you now?"

"That's what I said, isn't it?" Maggie replied, feeling like she was going to lose her patience.

Mother Superior gazed at her implacably. "A bath will only clean your skin, but deeper inside is where the dark part of womankind lurks." Her voice grew more sibilant. "Will you clean inside? Deep inside yourself?"

Maggie felt nauseous. She didn't want to know what this monstrous woman was talking about, but she thought she had some idea.

Mother Superior was clearly about to say a whole lot more, but Sister Bramley reappeared unexpectedly from the shadows. "I'll take her to the baths, Mother," the nun said softly. "You don't need to worry yourself about her."

Maggie turned gratefully toward Sister Bramley, her rescuer. But Sister Bramley's face now looked as cold and hard as Mother Superior's rings, her eyes black in the flickering torchlight.

"I'll take her to the baths, and I'll cut off her hair too," Sister Bramley continued, "and then I'll take her possessions to the furnace and burn them."

"Are you joshing me?" Maggie couldn't help but ask. She was very aware how alone she was in this place, and how far it was from London. She knew that her fear was evident in her cracking voice.

"We don't play games with little girls," Mother Superior spat. "And I won't brook lice at my school. They won't be tolerated. We shall disinfect your body tonight and start on your mind tomorrow." She half raised her hand as though she was going to strike Maggie across the face with her silver rings, but instead, she turned and addressed Sister Bramley. "Yes, burn her things at once. Shave her head. Do as you must. The will of God shall not be challenged."

"Yes, Reverend Mother."

Before Maggie could start screaming or crying about this injustice, she felt Sister Bramley's fingernails grip her arm again. Maggie was frozen by the unfairness of it all, unable to react quickly enough. Capitalizing on her momentary paralysis, Sister Bramley yanked her toward the darkness and away from Mother Superior, who stood there watching them, smiling with her lipless mouth.

Maggie and Sister Bramley entered into a dark hallway, lit only by a few candles on either side of the stone walls. When they'd gone several paces inside, Maggie felt Sister Bramley's breath in her ear as the nun whispered something to her: "Don't say a word. I'm not going to burn your things, or make you bathe, or cut off all your hair."

"But why—"

Sister Bramley pulled her arm harder, dragging her along violently. "I said, don't speak!" she snapped. Then softer, she added, "Reverend Mother will hear us."

It took Maggie a moment to understand that Sister Bramley seemed to be on her side. She wanted to ask more questions, but she kept her silence as they moved deeper into the bowels of the school. It was completely silent inside, so quiet that Maggie felt like she could still hear the noise of the train echoing in her ears.

When they were far enough away from the foyer, Sister Bramley stopped and turned to look at her. In the dim light, she was barely visible to Maggie, even though the nun's face was only a foot or two away from hers. "Don't ask questions, just let me explain. Our Reverend Mother has been touched by the hand of God in a terrible fire, and she's no longer like the rest of us. She exists on another plane now, a wholly spiritual one, and we follow her dictates as she gives them to us." Sister Bramley reached out and touched the cross around Maggie's neck. "In the last few years, we have bent away from the strict teaching of the Catholic Church, toward Reverend Mother's unique ways, like a reed bends to follow the light of the sun. Out here in the country, we are free to do as we please and forge our own path." She paused again, glancing back to see if Mother Superior had followed them. Then she continued sotto voce, "But sometimes she demands too much of us! I won't burn your things. I won't shave your head.

I said those words to appease her, girl. She'll forget all about them by sunup, because she has far weightier matters on her mind. And I didn't promise on pain of mortal sin, so God will overlook my transgressions. It's true you must bathe for lice at some point—but you can do that in the morn."

Maggie nodded. Sister Bramley sounded so rational now. Although Maggie was filled with questions about Mother Superior, she knew it wasn't the right time to ask them. She tried to put the nun's visage out of her mind.

"I'll take you up to bed. In the morning you'll be introduced to the other girls, and to your new life at St. Garan's."

Maggie thought to herself that she wasn't particularly interested in starting a new life, especially not in a place like this. The nun turned and continued down the hall, and Maggie followed.

"I'll give you a clean set of clothes for tomorrow, our school uniform. I'll put your others out to wash, and I won't tell Mother Superior about it if you don't. Mum's the word, all right?"

"Thank you," Maggie said gratefully.

"From London to Briarley in one day, eh?" Sister Bramley continued as they walked down the hall. "That will certainly make a girl tired, I'd imagine. We'll have you up soon though, for morning liturgy and a hot breakfast."

Maggie nodded again. She *was* tired, although the fatigue was still taking a backseat to her fears and worries. Morning liturgy sounded awful, because all Maggie wanted to do was get some rest and sleep in. She also felt like if she didn't have some time alone to think about everything, she'd go completely crazy.

"Right this way," Sister Bramley said, bustling toward a flight of stairs. "You girls lodge near the top of the house these days. It's not far."

Maggie trailed after her with her bags, pushing back strands of hair that kept getting in her face. Even though there was a war going on, and she knew that people all over England had it much worse than she did, she wondered if any of them felt quite so alone.

4

Confessionals

Maggie finally reached her destination, one step behind Sister Bramley, who was breathing hard from exertion. They'd climbed three flights of rickety stairs and passed through several long, dark hallways on their journey to the sleeping quarters. Along the way, Sister Bramley had retrieved a folded-up uniform for Maggie from a large empty room on the second floor, where she'd also stowed Maggie's knapsack and suitcase. There were many rooms with closed doors in the school, and Maggie wondered who, if anyone, was inside them. She wasn't sure where the nuns slept, whether it was here in the main building or elsewhere. These nuns were definitely not the typical ones she was familiar with from London; there was a Gothic, European quality to them. Maggie wondered what exactly Sister Bramley meant when she said they had split from the Catholic Church. She was sure she'd find out soon enough.

"Here we are," Sister Bramley managed to say as she reached a door and took hold of its handle with her swollen hands. "There's a bunk in the back for you, on the top to the left. It's a little crowded in there, but you'll make do. We all have to make do during wartime, don't we? England and Wales expect it of us." Maggie didn't disagree, so the nun turned the handle and swung the door open slowly. "Go on, then," she prompted. "I'll see you in the morning for breakfast. Sleep tight, Maggie Leigh."

Before Maggie could ask her any questions, Sister Bramley had already turned away and was heading back down the hall. Puzzled, Maggie sighed, and then took a tentative step through the doorway into the room where she was supposed to spend the night.

There was a dim blue light burning in one of the room's electrical sockets, like some sort of aquamarine night-light, and it cast underwater shadows on the stone walls. The light was buzzing loudly, and its noise and hue reminded Maggie of her train journey. For a moment she was back there, smelling the dust of the seats and watching the soldiers. But then the flashback faded, and she was solidly in the room once again, clutching her new uniform.

To Maggie's total surprise she saw that the room was completely filled with beds and bunks, and in each one was a slumbering body. She'd had no idea there would be any more than a handful of other girls inside, but there were at least sixty or more crammed into this relatively small space. The room had four thin windows, like in a castle, and the dim light of the moon shone in from outside, casting a gauzy glow alongside the blue light.

As Maggie looked around, she realized there was no sign of the empty bunk that Sister Bramley had mentioned.

She was suddenly really nervous again. She didn't know any of these girls. *Where did they all come from?* She moved farther into the room, trying to find a place to go, not sure how to fit in.

Suddenly a girl's voice cried out, "Shut that bloody door!"

Maggie froze. She couldn't tell exactly where the voice had come from. It had a rough burr to it, like the girl was from Manchester, or some other mining town in northern England. There were a couple murmurs of agreement, but most of the other girls remained either silent or fast asleep. Maggie reached back quickly and swung the door shut behind her, thinking that the last thing she wanted to do was get into a fight on her first night here.

She began maneuvering her way past all the folding metal bunks, trying to stay away from the side of the room where the angry voice had come from, and also trying not to bump up against any of the sleeping girls. She wondered if there was a nun stationed in the room somewhere, to keep an eye on everyone. Maggie heard the restless tossing of the girls, punctuated by the occasional semi-tubercular cough and the thrashing of covers. "Sorry," she muttered under her breath as she moved, annoyed that Sister Bramley hadn't warned her the room would be so incredibly crowded. At least it felt warmer inside, from all the contained body heat of its occupants.

Her foot touched something yielding, soft and fleshy, and she realized she was stepping on a girl's leg. Maggie recoiled, holding her breath; the room was so full, there were actually some girls sleeping right on the floor. She hadn't noticed them down there in the dark, but now she saw heads on thin pillows, and arms and legs sticking out of wool blankets. The girl she'd stepped on murmured and turned in her sleep, but thankfully didn't wake up.

Maggie managed to avoid stepping on any more bodies as she made her way to the back wall, where there was supposed to be an empty bunk, but wasn't. Clearly this place was not the orderly boarding school situation that Maggie had imagined. Instead, it seemed chaotic, the girls like beached seals.

Maggie stood there, embarrassed and not knowing where to go. She didn't want to wake anyone and ask what to do, and inexplicably there was no sign of a nun to ask for help. But she also couldn't sleep standing up, so she had to think of something.

Right then, she heard a voice whisper a few words in her direction. It was nearby, and very soft, so she wasn't sure she'd heard it correctly. Then the whisper came again, and Maggie managed to decipher it. It was a girl's voice, and it was saying, "Get over here." Maggie bent down, close to the floor, looking for the source. "Over here," the voice said again. "Are you deaf?"

Maggie moved nearer and discovered that a girl was sitting up, propped against the wall in the faint blue light, slumped against a pillow. Her eyes were open. "You," she said, beckoning with a finger. "That's right. Come here. I've got an extra blanket."

Maggie crawled toward the girl, slipping between two cots that were pressed close together, until she reached her. She could barely make out the girl's features, but saw that she was thin, with long wavy hair, large eyes, and a face that boys probably found attractive.

"What's your name?" the girl whispered. Maggie could tell from her accent that she was from London.

Maggie told the girl her name, then added, "I just got here tonight."

"Yeah, I can see that. Welcome to hell."

Maggie felt something being shoved into her hands and realized it was the extra blanket. "Thanks," she said.

"You can pay me back tomorrow. Give me your serving of mince pie at lunch."

"Deal," Maggie said, wrapping the blanket around her, thinking she was lucky, because she hated mince pie.

"I'm kidding," the girl added dryly. "About the pie. You don't have to give me anything." She continued speaking in a whisper: "I watched you come in. I can't sleep because I have insomnia. I'm up most nights, even when I'm knackered. Only whiskey works for me, and that's hard to get around here." She paused. "My name's Kate, did I mention that?"

Maggie had a million questions for the girl about life at St. Garan's, but most of them would have to wait until morning. She stretched out sideways, leaning back against the wall so her head was next to Kate's. She tried to focus on the most pressing issues she needed answered before sleep claimed her. "What's it like here really?"

"Horrible, just as you'd expect. You're here because of the war, like everyone else, right?"

Maggie nodded. "I wish I wasn't." The wall was hard against the back of her head, and she also wished that

Kate had an extra pillow for her too. She supposed she should just be happy she'd got a blanket. She took her folded uniform and placed it behind her head.

"Every day more girls get sent here. We're a very popular destination."

"My mum made me come—I didn't want to," Maggie said. She wasn't eager to explain that her mother had tricked her. *What kind of mother does things like that?*

"No one ever wants to come to a place like this. Please. It doesn't matter, though, because here we are, and there's no getting out of it."

In the gloom, Maggie surveyed the sleeping occupants of the dormitory. "How many girls are here?"

"At the school, or in this black hole of Calcutta?"

"Both, I guess."

"At the school, maybe a thousand. I'd say way too many in this shithole of a room."

The girl's unexpected profanity startled Maggie and made her laugh. She covered her mouth with both hands to stifle the noise before someone yelled at her for being too loud. It was extremely rare for a girl to utter a word like that, and Maggie was mildly shocked. But she was far more staggered by Kate's estimate. "A thousand of us?" she whispered. She couldn't believe there could be that many refugees way out here in no-man's-land.

"And growing every day," Kate said. "They can barely keep track of us all."

"Where's everyone else?"

"Upstairs, downstairs, and all around. The rich girls get better accommodations. But we have to fight over where to sleep every night, and how many blankets we get. The nuns know who's from rich families and who's from poor." As Maggie was digesting this information, Kate added, "St. Garan's isn't like a normal convent school. They're not normal Catholics here—they've got daft beliefs, have you realized that yet? Did they try to make you take a bath?"

"Sort of," Maggie said.

"It's awful. I've heard that Reverend Mother secretly watches the girls when they get naked and bathe. And her face is enough to make you swear off food forever—it looks like a rotten potato, doesn't it? Or maybe a moldy gourd . . ."

"Worse," Maggie said as she shuddered inwardly.

"Now listen," Kate continued, "you better get some kip because they wake us at dawn for breakfast and prayers. Me, I don't sleep, so it's no big deal. I just don't need to."

"I sure do," Maggie muttered back, thinking she had maybe four or five hours at the most until sunrise. She settled back against the wall in her blanket cocoon. She was glad to have found a compatriot here who was roughly her own age, and from the same part of England. "Thanks for the blanket, Kate," she said as she shut her eyes. She was asleep before Kate even had a chance to respond.

Morning came all too soon, as the gray light from outside grew incrementally brighter. Maggie was awakened by the sound of church bells pealing out across the Welsh countryside. Her eyes struggled open, the lids feeling heavy with fatigue. It seemed like she'd just gone to sleep seconds ago, instead of hours. The door to the room was open now, and a kindly looking older nun she hadn't seen before was standing there, blocking the opening.

"It's quarter past five, girls," the nun was saying in a singsongy voice. "You don't want to upset Reverend Mother. You don't want to be late for breakfast."

Maggie was thinking that she didn't give a flying fig about Reverend Mother's feelings, or breakfast. She just wanted to stay and sleep, even though her body was stiff from spending the night in such an uncomfortable position. She blinked and looked around. In the gray morning light she could now see exactly how crowded the room was. All around her were girls of various ages, from twelve to seventeen, all struggling to wake up.

She glanced over and saw that Kate was already standing. She was wide awake, but sporting black circles under her eyes. "Told you I wouldn't sleep," Kate remarked, sounding almost proud. The girl was even more striking in the light, and appeared older than Maggie, maybe by a year or so. She was tall and lanky, with an element of a tomboy about her, despite her good looks.

Maggie got to her feet unsteadily, clutching her blanket in one hand. She glanced down at it and saw that it was frayed and marked by old stains.

"You better hide that thing or someone's going to filch it," Kate told her. "I slapped a girl last month because she tried to take one of mine. She started crying, but no one likes a dirty thief, do they? I took mine back, and then I got hers too."

Maggie rubbed her eyes. "Nice." She reached down and found a nook under one of the beds. She stuffed the blanket under it as far back as she could, until it was out of sight. Then, self-consciously, she stripped off her outer layers and pulled her new uniform over her head. It consisted of an unflattering white blouse and a pinafore dress with a pleated skirt; there was also a navy jacket to go along with it. She transferred Aunt Joan's Ganesh statue to one of the pockets, hoping for much-needed luck.

"Come on, come on," the nun at the door was enthusing. "The Liturgy of the Hours waits for no man, woman, or child. Don't be pokey about breakfast and prayers." Maggie watched as some of the girls grumbled and began filing out of the room, their slept-in uniforms rumpled and creased. Maggie glanced at Kate again.

"We get to nosh first, then prayers," Kate said, understanding that Maggie was looking to her for some sort of guidance. "No one explains anything here. You just have to figure stuff out for yourself. There aren't enough nuns, and they don't really care either. They'll take anyone because they just want the tuition money." Maggie nodded. "And Reverend Mother's batty as a loon, but the nuns elected her abbess for life, so they can't do anything about it. Mostly they just try to tolerate her, like all of us do." Kate was saying this out of the corner of her mouth so that no one but Maggie could hear. She suddenly stopped talking and waved to two girls at the other end of the room, and the girls waved back. "Samantha and Eileen," Kate said. "They're farm girls from the north country. Cousins."

The cousins were looking at Maggie inquisitively, while most of the other girls were just ignoring her, wrapped up in their own dramas and private pain. Maggie gave them a little wave and smiled to let them know that she was friendly.

The taller of the two smiled back, but the other one looked away immediately, down at her feet.

"Samantha's the older one," Kate told Maggie helpfully. "She's a pal. But Eileen doesn't talk much—she got caught in a bombing and Samantha says she's been traumatized ever since. Her head's done in, although she was a little genius before that, from what I hear. But she saw her younger brother Brett get killed by shrapnel right in front of her, and she hasn't said much since then. When she talks it's in bursts, and she doesn't always make sense. She's only thirteen."

Maggie absorbed the litany of information. "That's awful."

"That's life."

Kate pointed out a few of the other girls to Maggie, but she was so exhausted it was hard to remember their names. She just kept nodding blearily as she tried to figure out how she was going to make it through the next three months. She wasn't used to being around so many other girls after her solitary life in London.

Kate pinched her own cheeks to make them look red; Maggie knew it was what some girls did to make it appear like they wore rouge. "Did they tell you about first confession yet?"

Maggie shook her head. "What is there to tell?"

"It's not like church in London. They'll make you confess today, probably right after breakfast. They'll make you tell them everything, and the penances are really extreme.

It's not just five Hail Marys and you're done with it . . ." She paused, brushing some of her hair back. "You'll see what I mean."

"Should I be scared?"

Kate laughed. "Don't take it seriously. This place isn't that bad if you can ignore all the religious malarkey and stay out of Mother Superior's way—which isn't hard to do because she's barely around. She hides in the day, like a vampire or something. I just try to do the least work possible in class and at chores, and hope that the war ends soon so I can go back home."

Maggie seconded that sentiment, thinking about her bedroom in Hudsworth Green. She was still furious at her mom for sending her to this place, and brazenly lying about it to boot, but she was also nostalgic for London, and wanted desperately to be back with all her comfortable and familiar things.

More and more girls were trickling out of the room now, so Maggie and Kate joined the flow. Maggie was glad she'd met Kate because a lot of the other girls seemed understandably sullen and churlish. *They probably don't want to be here any more than I do.*

Maggie fell into line behind Kate, and the nun at the doorway helped hustle them into the hall. She paused for a moment as she said to Maggie, "You're new from last night, then?"

Maggie nodded, thinking the nun would at least want to know her name, but the nun didn't show any interest in talking to her.

"Go get your breakfast," she said dismissively, as she

practically pushed Maggie into the hall after Kate. The two of them entered into the middle of a torrent of girls, flooding out of now open rooms and into the hallway. There seemed to be girls everywhere, Maggie saw, way beyond the capacity that the school was designed for. Most of the girls were quiet, but there was some talking and whispering, and the occasional laugh as the fluid, human procession moved farther along the hall and down the flight of stairs.

"We're in nowheresville," Kate said apropos of nothing as they walked. "As you probably noticed, there's nothing around here, not even any mining. Just this place." She paused. "You said your mother sent you here . . . What about your dad?"

"I don't really have one," Maggie whispered back, as she negotiated the crowded stairs.

"Pity. I do, but he spends most of his time in the local pub, and then he comes home drunk and pisses on the floor. My mum has to replace the hearth rug every fortnight. My brothers are in the RAF, one in Africa, one at the front."

"I don't have any brothers or sisters," Maggie said, knowing that made her a total anomaly, because most Catholics had huge families. But her crippled mom had been unable to bear any more children.

Kate was indeed surprised. "Only child? Lucky dog." She grinned toothily. "I've got two sisters along with my two brothers. We're all so scattered now, but I don't mind. I didn't get on too well with my sisters—they used to steal my lipstick and stockings."

Maggie realized then that Kate reminded her in some vague way of Aunt Joan. There was the same sparkle in her eyes that could display either an encouraging flash of attractive wit, or a disconcerting glimmer of instability. Maggie liked Kate, but she sensed that the girl might be a troublemaker. Still, Kate had been generous to her last night, and Maggie knew it was far better to have one imperfect friend than none at all.

Maggie and Kate accompanied the mob through another set of hallways and into a massive dining hall that was throbbing with controlled noise and activity. Large nuns in their habits patrolled a series of low dining tables, where girls ate in greedy packs, some protecting their bowls of oatmeal with both hands between bites. Maggie didn't blame them, because since the start of the war, pretty much every meal was something greatly anticipated. Maggie felt her own mouth start to water at the smell of the oatmeal.

Above everyone, at the end of the hall, hung the obligatory bronze crucifix, lit with a spotlight from below so that its gleaming contours caught the light and reflected it onto the ceiling in bright, jagged patches. Maggie glanced around the room, which looked like something from 1841 instead of 1941, and noticed that large woven signs had been hung like tapestries on all the walls. "Voluntary Humility for All," read one of them, and on another, the desperate phrase "Poverty, Chastity, and Obedience" had been inscribed in bloodred thread against a black background.

Kate noticed what Maggie was looking at. "That one's my favorite," Kate whispered sarcastically as she gestured at a nearby sign that read "Pray Without Ceasing, or Pay with Your Bleeding."

"Ugh, I haven't heard that one before," Maggie said, completely creeped out.

Kate chuckled at her discomfort. "It's homemade. These nuns are a rare breed of crazy."

The girls ahead of them abruptly halted, and Maggie realized that they were now finally in the queue for breakfast. But from the looks of things, it would be a while until they reached the front and actually got served any food.

"The rich brats from upstairs eat their grub later, so they don't have to wake up as early as us," Kate remarked. "The staff cooks up a whole other meal for them—eggs and ham, the works. They get treated like the cat's pajamas just because their parents donate money to the school. You'll see."

Maggie wasn't surprised that class differences played such a major role here, as they did all throughout Britain. "How typical."

"It sure is," Kate agreed. "But you know what? I don't even like eggs, or ham for that matter. I'd rather have some lumpy oatmeal any day."

"Really?"

Kate stared at her and then laughed. "God, you're gullible. Look, I'm lying of course. It's just what I tell myself to feel better about things. I'm bitter." She pouted.

Maggie shook her head, bemused. "So what happens after breakfast?" she asked.

"The Liturgy of the Hours, like at Sunday Sermon. Except here it's every morning. But that's for the rest of us.

Like I said earlier, they'll make you do a confession today 'cause you're new." Kate got distracted for a moment, waving and gesturing at two girls in line far behind them. More and more girls were pouring into the dining hall with every passing second.

The queue lurched forward again, and Maggie's stomach rumbled from hunger. It took another ten minutes until she was finally up at the front with Kate. They got their oatmeal and then found seats opposite each other at one of the long tables. Despite the noise and activity, most of the girls seemed well behaved. *They're probably scared of being caned by the nuns*, Maggie thought, which was the typical disciplinary tactic at most Catholic schools. Maggie started eating as soon as she sat down, washing the oatmeal down with a glass of warm, watery milk.

Kate introduced her to the girls they were sitting next to. "This is Miranda," she said, jerking her thumb in the direction of a short-haired girl who was engaged in a soft but intense conversation with someone else. "She's from Swansea. You know what that means."

Maggie had no idea, but she nodded as though she did because she didn't want to seem naive. She knew Swansea was a poor, industrial part of Wales, so she figured this was some sort of dig at Miranda. But she wasn't sure.

"And this is Bridget Bates," Kate continued, indicating the girl who was seated next to Maggie.

"Hi," Maggie said to her, feeling awkward. The girl returned her greeting, but with little enthusiasm, barely looking up from her bowl.

"You seen Daphne yet today?" Kate asked Bridget.

Alex McAulay

"Naw," the girl replied with a shrug, between bites. She didn't offer any more information. Kate looked at Maggie and rolled her eyes. Then she turned back to Bridget.

"Tell her I need to talk to her," Kate said insistently. "It's serious."

"If you say so," Bridget mumbled through a mouthful of oatmeal.

Kate peered at Maggie again. "It's about cigarettes. They're contraband, but Daphne's brother mailed her some, and she promised me a couple. She owes me because I stole a bottle of wine and shared a drink with her last week. We got totally blotto together. I can't wait to get my hands on some more alcohol and smokes."

Truly surprised, Maggie paused with the spoon halfway between the bowl and her mouth. "You smoke?" Smoking seemed so foreign to her, so grown-up. The only girls she knew in London who smoked were eighteen or older, except for the streetwalkers, and they had bigger problems than smoking.

"Sure, I smoke," Kate said, unfazed, although she spoke softly so the nuns wouldn't overhear. "Cigarettes and cheroots. It's glamorous, right?" She batted her eyes in imitation of a movie starlet and then laughed to show that she was mocking herself. Maggie laughed too, but she still didn't know whether to take Kate seriously.

Just then, a shadow fell over the table, and the girls nearby went silent, including Kate. Maggie looked up and saw a nun standing there. It wasn't Sister Bramley or the nun who'd let them out of their room in the morning. This nun was tall and imposing, and didn't look nearly as be-

75

nign as the other two. However, she didn't look as ravaged and frightening as Mother Superior either, so that had to count for something.

"Maggie Leigh," the nun intoned, her thick Welsh accent mangling Maggie's name. "You're done with yer eating, eh?" She obviously didn't want an answer because she continued to talk. "Stand yerself up and come with me."

Maggie looked at Kate, but for once Kate was looking away, down at her bowl, as though she didn't want to get herself in trouble. Maggie stood.

"Come this way, girl," the nun said. "Leave your plate and your tray." The nun began walking stiffly away, in the direction of the huge doorway, and Maggie followed with a backward glance at Kate and her other tablemates. There'd barely been a chance to talk to any of them yet.

"Where are we going, Sister?" Maggie asked as she followed the nun out of the dining hall and back into the long, wide hallway. She'd tried to ask the question as politely as possible, but the nun wasn't having any of it.

"Quiet!" she snapped at Maggie, without even turning around. "No impertinence! If I give you an inch, you'll take a mile. I know your type."

Maggie knew when to keep quiet, so she followed the nun down the halls silently, cursing the woman's rudeness in her head. She figured she was being taken to the confessional just like Kate had mentioned, even though it wasn't Sunday and she hadn't seen any priests around. She hated confessing because it always felt like an embarrassing intrusion. She never held anything back, though, and always told Father Hanley—their priest back home—about all the stupid, petty things she'd done that were wrong. It usually amounted to small sins, like thinking impure thoughts or telling a lie, and Father Hanley, who often smelled of booze, generally went light on the penances. But Maggie didn't know what to expect in a place like this.

She continued to follow the nun out a side door of the school into the cool morning air, and onto a stone path that cut through the briars and heather. They were slightly behind the body of the main building and were heading toward the entryway of the large, dark chapel. Maggie could smell the salt of the ocean from here, and she heard the faint cries of calling gulls. The water couldn't be far away, she knew, and was probably somewhere just below them. However, all around her were only wind-beaten trees and sharp granite rocks, reminding her she was in the austere wilderness of Wales and not at some seaside resort.

Maggie and the nun finally reached the heavy doors of the chapel, and Maggie followed her inside the building. The nun stopped and looked at her as soon as they were in the dark vestibule.

"My name is Sister Verrill," she finally said in her odd Welsh drawl, eyeing Maggie coldly. "I've brought you here to confess your sins, under the watchful eyes of Our Father. All who come and stay at St. Garan's must confess on their very first day, to cleanse themselves of sin before they begin their new curriculum." She paused, and Maggie felt unnerved by her stare, because the nun wasn't blinking and was just glaring at her.

"You've already made the acquaintance of Katherine Parris, I see," Sister Verrill continued at last. It took a second for Maggie to realize that she meant Kate. "You'd do well to stay away from her during your time here. She's a true hellion, and I believe she is a secret heathen as well." Her eyes were boring holes into Maggie's skull. "We admit too many girls these days, and I don't hold with that policy at all. I don't hold with many things that go on here anymore, but such is God's design, I suppose. Yet I won't allow our ways to be undermined by city folk, do you understand me?"

Maggie thought that Sister Verrill was lecturing the wrong person, because the last thing she wanted to do was undermine anything—she hadn't even wanted to come to St. Garan's to begin with. But trying to be logical with an angry nun was like trying to talk a wasp out of stinging, so she just nodded and said, "Yes, Sister. Of course."

Sister Verrill held out her robed arm imperiously, indicating that Maggie should follow her pointing finger and go into the chapel. "You may enter the sanctuary now, and you will find the confessional to your left. Don't dawdle, just tell your sins direct. I've got three other new girls after you today."

Maggie did as she was told, walking into the slightly ominous space, glad to be getting away from Sister Verrill. The building was very large for a separate chapel, and the only light came from a circle of tall white candles surrounding the altar. Maggie glanced back and saw that Sister Verrill was still at the door, watching her progress closely.

Maggie walked down the main aisle, past all the wooden pews with ragged hymnbooks on their seats. She imagined she'd probably be seeing quite a bit of this chapel over the next few months, and her stomach turned heavy with despair. As she approached the altar, she saw the wooden confessional booth on one side of it, as promised, and on the other, a raised pipe organ, with the door to the sacristy open behind it. She had a sudden, irrational urge to race over to the organ and push down a key or two, but she suppressed it. She imagined that would get her in trouble pretty fast.

Maggie walked all the way up to where the altar was, stepping into flickering pools of light from the candles. She turned left, conscious that Sister Verrill was still staring at her. When she reached the confessional, she saw that one of its doors was ajar. The other was closed, which let her know that the priest was already inside. Maggie knew that priests were supposedly God's emissaries, but she didn't like the idea of revealing intimate secrets to a total stranger. She wouldn't know whether he was nice or horrible until he delivered his verdict, and by then it would be too late to take back whatever she'd confessed.

Maggie sighed and climbed inside the confessional anyway, closing the door and latching it as she sat down. It was dark and clammy in the booth, and she felt like she could smell the sweat of all the other students who'd been inside over the previous decades.

Maggie turned to the mesh screen that separated her from the priest on the other side. Because the mesh was dark, she couldn't see through it very clearly, and only got the vaguest sense of a shadowy form beyond the lattice. Maggie thought to herself it was probably best to get this nonsense over with as quickly and painlessly as possible, so she began with the words she'd always said back home: "Forgive me, Father, for I have sinned—"

A harsh voice, like a guttural growl, cut her off immediately. "Hush!"

Maggie was so startled that her whole body twitched. She felt her face start to go red from surprise and embarrassment. *Did I say the wrong thing?* She didn't know what to do. "Father?" she stammered awkwardly, afraid of provoking another extreme reaction.

"No!" the voice said, the word sharp and curt, slicing through the mesh as though it contained a world of rage and hurt. "Not *Father.*"

It took Maggie a panicked moment to put the pieces together, because the situation was so shocking to her. Then all at once she realized who the voice belonged to. Indeed, it wasn't a priest at all, but Mother Superior herself. Maggie was so confounded that the breath got caught in her throat. It was inconceivable that a nun, even the Reverend Mother of a convent, would be hearing someone's confession. In fact, it went against everything the Catholic Church stood for. Sister Bramley had mentioned that this conclave of nuns had veered far away from tradition, but no one except a priest was ever authorized to hear confession. In fact, it was a mortal sin to pose as a priest to hear someone confessing their sins.

Maggie's confusion was giving way to anger. She was silent, trying to figure out if she should just open up the door and walk out.

"You're wondering why I'm here," the distorted voice continued. "Father Casey was indisposed, so I will be hearing your confession today. You may begin whenever you are ready."

Maggie's heart was racing with nervousness. "Mother Superior, I'm sorry—" She broke off. "Look, I think I need a priest, we can't—"

"There is no *we*," the voice said acidly. Maggie felt the nun shifting and moving around next to her and was glad the mesh was there so she didn't have to see Mother Superior's scarred face and demented eyes. "There is only me, the Reverend Mother, and you—a young child in the care of this convent. You will do exactly what I say without insubordination. Your safety and your life here depend upon my dictates, indeed to God. Do you understand me, Maggie Leigh?"

Maggie was stupefied. She wished that her mom, or Kate, or someone had given her more warning about what confession might be like here. "I understand you," she said, adding silently in her head, *I understand that you are stark raving mad!* Perhaps way out here, isolated in the Welsh countryside, Mother Superior had begun to truly lose her mind. Surely if the local archbishop discovered she was hearing confessions, the entire convent would be censured. Maggie had heard rumors at school about odd cultlike groups that supposedly existed in the barrens of Wales and Scotland—like the Oblates of the Immaculate, who worshipped the Virgin Mary and walked around on their knees—but she'd never expected to end up stuck in one herself.

"When was the time of your last confession?" Mother Superior asked, oblivious to Maggie's discomfort.

Maggie looked down at the floor, her eyes half shut, and hesitated only a moment before speaking. She'd decided she might as well tell this woman whatever she wanted to hear, because there wasn't much to confess anyway, at least nothing serious. Besides, she'd never confess any real doubts or problems; confession here would obviously just be a sham until she was back home with Father Hanley. She didn't think God would mind, and if He did, she'd try to make it up to Him somehow. "Less than one week, Mother."

"And how have you sinned against Our Father since that time, child?" The voice sounded cruel and unforgiving, almost mocking.

Maggie racked her brain for relatively harmless tidbits she could toss to the Reverend Mother. "I've thought about stealing," she admitted. "Stealing food from the bakery near my mom's house. Sweet cakes and pastries. And I've thought about stealing apples from the market too, just putting them in my pockets and running off, and eating them before anyone can stop me." All of this was true, because of the food rationing, but it wasn't that grave.

"The thought of sinning is as bad as the actual deed, sometimes worse," Mother Superior said sternly. "The thought of sin plants seeds in a young girl's mind, and they blossom into devilish plants." She coughed, a deep, phlegmy rumble that sounded almost animalistic. Maggie didn't know whether to pause, run away, or keep talking, until the nun recovered and snapped, "Continue!"

Maggie ran through the Ten Commandments in her mind, trying to think which others she might have broken, or contemplated breaking. "I spoke back to my mother," she said, which was also true, but not very damning. "I argue with her sometimes and we get in fights about silly things."

"What else?" Mother Superior sounded dissatisfied.

"I don't listen in school. I don't study the catechisms as much as I should. Sometimes I get really angry about the war." She thought about the unfair fate of her aunt and added, "Sometimes I hate my mum, and this stupid war, and what's happened to my life. I want to get away and leave it all behind. And I'm envious of girls in other countries. They don't have to suffer as much as us, at least I don't think they do, and I wonder why that is . . ." Her words trailed away as she thought, *I'm saying too much*.

Silence greeted her litany of supposed sins. Maggie wondered why any of this was necessary if Mother Superior wasn't even going to say anything in response.

"What frightens you, Maggie?" the nun's voice finally asked.

For a second, Maggie thought she hadn't heard her inquisitor correctly. "What?"

"I said, what are you most afraid of in this world? What frightens you the most?"

Maggie had never been asked this kind of question before in confessional. It was a provocative question, and she didn't have an answer. But she certainly wouldn't tell Mother Superior even if she did.

Maggie tried to think of some response to the question. The thought of suffocation—of being buried alive—came to mind, because of what had happened in the tube with

Aunt Joan. Yet that was too close to reality, and she didn't want to share something so private. So she said, "The water. I'm afraid of drowning. I always have been since I was a little girl." This was partially true, although the dread of being blown up by a bomb, or crushed during an air raid, had superseded this old fear. "I can't swim, and I don't want to learn. I hate the sea. It's always so cold."

This information appeased the Reverend Mother. It didn't seem to occur to her that Maggie might be lying or exaggerating. Maggie caught a glimpse of her shifting back against the seat like some great, ominous nesting bird, replete with rustling noises.

"The ocean," Mother Superior mused, turning the word over slushily in her mouth. "Yes." Maggie sensed that a smile had formed on her ravaged lips. "Are you ready to take your penance now, Maggie Leigh?"

Maggie hated the way she kept saying her full name, in such a weird manner, but she guessed there was nothing she could do about it. "Yes, Mother."

"You are to go down to the sea at once, directly upon leaving this confessional. You will speak to no one. The bay is below us, at the base of the seaside cliffs. There is a flight of three hundred steps, cut into the side of the cliff behind this chapel that will take you there. You will go down these stairs and over the rocks to the water's edge. There, you will disrobe entirely and bathe yourself in the water. The salt will scour you and wash away your fear, along with your many sins."

Maggie didn't know if Mother Superior was really serious. The water would be freezing, maybe forty-five degrees at best, and there was no way Maggie was going to take off all her clothes outside where people could see her. *Mother Superior really is crazy*, she thought.

"You will bathe in the waters," the Reverend Mother repeated breathily, as though entering a trance. "The ocean will become your bitter friend. Then you will dress and return to the convent. You will tell no one where you've been, or what you have done. Only then will your sins of envy, avarice, and wrath be forgiven." The voice grew louder, and Maggie sensed that Mother Superior's ruined face was creeping closer to the thin mesh. She didn't want to turn and confirm her suspicions, so she kept her eyes on the floor, hoping the experience would end very soon. "When you return to the convent, you will seek out Sister Bramley, and she will take you to your classes for the day." There was a brief pause. "I shall be watching you, Maggie Leigh, and if you don't do precisely what I say, then God will *not* forgive your sins. And neither will I, which will mean severe punishment . . ."

Maggie braced herself for more lunacy, and for the litany of Hail Marys and Our Fathers she fully expected was coming in addition to this bizarre penance. But it never arrived.

"You are dismissed!" Mother Superior cried abruptly.

Thank God, Maggie thought, and she wasted no time in pushing open the confessional door and bursting back into the candlelit confines of the chapel. For all of Mother Superior's talk of cleanliness, this false confession had just made Maggie feel somehow dirty. She wanted to get outside and away from this place. She had no intentions of doing what the nun had instructed—she decided she'd just walk down to the ocean and then back up, pretending that she'd bathed. *Maybe I can splash a little water on my face or something*, she told herself. *Just for show.* Maggie looked up the aisle and saw that Sister Verrill wasn't there anymore. *Good.* She began walking toward the gray daylight and fog waiting for her beyond the imposing front doors.

5

Deep Water

Maggie reached the doors and went outside, stepping onto the pathway beneath the cloud-filled sky. It was easy to find the path that Mother Superior meant, because it wrapped around one entire side of the building in the direction of the ocean. She'd suspected the school was on top of a cliff all along, and indeed, when she neared the end of the path, she saw that the land just dropped away into nothingness. The salty wind was cold and sharp here; it cut at her skin through the fabric of her uniform and made her long hair whip around behind her head. She peered out at the horizon and the vast, black Atlantic Ocean below. The stairs were right in front of her, a steep-looking set of stone steps with a rusty iron railing. It appeared as though they zigzagged sideways back and forth down the face of the cliff. They were precipitous, and Maggie thought to herself it was a very good thing that she wasn't afraid of heights.

From behind her she could hear the distant sounds of girls and nuns moving around the school and its grounds, still heading to breakfast. No one else seemed to be nearby, and the path and stairs were currently quite empty. Gritting her teeth and steeling herself against the wind, she stepped forward and took hold of the railing. It was cold and damp from the fog. She glanced back once at the chapel to see if Mother Superior really was watching her, but the thin windows reflected the light back, making it impossible to tell.

However, to her surprise, she did see another girl heading in her direction through the heather, and it took her a second to realize it was Eileen. Maggie wondered if Mother Superior had sent the girl to help guide her down the steps, or maybe to spy on her, but that didn't seem to be the case. Perhaps Eileen had just been wandering this way herself, Maggie thought.

"Hullo," Maggie said as Eileen neared, but the girl stared at her blankly. Maggie thought that Eileen's eyes looked like those of a frightened cat, both scared and feral. "I'm going down to the ocean," Maggie said. "Mother Superior is making me go as penance." There was still no response, but Maggie sensed that the traumatized girl understood. "Are you going down there too?"

For a moment, Eileen continued to stare, but then, shyly, she nodded. Maggie thought this was progress.

"Do you want to come with me? We can go down together."

After a moment's hesitation, Eileen nodded again. Relieved to have company, Maggie said, "Watch your step—it looks really slippery." She then began to descend the steps carefully, trailed by her new companion, all the while thinking that this was a particularly unsafe endeavor for both of them. She wondered how many times Eileen had come this way before, if ever. *Do the nuns really let a girl as barmy as Eileen just roam around aimlessly near a cliff, without supervision?* It seemed hard to believe.

When Maggie dared to look down—which she only did once—she got vertigo, because the rocky beach and crashing ocean seemed to be contracting and expanding miles beneath her. The cliff had to be at least a hundred feet high, she thought glumly. Gulls circled overhead, cawing mindlessly at one another in the gloom. This rural, wintry scene was as far from home in London as Maggie could have imagined, and it was shocking to think that she'd been in the city just one day earlier.

As she continued downward with her mute partner, Maggie mulled over her strange fate. She didn't really understand Mother Superior's idea of penance, which seemed to be closer to torture than scripture. The waves boomed furiously against the rocks below, the sound echoing up toward her. She took her time getting down to the bottom, gripping the slick railing, afraid that she might slip and tumble down onto the rocks. Several times she glanced back at Eileen, to make sure the younger girl was okay.

When the two of them finally got close to the bottom, Maggie exhaled, realizing she'd been periodically holding her breath from fear. She walked down the last stone steps and onto a slab of concrete that looked like the beginning of a partially completed jetty. The concrete only ran a short distance, not even all the way to the water, the foaming edge of which was thirty feet ahead of her. Beyond the slab, and all around it, were piles of jagged rocks with little patches of black sand in between. The beach continued this way on either side of them for miles, deserted as far as she could see. Eileen shuffled out onto the concrete behind her, and Maggie looked back.

"Well, we made it," Maggie remarked, just to say something.

Eileen nodded ponderously as she gazed out to sea.

The noise of the ocean was loud and constant, and Maggie guessed there had to be a storm somewhere to produce such roiling, violent waves. The air was filled with ocean spray, and she felt it on her face and on her hands. She joined Eileen in staring out at the dark, churning water. *Mother Superior must want me to drown*, she thought to herself. Any attempt to go bathing in water like this would probably result in a quick death.

Maggie was so occupied with her own thoughts that at first she didn't hear the strange voice speak out from behind her, over the noise of the ocean. And when Maggie did hear the voice, for a second, she thought it belonged to Eileen. She glanced back, expecting to see the girl right there at her shoulder. But Eileen had turned in the other direction and was staring at the base of the cliff near the stairs. Maggie followed her gaze, and when she saw what Eileen was looking at, her chest tightened all at once, as though the salty air was suffocating her.

Sitting in a crevice in the rocks at the bottom of the cliff wall, facing her and Eileen about twenty feet away, was a man dressed in a soaking wet gray uniform. She saw the metallic glint of a pistol in his hand, the barrel of the gun pointed roughly in her direction. She realized that he was calling out to her and Eileen, but Maggie couldn't understand a word he was saying. In a way, it didn't matter, because she realized in horror—from his uniform, demeanor, and weapon—that he was a German soldier. Her better instincts told her to grab Eileen and run as fast as she could back up the stone steps, but her body completely refused to move.

Maggie stood there as the German mouthed words at her and weakly flourished his pistol. She had no idea how this Nazi soldier had come to be here on this bleak stretch of Welsh coastline. In all her thinking about the war back home, it had never once occurred to her that she'd encounter the enemy so directly in real life. To her, Germans were either invisible monsters in the sky, dropping bombs over London, or prisoners of war, paraded about in the local papers and newsreels. To actually encounter a German on this beach felt like discovering an alien life-form that had just landed from outer space. *How can this be happening?*

The gun kept Maggie mesmerized and held her prisoner. She wasn't very far away from the man, so she couldn't risk running in case he fired his weapon. She also couldn't leave Eileen behind, but she didn't know how to communicate or strategize with the girl with the German sitting right there. So Maggie just stood there staring at him, the skirt of her uniform flapping in the wind as the water crashed relentlessly behind her.

Keeping the gun trained on Maggie, the German beckoned to her and Eileen with his other hand. He looked very pale and cold, and he was holding himself stiffly, as though he was injured. Maggie glimpsed something red on the side of his neck and wondered if it was blood. She didn't want to approach him, but she realized that she didn't have much choice. There was no way to get past him back to the stone steps, and no way to seek shelter on the beach from the gun. Out here, she was as exposed as the granite rocks that lay all around her like fallen tombstones.

The German continued to beckon and call for them. Maggie could barely hear him over the water, but finally realized that he was saying, "Come here, come here," in English. She could only really tell because she was looking at his lips move. It was becoming clear to her that her life, and Eileen's, were truly in danger. It was a different feeling from when the underground station was attacked; she'd felt so panicked and desperate then, but now she just felt a numb sense of despair.

Maggie suddenly remembered Mother Superior's claim that she'd be watching her. She dared to look away from the German for a moment, to stare up and around, hoping someone could see them. But because they were at the base of the cliff, nothing at the top was visible from their angle. Maggie thought about screaming for help, but even if she could shake her paralysis, she knew that over the noise of the water, no one would hear.

She looked back at the German and saw that now he'd inexplicably lowered the gun a little bit, so it wasn't pointing directly at her or Eileen. Yet he continued to motion with his other hand, in a peculiar little waving gesture. Maggie took a small step off the concrete toward him, bending down a bit to navigate the rocks so they didn't lacerate her legs. She looked over at Eileen, who was doing the same thing. The girl seemed to just be following her own actions, mimicking them.

The German lowered the gun even more, finally resting it on his lap. He made a strange expression with his face, like he was trying to smile but could only manage a grimace of pain. Maggie took another cautious step forward. Now that the gun was lowered, she thought it might be possible for her and Eileen to start running when they got right up close to him, and head for the steps. Still, he might be able to shoot upward and get them, and besides, she didn't know how she and Eileen could coordinate their plans. She also didn't know how accurate a shot the German was, or if his gun even worked. People said all kinds of disparaging things about the Nazis, and rightfully so, but no one ever said they didn't know how to shoot.

Maggie crept closer still, moving toward the German and his hiding place in the rocks. She was now only seven or eight paces away, trailed tightly by Eileen. She was so close that even in the gray light she could see that the color of his eyes was an icy, crystalline blue, so different from hers.

"You there!" the German called out in heavily accented English, as Maggie crouched down near him in the rocks. She was freezing, and could only imagine that it was much worse for him because of his wet uniform, and possible injuries. *That might give us an edge*. He didn't raise his gun again, so Maggie primed her legs to start sprinting past him and toward those steps, in case the opportunity arose.

"You will help me," the German continued, looking right at Maggie. "Listen to me! You girls will help me, okay?" He sounded a little delirious, but at the same time demanding and didactic.

Maggie saw his fingers tighten around the gun again, which meant there was no chance to run, at least for now. She knew she had to muster up the courage to talk to him, maybe ask a question or two. If she kept him talking, it would hopefully keep him from shooting at her and Eileen, and possibly give them a chance to escape. She still couldn't believe that in a school with a thousand girls, this awful experience was happening to her, and on her very first day.

Maggie glanced at Eileen, whose face had gone even blanker with catatonic shock. Maggie doubted Eileen would be capable of running anywhere even if the German gave them a free pass. "Where . . . where did you come from?" Maggie finally asked.

The German pointed up at the sky and finally managed a smile, which looked more like a snarl, because it showed the white of his crooked, broken teeth. He looked back at Maggie. "I am a pilot. The engine failed. I crashed." He paused, each word causing him pain. Maggie wondered where his plane was in that case, but he continued with his explanation, almost as if he wanted to talk to her. "I crashed in the water, and I floated with the plane. For many miles. I see this beach, and I swim for shore.

Almost, I didn't make it." He paused again, heaving for breath. "Your name, fräulein?"

"Maggie," she told him reluctantly. She didn't know if he was telling the truth or not. *Wouldn't someone have heard a plane crash?* she wondered, but then realized maybe not, if it was far enough out to sea. She didn't see any wreckage, but the brutal waves could have easily carried it under.

The man glanced at Eileen. "Your name too."

There was silence, so Maggie said, "She doesn't speak. She's not well."

The German nodded. "Okay. Fine. Tell her to come here."

There was no need for Maggie to say anything, because Eileen heard and shambled toward the man like a sleepwalker, brushing past Maggie. The German motioned for her to sit, and she did so nearby on the rocks.

"You two must help me," the German instructed Maggie, turning back to her. "I need food. Supplies. You will get them for me."

"I can't do that," Maggie said over the noise of the waves, feeling her panic rise. "I'm a refugee. I'm at the school here—"

The German cut her off. "You get me milk, bread, Marmite, and water!" he said, as though reeling off a grocery list to a servant. "You will bring them here to me. I will keep your friend until you return." He glanced at Eileen as he flicked wet hair off his forehead and said to her, "Yes, correct. You stay with me." Eileen's eyes carried a distant look, as though her mind had drifted far away as a protective mechanism. The German returned his gaze to Maggie and said, "Get food and come back. Then I will give you this girl. Tell no one I was here."

"I can't get those things you said," Maggie replied over the knot in her gut, trying to sound normal. "There's rationing. We don't have much food. Besides, I don't know where to find it."

The German dismissed her concerns with a flourish of his gun. Then he winced and doubled up, as though having a cramp. Maggie almost lunged forward right then, but she wasn't confident enough she could get the gun in time, and she didn't want to put Eileen in jeopardy. *God, what do I do?* she agonized. The cramp ended quickly, and the German uncoiled his body again, the pistol outstretched in his hand.

"No time!" he gasped. "They will find me soon. You go now, and bring everything I told you. If not, I shoot your friend in the head. Then I shoot anyone who comes for me. Then I shoot myself. All these deaths, because of you."

He said the words so matter-of-factly that Maggie wondered if she was hallucinating. No one could speak like this about killing people, but yet, there it was. She had no reason to doubt what he was saying. His demeanor, and the look in his eyes, made it perfectly clear that he was willing to carry out this plan if he had to. It was a look way beyond desperation. Maggie glanced over at Eileen, but Eileen was still far away and hadn't heard, or at least pretended like she hadn't.

"I give to you twenty minutes," the German continued in his fractured English. "If you do not return by then, I start to kill. I have killed sixteen men in combat. I will kill more."

He stopped for a moment. "Milk is most important, and needed above all else."

Maggie tried to think of something to say to that, but she couldn't formulate a logical response.

"Go!" he spat. "Twenty minutes. The clock has started, tick tock." He gestured with the gun maniacally, and then pointed it at Eileen's head. "Keep her alive."

Maggie knew if she thought about it too much, she'd remain frozen like a statue, so she numbly began to creep away from the German. "I'll come back for you, Eileen!" she called. "Don't worry. I'll keep you safe." But Eileen wasn't looking at her. Maggie picked her way across the rocks to the steps, gaining speed as she got farther past the German. When she reached the first step, she looked behind her and saw that the German still had his gun trained on Eileen.

Maggie began hauling her body up the steep stairs as quickly as she could, using the railing to help her. Her mind was racing even faster, trying to figure out what to do. *The smart thing is to run back to the school and tell the nuns*, she thought. Yet she'd seen the perversely determined look in the eyes of the fallen Nazi pilot. If she told the nuns, they'd presumably summon the constable, or perhaps try to deal with the German themselves. Maggie knew that the German would kill Eileen before anyone else could get to him. He had nothing to lose, and was therefore willing to throw everything away—including his own life, and whatever shred of humanity he had left.

The other option was to do what the German had said and tell nobody. This was far scarier for Maggie, because it

97

meant stealing food and bringing it back to him. And there was no guarantee that he would keep his word; he definitely hadn't shown any signs that he might be trustworthy. For all she knew, he'd shoot her and then Eileen, eat all the food, and be on his way once he'd recovered. Her life was almost certainly a disposable one to him.

Yet Maggie knew that while the Nazis had few ethics or morals, they were also coldly rational creatures. If he shot her and Eileen, then they would lose their usefulness. Also, the sound of gunshots could echo off the cliff and be heard by someone. It might be in his best interest to let them live, if they promised not to tell anyone. Maggie wondered what Aunt Joan would do in such a situation. *Probably grab the German, take his gun, and march him up the steps like the prisoner of war that he is.* But Maggie lacked her aunt's size, and courage, so there was no way she could do anything like that.

By now Maggie was nearly at the top of the stairs, out of breath and freezing, and she still hadn't come up with a decent plan. She thought about praying, but there was no time to stop and think. If she was going to tell someone, she had to do it as soon as possible, before the time ran out. But if she was going to get food for the German, she had to act swiftly too.

What the bloody hell should I do? she thought desperately. Where was Mother Superior? Why wasn't she watching, like she'd threatened? *Then I wouldn't have to make these hard choices on my own.*

She knew any decision she made would require her to go into the school, so when she got to the top of the cliff, she began running through the brush toward the large stone building. As she got closer, she saw a clump of girls in the distance, clustered around a nun. For a second she was certain she was going to run toward them and scream for help, but then she veered away, around the other side of the school. To her dismay, she realized she just couldn't tell the nuns after all. She didn't want to be responsible for Eileen's death, not after what had happened to Aunt Joan. It was probably a bad decision, she knew, but it was the one she was making. She'd already seen too much destruction and death. At least if she got food for the German there was a chance he would let Eileen go.

Conscious that time was growing short, Maggie increased her pace, her legs burning. She was worried a nun would stop her, but no one did. Like Kate had said, there just seemed to be too many girls at the school for the nuns to worry about any single one of them. Maggie wished she could find Kate—the only person she knew here—but there was no sign of the girl.

Maggie reached the side entrance to the building and pulled open the heavy oak door. Inside it was much warmer, and to her freezing skin, it nearly felt hot. She scooted inside the dark hallway and made her way through the halls to the dining area, from which there emanated a hubbub of noise and intoxicating smells. She'd been hoping the place would be less crowded, but she realized this must be the time when the wealthy students got their special meals. Unable to slow her momentum, she turned the corner and stepped directly into the path of a tall nun, almost plowing straight into her.

"Halt!" the nun snapped, startled and angry. "No running in the halls!"

"Sorry," Maggie managed to choke out, her chest heaving from exertion. The nun glared down at her through thick square spectacles.

"Name?" the nun asked in a brittle voice.

Maggie swallowed and told her.

"And where on God's green earth did you come from?"

"I'm new here," Maggie said, trying hard to slow down her breathing, even though being detained like this was wasting precious time. "I just got here last night from London. I'm really, really sorry."

"You *are* sorry." The nun looked at her haughtily. "A sorry whippet of a girl. Why is your hair like that?" Maggie reached up a hand and tried to smooth it down, but realized it was all wet and tangled. "You can't race in here, knocking people over, looking like something the cat dragged in." She sniffed, like Maggie smelled bad. "Who raised you? Jackals? And what are you doing in the dining hall at this hour of the morn?"

The last thing Maggie wanted was to get into any sort of argument with the nun. "I'm doing my penance," she blurted out in a burst of divine inspiration. "That's why I'm like this. It's part of penance for my sins." The nun looked at her oddly, as though trying to figure out whether Maggie was lying or not. Maggie forged ahead: "I just had my first confession here this morning, and I've been sent on a journey for redemption. Don't mind me, Sister. But I need to get to the kitchen or else I'll break the holy sacrament.

I made a promise to Mother Superior that I'd do this for her."

Her story must have sounded convincing enough, because the nun stepped back. Maggie guessed that Mother Superior had sent students on plenty of peculiar errands and penances over the years, and now the woman's eccentricity was actually working in Maggie's favor.

"Fine," the nun said dismissively. "Go about your business, then, but do it more peacefully. Life is not a scavenger hunt. I'll discuss your behavior later with Reverend Mother myself."

"Thank you, Sister," Maggie said, trying to sound as humble as possible, while secretly just wanting to shove the nun out of the way and get into the kitchen. For a moment she thought she might have to do just that, because the nun continued to stand there, dawdling and looking at her, but then she started moving forward again, away from Maggie, with a final glare. Maggie slipped into the dining hall.

Right away, she saw the rows of rich girls seated at the long tables. They didn't look too different from her and the others, except their uniforms seemed to fit better, and Maggie didn't doubt they were of a more expensive cloth. The way the girls held themselves was different too—more confident and grown-up, like they belonged there. Some even wore jewelry.

Maggie noticed all this in the few seconds it took to sneak past them and into the first entryway leading to the kitchen. The kitchen presented an ironic inverse of the sophisticated girls in the dining hall. Here, it was old, fat Welsh countrywomen who were making the food, and there wasn't a nun or an upper-class brat in sight. The Welsh women gave Maggie curious stares, but didn't say anything. They were the ones who cooked all the meals and undoubtedly cleaned all the rooms in the school. Here they were working hard, beating eggs and baking bread in the heat of the stone kitchen. Maggie was transfixed by the sight of so many eggs—a rationed item—not to mention the large pitcher of honey she saw on the edge of a metal table. There were no windows in the kitchen, and only a tiny wooden door at the back, so the room was filled with a hazy smoke. Despite the aroma of cooking food, it didn't look like a very pleasant place to work.

Maggie figured there probably wasn't much time left. She had no idea where these women kept their milk or bread, let alone something as exotic as Marmite, and she realized she'd have to ask someone for help.

She saw a kindly looking old lady gazing at her from over a baking tin, so she walked right up to her, emboldened by urgency. The old woman's dark blue uniform was covered in patches of flour, and stained at the cuffs.

"Excuse me, ma'am," Maggie said loudly. "Could you help me for one moment, please?"

"Eh?" the woman asked, looking confused, the smile slipping from her face. Maggie could feel the eyes of the other cooks hard on her back.

"I need your assistance," Maggie continued. "I need some milk and bread, and Marmite too." She took a deep breath, preparing herself to lie. "It's for Mother Superior. She told me to get this stuff and bring it to her, right away."

"Picau ar y maen, vach?" the old lady said, looking at one of the other cooks. Maggie realized she was speaking Welsh, although it was the first time she'd actually heard the language spoken aloud. It had a comforting sound, like something from a fairy tale or ancient manuscript. Still, Maggie couldn't understand a single word of it, so it wasn't much help.

"Please," Maggie said, feeling the time limit pressing in on her. "I really need these things or I'll get in big trouble."

"I can help thee," said a voice from nearby. Maggie turned and saw that one of the other cooks was addressing her. This woman was slightly younger, with her long red hair pulled tight in a bun above her wide freckled forehead. She pointed at the old woman. "Olwyn only speaks Welsh, but I can do for thee, *vach.* What do you need?"

"Milk, bread, Marmite," Maggie reeled off again. "Water too, if you've got a jug."

The woman eyed Maggie curiously. "Reverend Mother needs all this? Food and a jug of water?" She sounded gently skeptical. "For why?"

"I don't know," Maggie said, bluffing her way through. Her mouth was so dry from nerves at this point it was hard to talk, or act normally. She prayed that the German hadn't taken action yet. "Mother Superior just told me to come in here and get it! I was afraid to ask her any questions."

The woman's eyes danced and sparkled, and then she said, "Aye, I'm also afraid to ask her questions. Best not to know what she's up to, I suppose." Before Maggie could respond, the woman turned and called out a few sharp instructions in Welsh. Some of the other women began bustling around, and Maggie realized they were inexplicably getting the items together for her. She was relieved beyond words.

"You're from London?" the woman asked her.

"Yes," Maggie nodded, watching one of the other cooks decant some milk into a glass bottle. "Hudsworth Green."

"I've never been there meself," the woman continued. "To London. Terrible what's happening to it now."

Maggie nodded, but she was thinking that she'd do anything to be back there right at this moment, even with the bombs and her mom. At least in London, she'd never had a gun drawn on her by a crazed Nazi.

"Ah, well, here you go, then," the Welsh woman declared, as two of the cooks brought Maggie the milk, half a loaf of doughy bread, a flagon of water with a rubber stopper in it, and a small container of Marmite that looked like a medicine bottle. "I hope this satisfies Reverend Mother, I do."

Maggie took all the items and wrapped her arms around them. "Thank you," she told the woman who'd helped her. "Thank you so much!" She started backing away, out the door of the kitchen and into the dining hall. The Welsh woman was still watching her, like she knew something might be wrong but couldn't quite put her finger on it. "Thanks ever so much," Maggie called out one last time, and then she was gone, back into the dining hall.

She knew if she started running, she'd catch the attention of the nuns again, so she just tried to walk as rapidly but naturally as she could. She passed a table of flaxen-haired girls and heard a round of derisive laughter. She wondered if they were laughing at her and thought, *Bugger them all*. She didn't really care what she looked like or what anyone thought of her, because she had much bigger problems than snobs to worry about.

Maggie only started running once she got outside the convent. She looked around in all directions as she ran, trying to see if there were any nuns lurking in the bushes, waiting to stop her. Fortunately, she saw no one. The wind had picked up at the top of the cliff, and she was afraid it would make descending the steps even more difficult than last time. She also worried that it would be hard to get back down to Eileen and the German with her arms full.

When she got to the steps, she paused for an instant and looked down, but couldn't see any sign of Eileen or the Nazi from her vantage point. *I hope I'm not too late*, she thought desperately. As fast as she could, she began her descent, moving carefully but swiftly down the steps toward the beach and the water. The wind, which was now howling in her ears again, had whipped the waves into a frenzy, and white-tipped breakers crashed on the rocks. To Maggie, it seemed like it took an hour to get down to the beach, but it couldn't have been more than a few minutes. Before she knew it, she was standing there at the base of the stairs.

She turned around, clutching the items the German had requested, looking for him, and most of all for Eileen. At first, she didn't see them anywhere, and all kinds of awful thoughts swept into her mind. Maybe he'd taken Eileen off with him somewhere, and sending Maggie to get milk and bread had just been a ruse. *Maybe he wanted to hurt or rape Eileen,* Maggie thought, *and then run away.* Yet he'd seemed very frail, and it was doubtful he'd get too far on his own.

"Eileen!" Maggie called out, the noise of the surf devouring her words. "It's me! It's Maggie!"

Her eyes caught movement, and she saw a head poke up above the rocks. It was about twenty yards to the west of where she'd left Eileen and the German. At first, she thought the head belonged to the German, but then she squinted through the gloom and fog, and realized it was Eileen. She felt a massive rush of relief that the girl was still alive.

"I'm coming to you!" she yelled, knowing that Eileen probably couldn't even hear her words. Maggie began scrambling over rocks, painfully crawling her way toward Eileen. "I got the milk!" she yelled, just in case the Nazi was planning to do anything rash. "I got bread too!" *He has to be out here somewhere,* she thought as she continued forward. "I did everything you said!"

Maggie finally reached Eileen, who was crouching alone behind a pile of rocks.

"Eileen, are you okay?" Maggie gasped, collapsing down between the boulders in a natural enclave, nestling the food and drink between her legs, trying to keep it safe. She was looking around everywhere, searching for the German, who she'd suddenly realized wasn't anywhere near Eileen. In fact, there was no sign of him.

Eileen turned to face Maggie, her face looking ghostly pale in the odd light, and she opened her mouth. "He's dying now," she suddenly said, her voice unexpectedly crisp and bright, like a bell.

Maggie didn't know what shocked her more: the fact that Eileen had just spoken, or what she'd said. "Dying? What do you mean? Where is he? And I thought you didn't talk . . ."

"I'm fickle. I do what I want to." Eileen raised her arm and pointed to her left, farther down the beach. "He went away to die. I didn't follow."

Maggie wished Eileen could have been this articulate earlier, but she was just relieved the girl was okay and had started talking again, although she had no idea why. *Maybe the trauma of the Nazi shocked her back to her senses.*

"What happened to him?" she asked Eileen. The German had been fragile, no doubt, but he hadn't seemed ready to give up the ghost quite yet. Maggie was guessing he must have suffered some hidden internal injury in the crash, and that it had finally caught up with him. But the next words Eileen spoke changed all of that for good.

"I killed him," Eileen said, sounding very calm as she looked at Maggie with remarkably clear eyes. Maggie thought the girl was kidding around for a second, until Eileen elaborated. "I mean, he's not dead yet. Not all the way. But he will be."

"What are you talking about?"

Eileen sighed, as if Maggie was stupid for not understanding. "My daddy makes guns. I learned to shoot when I was eight. It was very important to Daddy. My cousin Samantha too. She's an ace with a pistol, much better than me." Eileen's little-girl voice was unnerving, and Maggie didn't know if she was lying or not. "That man was going to hurt us. He wasn't very careful. He put his gun down, so I took it and shot him in the tummy. Then he started screaming and he crawled away."

Maggie listened in stunned silence, one hand still resting on top of the milk bottle. Eileen had gone from being mute to babbling like a lunatic. "You're serious?"

"I'll show you." Eileen began moving over the rocks with something close to childlike abandon. Maggie was totally horrified, but also felt a visceral fascination at this strange turn of events. "I found him!" Eileen called out. "Over here!" Maggie finally reached her and saw the man's body sprawled between two boulders.

The German was lying faceup, gasping for air, a massive wound right in the center of his abdomen, just like Eileen had said. His eyes were shut and his hands and legs were moving around sleepily, like he was having a bad dream.

"Jesus Christ!" Maggie swore, not even caring that she was taking the Lord's name in vain. "What did you do?! I thought you were lying . . ."

"I never lie. It's a sin, you know."

"So's murder!"

The German heard their voices, and his eyes fluttered open. Maggie took a step back, afraid he was going to stagger up and attack them. "Where's the gun?" she suddenly asked Eileen.

"I hid it under a rock, near where you put the milk."

Maggie kept looking down at the German. Less than

twenty minutes ago he'd been threatening to kill them both, and now he was the one who was dying.

"I got your things," Maggie told the prone figure, partly because she didn't know what else to say. She knew he was the enemy and she should loathe him on sight, but part of her hated seeing another person in pain like this. It reminded her of her aunt, and all the other victims in that underground station.

"I did not want . . . to go to war," the German replied, bloody foam bubbling from the corners of his mouth like red soap suds. "My father—" He stopped to heave a shuddering breath before continuing. "My father . . . is a famous pilot. No choice to fight—" He coughed weakly, and very bright blood leaked out of his nostrils, forming a grotesque sort of mustache on his upper lip. His eyes rotated slowly in their sockets and found Eileen's face.

"I would not have hurt you . . ." he murmured to Eileen. "The gun was . . . to scare only."

Eileen just looked down at him, her face as expressionless as a ballroom mask. "Sorry," she said blandly. Maggie didn't know whether she was sincere or not, but knew it didn't matter. This German was going to die anyway, and the sea would claim his body as soon as the tide rose.

The German's eyes moved around again and lit upon Maggie. "They will come for me. My father . . . will make them come. They will bomb you. They will destroy—" He broke off for another coughing spell. His face and chest were now totally covered in blood. When he recovered, he yelped more weakly, "Damn Hitler! Damn Hitler!" and then he started to laugh, his face wrinkling so hard that tears leaked out his eyes.

"We shouldn't watch this," Maggie said, terrified. She was worried not only about herself but for the younger girl too.

"I want to watch," Eileen said, almost cheerfully. "I was with my brother when he died, but I wasn't watching then. I've seen animals die. Dogs, pigs, chickens, rabbits. But I want to see a human being die. I bet it's different from when an animal dies, because people have souls." She bit her bottom lip pensively. "I don't know if Nazis count, though." Maggie reached out a hand to try to cover Eileen's eyes, but Eileen pushed the hand away. Maggie wondered if Eileen was some kind of budding psychopath, or just really confused.

"Killing is wrong," Maggie said, knowing that she sounded totally ineffectual.

"Daddy says all Nazis are evil and their hearts are black, like pieces of coal."

Maggie looked down at the Nazi. He didn't seem evil or black-hearted at this point in time, only completely pathetic. He was now mumbling to himself in German, his eyes shut again. Maggie thought about going up and finding a nun to come and help, but she sensed that the end was near and that no sort of medicine would prolong his life.

He rallied one last time. "You have the milk—" he said. He was gasping now, taking sandpapery final breaths.

Maggie didn't know why it mattered anymore, but she said, "Yes."

"Go behind the rocks . . . where you found me . . ." He

struggled for air through the blood. "There is a crate . . . look inside, you will understand . . ." He opened and shut his eyes, blinking frantically. "I was running from Deutschland . . . seeking asylum . . . Now you must find . . . my secret . . . for me . . ." His words had become a fractured jumble as he lapsed into total incoherence. "Jesus God . . . my son . . ." He mumbled a few more things, all in German. With Maggie and Eileen staring down at him, he finally stopped talking altogether, and his limbs grew still.

It took Maggie a few moments to realize he had also stopped breathing. As the wind whipped around them, Maggie turned to Eileen and said, "Oh my God, I think he's dead."

"Aye-up," Eileen said back, not looking away from the body. "I told you I'd killed him. It just took some extra time for him to die." She sounded a little disappointed. "It wasn't different from an animal after all. I thought more would happen."

Maggie was thrown by Eileen's attitude—the girl didn't care that she'd just killed someone? Frankly, Eileen was giving her the creeps. "He said he was looking for asylum. Maybe he was defecting to our side." A few Nazis had done that so far: not many, but a few who didn't agree with Hitler's policies. One had even been a pilot, just like this man.

"Nazis will say anything, that's what my daddy says," Eileen maintained, dismissing Maggie's attempt at logic. "They've got silver tongues, like the devil. I think sometimes their feet are cloven. We should check."

"I don't think we have to worry about his feet anymore."

Maggie crouched down for a closer look at the man and could tell that he really had passed away. Her shoulders slumped. She felt a mixture of relief and horror. "He said he had a crate with him? Did you see anything like that?"

Eileen pointed behind them, back at the cliff wall. "It's mostly hidden, but I saw it."

"We better take a look, then. Show me where it is." As Eileen led the way back to the cliff, Maggie wondered what they should do next. She supposed they had to get back to the convent and find one of the nuns as soon as possible, and explain the situation. She wondered if the nuns and the other girls would be shocked by their story, or if events like this happened all the time out here. Somehow she doubted that they did.

"Here it is," Eileen said as Maggie reached her. Just as the German pilot had promised, there was a wooden crate secreted behind two rocks in the sand, with just one corner poking out. Maggie stepped over and examined it. It was about the size of an apple crate and was made of thick, wet pine slats, with a row of small holes punched in it around the top.

Maggie knew it was theoretically possible there were explosives inside, or something even worse, but she had a feeling that there was nothing in the crate that would hurt them. She guessed it contained war papers or information that the German hoped to trade for his freedom and a new life in England. Maybe there were even secret German documents or codes inside that might help the British government win the war.

But then, as Maggie leaned down a little closer, she

heard a faint sound. It made her jump back with a startled cry because it was so unexpected. "Did you hear that?!" she practically yelled at Eileen. From inside the crate was coming a strange, piteous mewling noise, along with odd scrabbling noises, increasing in intensity. "What in God's name is in there?" Maggie asked Eileen urgently, wondering if she'd finally gone mental from all the stress. *Could I be imagining things?*

Yet when Eileen looked back at her, her eyes were huge with surprise, and Maggie knew the girl had heard the noises too. "There's something alive inside," Eileen whispered. Her voice didn't sound so matter-of-fact anymore. "I told you Nazis are the devil. There's a demon inside that box, sent to us straight from hell! We have to run or we're going to get killed!"

Maggie eyed the crate warily, ready to take flight as she listened closely to the sounds coming from within, barely audible over the waves. But as she listened, she realized there was something awfully familiar about their pitch and cadence. Before she could stop herself, she knelt down next to the crate on the rocks. She pressed her ear against the wood as she looked up at Eileen, who was cowering in fear. "We better open this crate right now," Maggie said firmly. "I think I know what's inside, and it's definitely not a demon . . ."

While Eileen stood far back, Maggie attacked the front of the crate with a fist-size rock and her chipped fingernails, trying to pry it open. It was difficult and took several minutes of struggle, but when it was over, the crate was open, and both Maggie and Eileen gazed in stupefaction at what lay inside.

Eileen made the sign of the cross, stunned back into speechlessness. Even Maggie didn't know what to say, although she'd correctly predicted what they would find. "This is insane," she finally managed to get out. "How can this be?"

Swaddled in wool blankets and pillows, red-faced and screaming, was an infant dressed in a blue jumpsuit. Its tiny fists were balled up angrily next to its face, and its squarish head was covered with a miniature gray knit cap bearing a stark, red swastika. Maggie had no idea how old the baby was, but guessed it had to be under six months. She also had no clue how the baby could have survived the plane crash in the water, and been brought safely to shore. She smelled the tang of urine mixing with brine and wondered how long the baby had been hidden inside this box.

"I never . . ." Maggie muttered, unable to complete a coherent sentence. She forced herself to concentrate. "I bet it's cold. We better get it and take it to the nuns. The poor thing might be hurt, or sick." She looked back at Eileen, seeking confirmation. For a moment, she was afraid that Eileen had been permanently driven into silence again, but then the girl piped up, albeit nervously.

"It could still be a trap."

"I don't see how."

"It could be a demon disguised as a baby."

Maggie shook her head. "It's a baby." She thought about the dying man's incoherent ravings and realized what he'd presumably been trying to tell them. "I think this is his son—his secret. He was fleeing Germany with him. Maybe he put him in this crate to hide him from the authorities and smuggle him out—"

Eileen wasn't listening. "There could be a bomb hidden in the blanket," she interrupted. "Nazis don't care about life. They'll kill babies. They'll kill anyone who isn't one of them."

"Look, I really don't think it's a trap. There's not enough room inside for a bomb, and this baby needs our help." The baby continued to cry and wail in the cold as the two girls debated.

"Daddy said to never help a Kraut," Eileen proclaimed, but then abruptly softened, adding, "But I guess babies are innocent. They can't hurt anyone, not really. Although they're born of sin, they have not yet sinned."

To Maggie it sounded like Eileen was reciting lines she'd heard from her father, or maybe from a nun or a priest. There was, in fact, something about the girl's odd voice and waxen face that reminded her of a ventriloquist's doll, like Eileen didn't have a mind of her own yet. There wasn't much evidence that Eileen had ever been a little genius, like Kate claimed. Maggie didn't really care, because at least now she and Eileen were on the same page when it came to the baby.

"Do you think it's his child? Maybe he stole it," Eileen said, suddenly getting agitated again.

"I think it's his," Maggie replied. "I'm going to reach in and get him. Then we'll take him to the nuns. They'll know what to do."

Maggie didn't really know how to hold a baby, because she'd never had any experience, and Eileen apparently wasn't going to help her. Maggie bent forward and reached into the crate to extract the angry, soaked infant with both hands. He kept screaming as she brought him out into the cold, the wind whipping his cries away.

The baby was very small and felt incredibly light. Maggie clutched him close to her chest, even though he was soiled. The baby's eyes were shut as though he was trying to block out the world, and Maggie didn't blame him. She wondered if the infant was okay, or if he was in pain. He was cute, with chubby cheeks and little ears that stuck out, and Maggie was afraid she might drop him.

"The milk," she said to Eileen, suddenly realizing. "That's why the German wanted it so badly. Not for himself, for the baby, of course. Probably the Marmite too, because I think it has vitamins in it."

"I already figured that out," Eileen replied, but it sounded like a lie. She was still eyeing the box suspiciously, like it was going to explode. When it didn't, she looked at Maggie and said, "Here, give him to me. Let me hold him—I won't do anything bad. He reminds me of my brother Brett when he was little. I helped raise him."

Maggie awkwardly handed the tiny, crying bundle to the other girl, and Eileen took the baby in her arms, cradling him gently. Maggie was worried for an instant, but Eileen actually appeared to know what she was doing. She held the infant in her arms and began rocking him back and forth, as the howling wind blew relentlessly.

In a grating, off-key voice that startled Maggie, Eileen began to sing to the baby: *"Hush-a-bye little one, have no cares / Free from harm, and safe with me / Down in the valleys and up on the hills / The shine of the Lord is plain to see . . ."* She glanced up at Maggie and said contentedly, "He's gone calm." Then she added, "I used to sing that song to my brother. It always helps babies."

Unfortunately, any evidence of that fact seemed to be in Eileen's head. The infant was still screaming like crazy, and his face was redder than before, nearly purple. He struggled and kicked his tiny limbs against the blankets and Eileen's chest.

"Let's get back up to the school," Maggie said in dismay. "We need to give them the baby and tell them about the German. He said others were coming to look for him, and to bomb us, remember?"

"Okay," Eileen said, nodding, as she turned her attention back to the baby.

Maggie was going to ask to hold him on the way up, but then realized perhaps he was safer with Eileen after all, because she'd had a baby brother of her own. It was true that Eileen's song wasn't working, but Maggie didn't even know any songs to try. So she went back over and retrieved the milk and the other items as Eileen continued to sing and coo.

When she returned, she put her arm around Eileen's shoulders for balance, and to protect the girl and the baby from the wind. "It's time to go," she said, and Eileen didn't disagree.

Maggie guided Eileen and the infant toward the stone steps, passing the German's corpse on the way. Maggie didn't know if it was right to just leave him lying there, but she imagined the German would have wanted them to take care of his baby rather than worry about his body. The important thing now was to get the baby to the nuns, who would hopefully bring in a doctor to take good care of him.

Very slowly, Maggie and Eileen made their way up the steps. A light drizzle had begun, and Maggie felt occasional cold droplets on her forehead. Eileen had covered the baby's head with one edge of her coat so that his face was somewhat protected.

When they finally reached the top, pausing for breath, Maggie scanned the fog-covered landscape. In the distance she could see a large group of girls being led by a robed figure from one building to another. She wondered if

the nuns even realized that she and Eileen had been missing for so long. *Probably not*, she guessed.

"Let's try to find Sister Bramley," Maggie said, naming
the sole nun who seemed to be relatively sane and decent.

But Eileen frowned, holding the swaddled infant tighter.
"Not her, never. She caned me once in a history lesson.
Because I wouldn't speak."

"We just need to find someone else, then. Anyone."

"You haven't been here as long as me," Eileen said,
sounding both worried and prissy at once. "You don't know
the sisters. Sister Bramley and the others won't do right by
the baby, or by me. But there's Sister Hatton. She's taken
a liking to me, on account of I'm quiet. We can take the
baby to her. She's cloistered, and she lives up in the abbey.
She's almost ninety years old."

"Are you sure that's a good idea? A ninety-year-old
woman?"

"Trust me. The nuns here, they're mean. Sister Hatton
is different. We'll take the baby to her."

"Okay, okay." The baby had started crying and flailing
like mad, like he was about to have a seizure, and Maggie
just wanted to get him inside and safe.

Eileen paused, chewing on her lip like she was thinking. "Only . . . you shouldn't come with me when I see Sister Hatton. I should take the baby to her by myself."

This sounded strange to Maggie. "Why's that?"

"Sister Hatton won't like you. She doesn't like Londoners. She says city folk put on airs, just like Daddy tells me
too. I'll take this baby to her myself. That way you won't get
in trouble, and neither will I."

"Why would I get in trouble?" Maggie asked, even more puzzled and wary.

"Because you got food for that Nazi . . . You helped him, Maggie."

"Only because I had to!" Maggie was startled by Eileen's peculiar logic. "He had a gun. I helped him so he wouldn't shoot you, or don't you remember that part? I didn't have a choice!" Then she added, "Besides, you were the one who shot him. You killed him, Eileen. That's much worse than what I did."

"His death is another victory for England. Besides, I'll tell Sister Hatton everything. She'll understand, and she'll help us. The other nuns, they won't believe what you say. Mother Superior sure won't. She'll lock you away for being a Nazi-lover. Let me handle it, and things will be fine. I'll go to Sister Hatton like I said."

While everything Eileen was saying sounded vaguely legitimate, some element of her bright voice and demeanor didn't seem at all right to Maggie. It was as though Eileen wasn't telling the truth about something, although Maggie wasn't sure what. The thought crossed her mind that maybe Eileen was thinking about hurting the baby, or telling Sister Hatton a bunch of lies about the shooting. Yet there was no real reason for Eileen to do any of these things, and Maggie knew that Mother Superior was, indeed, totally crazy. She could imagine all too well what would happen if she got on her bad side. Still, Maggie couldn't shake the sense that Eileen was trying to outfox and manipulate her. Reluctantly, however, she handed over the milk and the other provisions.

Eileen stepped away from her, juggling the crying infant and the other goods as she stroked his forehead with her thumb, just below his knit cap. "Sister Hatton will know what to do . . ," she reiterated. She kept taking steps away from Maggie, moving backward in the direction of the school, through the bank of fog welling up from the cliff.

Maggie knew she should go after the girl, but for some reason, she didn't. Maybe it was because she was afraid of getting in trouble after all, or maybe because Eileen knew more about babies and knew the ways of the convent school too. Or maybe Maggie was still in a little bit of shock from her journey to Wales, and from the unexpected appearance and death of the German. But she just stood there as Eileen slowly walked away, cooing and talking to the baby in a gentle, tinkling voice.

What a bloody awful place this is, Maggie thought to herself. She felt a pang of longing to be back home by the hearth, knitting or reading a book while her mom listened to war reports on the wireless. Out here in Wales she felt disconnected from her own life, and from what was going on in the rest of the country. Everything was eerie and different, and worse than home in almost every possible way.

Maggie watched as Eileen got farther and farther away, finally disappearing around the edge of a building, presumably heading to the abbey and Sister Hatton. The girl's rapid exit surprised her, and she felt herself taking a step forward in Eileen's direction, as though she wanted to follow. But then she stopped, unsure of herself. She realized it was best for her to go back inside and find a nun to talk to right away. So, brushing sand off the front of her uniform, she headed through the cold, damp air toward the school.

When she got inside, she didn't have to look far to find one of the sisters. Waiting for her in the hallway, scowling through squinted eyes, was Sister Bramley. She didn't look friendly like she had before. In fact, now her expression carried great anger.

"Maggie Leigh!" she practically screamed. "I was told you nearly knocked Sister Harrison over in the hall after breakfast. What would your mother think, child? She raised you better than that. I should know, because I helped raise her. Even if you're on an errand for the Reverend Mother, you must display grace and discipline at all times, understand? That's what befits a girl of your age. Just because you're in the country doesn't mean you're in a barnyard."

"Sorry, sorry," Maggie said, wanting Sister Bramley to calm down so she could tell the nun about the Nazi and the baby. "But something terrible just happened to me and Eileen, down on the beach."

The scowl persisted. "You're not hearing me! You can't run around here scot-free. This is a place of God. We're here because of His Divinity, and God likes order and discipline. You must listen to and obey your betters, Maggie."

You're the one who's not listening! Maggie wanted to yell, but instead she took a breath and said, "Eileen and I went down to the beach this morning, and we found a German—a Nazi pilot who'd crashed, and he had—" Before

Maggie could finish the sentence, Sister Bramley's hand whipped out and struck her directly in the mouth.

Maggie was so surprised, she couldn't believe it had actually happened. She stumbled backward against one of the brick walls, pressing her hands to her lips. The shock made her face go momentarily numb, but the sensation quickly gave way to jarring pain. One of Sister Bramley's rings had connected with Maggie's bottom lip and lower teeth, and when Maggie brought her hand away from her mouth, there was blood on it. Maggie realized she was about to start crying. *Why the hell had Sister Bramley done that?*

"You weren't listening to me," Sister Bramley said, almost apologetically, her hand back at her side like it had never strayed. "You were running your mouth. I won't tolerate hysterical girls in this school, Maggie."

Maggie was still trying to fight back tears, and she felt her eyes getting damp, despite her best efforts. Her lip was throbbing and starting to feel huge. She'd never been hit like that before, not by anyone. Her mother had slapped her on more than one occasion, and Maggie's knuckles had been rapped by overzealous nuns back in London multiple times. But this was something different. This had been a punch, a real one that was totally unexpected. "I thought you were nice," Maggie finally mumbled, without really even meaning to say the words out loud. It hurt her mouth to talk, but her heart ached more.

"I'm not here to be nice," Sister Bramley said, the model of calm patience again. "I'm here to guide you and strengthen your character, as your mother wanted, and as the Lord wants too. I don't want to hear any talk of Nazis this, and Germans that. You're fantasizing things, Maggie. In Briarley the war rides in the boot, and the Lord and His servants are in the driver's seat. There are no Germans on our soil—this is Wales, not Poland. You'd do best to fix your mind on improving your manners rather than daydreaming about Nazis. Wars come and go, but eternal life is forever."

Maggie wanted to retort, *So you're as crazy as everyone else here,* but she knew better than to say anything remotely critical to Sister Bramley now. She didn't understand the nun's inexplicable rejection of historical fact: Britain was at war, and not mentioning the Germans wasn't going to change anything. It was especially bizarre given that back home at school, the nuns often discussed the war and led classes in bomb-safety drills. The aberrant nature of these Welsh nuns made them more like some sort of pagan cult than a legitimate convent.

"You need to stop running around like a chicken with its head lopped off," Sister Bramley continued. "You're so unlike your mother at your age, but I suppose that's why she sent you here, isn't it? Come along now and clean up your face. You mustn't get blood on your new uniform—we only do laundry once a fortnight here. I'll take you to the upstairs bathroom, and then we'll get you settled in a routine. I can see I'll have to keep a closer eye on you from now on . . ."

Maggie was beginning to understand why Eileen had wanted to take the baby to another nun, and could only hope that the girl was having far better luck than she was.

Massaging her aching chin, Maggie nodded. She decided not to say anything more at all to Sister Bramley, because she wasn't sure what words might precipitate an outburst. Her silence didn't seem to trouble the nun. In fact, it was the opposite. Sister Bramley chatted away happily as she led Maggie through a maze of halls and stairs to a small upstairs toilet.

"Don't take long," Sister Bramley cautioned, positioning herself outside the door. "Prayers are soon."

Maggie stepped into the small bathroom and latched the door, shaking. She looked at herself in the tiny, circular mirror above the porcelain sink and touched her swollen lip with her index finger. It was sore, but she knew she'd recover from the physical pain quickly—it was the fear and emotional hurt that would leave a deeper, more permanent mark. She kept staring at her face in the mirror. She wondered if Sister Bramley had ever hit her mom like that when she was young. Probably not, she mused, assuming her mother had been as obsessive about religion back then as she was now. *But who knows for sure?*

Maggie turned on the tap and a thin stream of freezing water trickled out. She bent over and washed her face gently in it, rubbing away the blood. As she worked, she wondered what to do about the dead German on the beach, and the baby, both of whom were now starting to seem like some sort of hallucination. She briefly entertained the idea that maybe Sister Bramley was right, and it hadn't really happened—or that maybe the German and the baby had been ghosts—but Eileen's presence verified their existence, and she knew they were all too real. As she stood back from the sink, she realized she didn't really have to do anything about the situation. Presumably Eileen would make sure the baby was taken care of by Sister Hatton, and the body on the beach would get washed away by the tide. She didn't know what would happen after that. *Maybe things will just calm down.*

Maggie heard the doorknob rattling, and Sister Bramley called out, "We haven't got all day, child!"

Maggie sighed and wiped off her face. There was no more blood now, only swelling and pain. Part of her wanted to pop Sister Bramley back, right in the jaw, but mostly she just wished she'd never come here. Maggie opened the door and stepped into the hallway.

"Much better," Sister Bramley decreed. "Let's avoid any more unpleasantness in the future, shall we?"

"Yes, Sister," Maggie muttered, avoiding her gaze.

The nun led Maggie back downstairs, all the way extolling the virtues of St. Garan's. Maggie deliberately didn't listen, but instead looked around as they walked, trying to soak everything in. The building seemed to go on forever, and she could hear the noises of girls in the distance as usual, echoing through the chambers of the vast school. She didn't know who to tell about the German and the baby now. She definitely wasn't going to risk telling any more nuns because they would either disbelieve her or punish her, or both. She hoped she'd get a chance to see Kate soon, because she'd definitely talk to her about it. She knew Kate didn't have any more respect for the nuns than she did.

Downstairs was a mob of girls, all in their blue uniforms, so that they formed a unified, monochromatic mass. Prodded by Sister Bramley, Maggie fell in with them, joining the crowd.

"Time got away from me!" Sister Bramley cried out above the hubbub of the girls. "Prayers are here already. To the chapel with you lot!" She flitted away to join two other nuns near the doorway of the school's main entrance, and Maggie was left standing there. She felt alone, despite the fact she was actually near the edge of a large crowd; she saw some girls look at her and then glance away. Maggie felt self-conscious and wondered if anyone could notice her swollen lip. She stared at the front doors just as two more nuns swung them open from outside, letting shafts of light fall into the school's massive foyer. The group of girls began to move forward and flow out of the building and down the front steps, like a human river. Caught up with the crowd, Maggie moved along with them.

She was nearly at the doors when she felt a hand tap her on the shoulder. For a moment she was afraid it was one of the nuns, but to her absolute relief, it turned out to be Kate.

"Kate, thank God," Maggie said. "I've been dying to find you."

Kate moved up closer so that she was next to Maggie, shamelessly elbowing another girl out of the way. "So, how was confession?"

Maggie whispered her response: "Bloody awful!" They reached the doors and got outside into the cold.

Kate laughed and said, "Awful sounds about right. Was

it Father Casey? He tried to put his hand up my skirt once and squeeze my thigh."

"There *was* no priest. Mother Superior heard it."

"What? How is that possible? Nuns don't hear confessions."

"They do now. She told me the Lord instructed her to do it."

The two girls were now near the back of the crowd, walking slowly under the gray sky in a procession leading to the chapel. They were both talking urgently, but softly, because Maggie didn't want anyone to hear.

"Mother Superior's as nutty as a Christmas cake," Kate chuckled. "She's gone round the bend, but I guess we knew that already, just from looking at her."

"Listen," Maggie said insistently, turning to Kate. "None of that matters anymore, not really. Something worse happened."

Kate smirked. "What could be worse than Mother Superior's face?"

"Look, I went down to the beach with Eileen, and we found a Nazi, a downed pilot." She didn't know how to explain everything without it sounding completely preposterous, so she just said, "The German had a gun, and he made me go smuggle him food, but Eileen ended up shooting him. Then we found out that the German had a baby with him—"

Kate interrupted, looking startled. "Are you joking?"

"No. I'm serious."

Kate looked like she thought she was being teased.

"You swear? On your life?"

"Please, I'm not kidding at all. I swear it, cross my heart."

Kate must have realized Maggie was telling the truth from her tone of voice, because she muttered softly, "Jesus, this sounds scary. Are you okay?"

"Kind of." They were halfway to the chapel already, so Maggie spoke quickly and quietly, telling Kate everything. "Eileen shot the Nazi, and he died. But he had his baby son with him, hidden in a crate, and somehow it survived the crash. I was going to take him to the nuns and tell them everything, but Eileen said she'd take the baby to Sister Hatton, so we wouldn't get in trouble."

"Sister Hatton?" Kate managed to ask. "Who's that?"

"Eileen said she was one of the only good nuns here, that she'd know what to do with a baby, and she'd take care of things for us."

"Oh no."

"What?"

Kate turned to her and clutched her arm. They were almost at the chapel now. "Maggie, I've never heard of a Sister Hatton at St. Garan's. I think Eileen made that name up."

Maggie was startled. "Are you sure? She said Sister Hatton was ninety years old and lived in the attic or something."

"That sounds really dodgy. I've been here two months, and I know all the nuns. I think Eileen lied to you."

"Why would she do that?"

"Because she's troubled. I told you. The bombs tangled her mind, and she's not right in the head anymore."

The group had reached the chapel and was moving inside, so Maggie and Kate went with them. Sister Bramley was standing near the door in the darkness, and the two girls had to stop talking for a moment. Maggie's thoughts were in turmoil. She knew there'd been something extremely weird about Eileen taking the baby so suddenly, and now she wished she'd gone after the girl instead of waiting around like a dupe. *What was I thinking?* Maggie wondered. *I handed off a helpless baby to a murdering, lying mental case!*

Maggie and Kate entered the depths of the familiar, candlelit chapel and found seats in the pews near the middle. The front areas were all taken up by the rich girls. Maggie turned to Kate and whispered, "Why would Eileen even want to run off with the baby? What does she need him for?" All kinds of horrific images were passing through her mind, a parade of carnage. Maybe Eileen was going to kill the baby, or had already done so—Eileen certainly hadn't seemed troubled by the fact she'd shot and killed the Nazi. Of course, there was a huge difference between killing a German soldier who'd threatened their lives and killing a helpless baby, so Maggie hoped that difference would be enough to stay Eileen's hand.

"I don't know why she did it," Kate murmured in response to Maggie's question. One of the nuns had begun playing a hymn on the organ, and the girls rose en masse.

Maggie scanned the crowds, looking for Eileen, but saw no sign of the girl anywhere. She nervously fondled the Ganesh statue in her pocket, flicking it back and forth between her fingers. *Bring me some luck here.*

Further conversation with Kate was made impossible by the fact that the organ rose in volume, and Maggie realized most of the girls had started singing along to the hymn. She mouthed the words listlessly as she continued looking for Eileen in vain. She couldn't wait until the hymn was over so she could be out of the chapel and planning her next move. *Surely Kate and I can think of something*, she told herself. *No matter what, we have to find that baby and save him from Eileen . . .*

But everything did not go according to plan, and there was no easy resolution to the disappearance of Eileen and the baby. After the hymn staggered to its conclusion, one of the nuns delivered a nearly incoherent Latin mass, to which few of the girls paid any attention, including Maggie. And when the service finally ended, Maggie and Kate found themselves back outside, being led into the school for classes. Maggie felt like the nuns were watching her, so she couldn't talk to Kate, and inside the school, they quickly got separated.

Although the two girls strategized every chance they got for the rest of the day—between classes, and during lunch and dinner in the refectory—they couldn't come up with a way to find the baby, or to tell the nuns about Eileen without getting in trouble themselves.

By day's end, Kate seemed to be giving up on the idea and accepting the deranged situation, which was something Maggie couldn't understand.

"The longer we wait, the worse things will be," Maggie said quietly but vehemently. They were back in their tight sleeping quarters, wrapped in their thin blankets. "We have to do something! What if the baby dies?"

But Kate cautioned against doing anything except biding their time and covertly trying to search for Eileen without attracting attention to themselves. "The nuns torture girls here," Kate whispered back. "I've heard stories . . . you don't want to know."

"Sure I do," Maggie pressed, trying to ignore the sounds of the other girls around them. "Tell me everything."

Kate sighed and added, "They lock girls in the basement with no food, chaining them to the wall for days at a time and lashing them on the back—sick things like that. Listen, I like food. I don't want to let some crusty old witch in a habit take my meals away, do you? And I definitely don't want to get chained or whipped." She paused. "And girls sometimes disappear from here. They do one thing wrong and then you never see them again . . ."

Maggie shuddered. She had no doubt that Mother Superior was crazy enough to enact brutal punishments. But Eileen might be even crazier. "Then what do we do? That baby needs our help."

"We wait until something happens. Trust me, Mags, eventually something will, and then we make our move. If Eileen wants to hurt the baby, we're already too late. We're stuck for now, okay?"

After that second night at St. Garan's, Maggie realized she was indeed stuck and had no choice but to drift into the uneasy rhythms of life at the convent. She knew it was cowardly of herself not to make more of an effort, but without Kate's support, she didn't really know how to take the next step. She thought about trying to tell one of the other nuns, but doubted anyone would believe her story. So she decided to watch and wait, and try to acclimatize herself to her new surroundings.

The daily routines at the school seemed to be the same: after morning mass always came class—the tedious recitation of catechisms in large, dusty rooms—and following that came chores, and a meager lunch, and then more classes. It wasn't so different from the routines back home, only slightly more chaotic and much more meaningless. The nuns who taught the overcrowded classes seemed disengaged to Maggie, like they had contempt for their students, and the chores mostly involved cleaning the convent and folding laundry downstairs.

Maggie didn't try to talk much to anyone except Kate, but she was often separated from her friend by other groups of girls, none of whom were particularly friendly. If it hadn't been for the German and the baby, she might have made more of an effort to assimilate, but she was too nervous and scared. Hanging over her head was the constant fear that her role in the death of the German, and the disappearance of Eileen and the baby, would be discovered. Keeping such a heavy secret was almost unbearable, and she felt like it isolated her from everyone but Kate. *Thank God I've got her*, Maggie thought. Without Kate, it would have been intolerable to hold the secret all to herself. *I think my heart would just explode.*

Maggie felt bad enough as it was—always having to look over her shoulder to make sure the nuns weren't going to come down on her. She just hoped that the baby was still alive, and that Eileen was okay, wherever the two of them were. But deep down she knew what had happened on the beach that day would eventually catch up with her. *I'm innocent*, Maggie told herself. *Whatever they say or do, I know I tried to do the right thing* . . . But those thoughts didn't make her feel any better.

7

Escape

It was on the morning of Maggie's fifth day at St. Garan's, as she and Kate prepared themselves to sit through another post-breakfast mass, that Maggie's worst fears finally came true.

As usual, girls were drifting in late, and taking seats on the floor because there wasn't enough room for everyone. There seemed to be an element of organized chaos to the proceedings, like everything else at the school. But today, a nun who Maggie hadn't seen before stepped up and onto the dais and stood there scowling, surrounded by the altar candles.

This was a change in the typical pattern of events, and Maggie was immediately suspicious. *Do they know something?* She glanced over at Kate, who was sitting next to her, but Kate didn't look too concerned.

"Children, children," the nun called out in a shrill Welsh brogue, which cut through the air and brought about an immediate silence. "We have a terrible crisis on our hands today. A crisis of evil!"

Instantly the silence gave way to a multitude of chattering voices, and the nun exploded in anger. "Silence in the house of God! Gossip is the devil's tongue—I'll silence you myself if need be!"

"This oughtta be good," Kate muttered to Maggie. "She's all het up about something—I hope it's not your Nazi."

Maggie could only nod mutely, feeling afraid. Part of her wanted to run from the chapel and hide. The other part wanted to stand up and call out to the nuns, and tell them what had happened. But before she had a chance to act, the nun at the altar cried out again.

"Today we will not be holding morning prayer. We face a critical threat, and the Lord needs us to help Him right away." She inhaled deeply and dramatically. "There is a traitor in our midst—someone who is working against the aims of this school, and therefore against the Lord Himself." The crowd of girls started to murmur again, and the nun waved her hands around to indicate silence. "We have evidence that someone here smuggled precious food from our kitchen to an enemy, and abetted this enemy in planning to destroy all we stand for. They have done the unthinkable and brought matters of the outside world to our safe haven."

Maggie knew right away that the nun was talking about her helping the German, and she felt like she'd entered some kind of waking nightmare. *How much do they know?* She hadn't been too subtle when she'd got the food from the kitchen. The nuns would only have to interrogate one of the Welsh cooks to figure out who was responsible, if they didn't know already. Maggie wondered if they'd got to

Eileen and found the baby. *Maybe Eileen told them a bunch of lies about me*, she thought. *Eileen doesn't really seem to have a conscience*. She slunk down lower in her seat, and Kate reached out a hand and clutched one of hers.

"I ask now," the nun continued, "that this traitor stand up and reveal herself. We already suspect the identity of the villain." The girls were buzzing all around Maggie and Kate, murmuring with a mixture of shock, anger, and crazed delight at this unexpected reprieve from a tedious prayer session. "She will be punished, but if she comes forward now and confesses, we will take her repentant actions into account." The nun stared out across the sea of girls. "Repent!" she shrieked suddenly, making some girls yelp from fright over the din. "Repent or be damned! Reveal yourself now, and you might just avoid the torments of eternal brimstone . . ."

Maggie remained perfectly still in her seat. She felt Kate looking at her and squeezing her hand for support, but she didn't want to return the glance in case it made her look suspicious. Many girls were still muttering, and Kate took advantage of the noise to whisper out of the corner of her mouth, "Stay strong, Maggie. I won't say a word."

Maggie just nodded in response; she couldn't risk talking. She hoped that the nun was just bluffing and had no idea it was her. *Please God, if they found Eileen, I hope she didn't talk, and I hope the baby's okay*. There was no way Maggie was going to stand up and reveal herself and get punished for something she'd had no choice in. So she just stared straight ahead, trying to be anonymous and blend in with the crowd.

After a momentary pause, once the noise had quietened, the nun at the altar spoke again. "So, you will not confess. Then may the Lord have mercy on your soul. I now cede judgment of this matter to the Reverend Mother . . ."

At those words, the buzzing of the girls grew instantaneously louder, and the nun stepped out of the circle of candlelight, retreating swiftly to the rear of the dais. Maggie heard a rustling sound, and a dark, robed figure began to move forward, emerging from the shadows as though it was part of the darkness itself. The figure resolved into Mother Superior, shambling hunched and hooded toward the altar, her scarred chin jutting out. The flickering candles seemed to dim for a second, as though acknowledging her presence.

"Old bag," Kate whispered in derision. Maggie flinched, because she just wanted Kate to be quiet and not draw any attention to them.

Mother Superior gazed out at the sea of girls, as though looking for a particular face. Maggie kept her eyes down at the hymnals and the stone floor. If it wasn't a bluff, she guessed it was only a matter of time before Mother Superior called her out. She knew that in this atmosphere, in this church, there would be no way for her to explain herself.

"Girls, one of you has betrayed our faith," Mother Superior began softly, almost delicately, in her raspy voice as the students strained to hear her. "This traitor has refused to show herself, which worsens her sins. Yet she will begin to understand the meaning of true justice soon enough." The Reverend Mother turned and peered back into the area of darkness located behind the altar. "Bring them out!" she hissed to some unseen cohort. "All of them!"

Maggie watched as the group of Welsh cooks from the kitchen was led slowly from the darkness by one of the nuns. *Oh God, no*, Maggie thought desperately, realizing the game was almost up. Most of the Welsh women looked somewhat befuddled to be up on the dais, while some just looked irritated. Maggie saw the woman who had helped her near the center. Several other nuns stepped up on either side of them, to shepherd the group along, as though the cooks had become prisoners.

A confused silence fell within the chapel, and Maggie could tell most of the girls were just puzzled and curious. But Maggie suspected she knew what was coming next.

"These menials have disgraced our school by assisting the traitor," Mother Superior continued, her eyes catching the candlelight and gleaming outward from her scarred face like two marbles pressed into a slab of granite. "They gave the traitor food and water so that she could help the enemy. Yet they claim they do not know the name of the traitor, and cannot adequately describe her. I think they merely need greater persuasion . . ."

Inexplicably, Mother Superior held her hand out over one of the candles. For a moment, Maggie thought she was going to burn her own flesh, but then she realized that the Reverend Mother was just holding her silver rings over the flames. She held them there for a while, with Maggie and the rest of her audience mesmerized by the peculiar scene unfolding in front of them. Mother Superior's mouth was moving as though she was praying silently to herself.

Then, without speaking, she swung her arm around and slammed her hand against the face of one of the Welsh women, right on the cheek. Heated by the flames, the rings were scorching hot, and the cook let out a squeal of pain and outrage as the rings seared her skin. Before the other cooks could react, nuns swarmed from the edges of the dais, as though all of this sadistic torture had been planned in advance. They were clutching ceremonial knives and candlesticks like weapons. "Today is the beginning of a new age at St. Garan's!" Mother Superior declared, as the cook she'd burned staggered back, clutching her face and sobbing. "These scrubbers will pay for the sins of the traitor. I will not stop until there is justice for the Lord! I will burn them all!"

Maggie was beyond terrified and tried to suppress the urge to scream. She had no idea why the cooks would defend her by not speaking. Maybe they really didn't know her name, or perhaps they hated the school and were stonewalling the nuns. Either way, Maggie had seen more than enough and knew that for once, she had to take action and stop the Reverend Mother before things got worse. She knew she was putting herself in a position to receive the same treatment, but she refused to sit back and let innocent people get attacked for something she'd done. She stood up, surprising Kate, who hissed, "Don't do it!"

But it was too late. Eyes were turning toward Maggie, both from the dais and from the other girls in the crowd. "It's me!" Maggie yelled at Mother Superior, hoping to prevent anyone else from getting hurt. "I helped the German because he had a gun, and he made me! Stop hurting them! You're crazy! It's me—I'll tell you everything!" There was a millisecond of stunned silence, during which Maggie's words hung in the air. It was just enough time for Maggie to wonder if she'd made a huge mistake.

Then Mother Superior unleashed a scream of "Traitor!" and the chapel exploded into a frenzy of noise and motion. Except for Kate, the girls surrounding Maggie scrabbled desperately to get away from her, scrambling over pews in their haste, like she had the plague. Everyone was yelling, and the nuns were moving through the crowded rows trying to get to Maggie. It was almost like they were afraid she was going to bolt, but there was nowhere for her to run in the chapel, and she knew it. She just stood there, with Kate at her side, waiting for them to reach her, her whole body cold with fear and shock.

"Evil! Evil! Cast it out!" one of the nuns was shrieking as she clawed her way toward Maggie, knocking girls out of the way in her agitation. Other nuns joined in the chant. Maggie didn't know what would happen next, but she guessed it would be terrifying, and probably painful. She grabbed at Kate's hand again, and Kate grabbed her back. "Oh bugger," Maggie whispered as the nuns closed in, blotting out the world.

Many hours later, Maggie was still waiting for the torture and punishment she'd assumed was inevitable. After the scene in the chapel, the nuns had grabbed her, Sister Bramley among them, and hustled her roughly back into the main building of the school. One of them had held her by the collar and dragged her, like she was a wayward dog, or a child having a temper tantrum. Their faces were distorted in anger, and they barely spoke to her, other than to offer epithets delivered in scornful tones.

"You're going to pay penance forever, Maggie girl," one of them hissed, as they pushed and dragged her through the halls and up the narrow stairways to the top of the school. They ended up locking her in a small, dusty attic without any windows.

Maggie hadn't cried or pleaded with the nuns for leniency, and not because she didn't want to. It was because she'd recognized in their eyes the same zealous look she'd seen so frequently in her own mom's eyes when it came to matters of faith. The isolation of the nuns and their apparent devotion to Mother Superior meant they weren't going to listen to reason. They'd made up their minds, and there was no way Maggie was going to change them.

When they'd locked her in the room, Maggie assumed that Mother Superior would visit her soon, probably with a phalanx of nuns bearing torture implements, but so far, she was still waiting. She spent her time curled up against the back wall of the room, staring in fear at the wooden door while she tried to think of a plan. None came to her traumatized mind, and she cursed her decision to turn herself in. Still, on another level, she was proud of herself for doing the right thing. She hadn't been able to act and save her aunt in the tunnel, or the baby from Eileen, but she'd been able to halt the random cruelty of the nuns, albeit briefly. *What are they going to do with me now?* she wondered. Would they ring her mom? Would she be expelled, or receive a much harsher punishment? Expulsion sounded good to her.

Eventually, just as she decided that no one was coming for her yet, and that being left alone was part of the punishment, she heard a key turn in the lock. She struggled upward, the fear surging, her back pressed against the brick wall. She had no idea who was going to come through the door, but fervently hoped it wasn't the Reverend Mother.

"Maggie?" she heard a familiar voice whisper as the door opened a crack. "You in there?"

"Kate!" Maggie half cried and half whispered with relief, as her friend opened the door and passed through the darkened doorway, holding a small oil lamp. "But how—" Kate held a finger to her lips and slipped all the way into the room, shutting the door behind her.

Maggie moved quickly across the room and hugged the girl tightly. She noticed that Kate was wearing a scarf and had dressed for the outdoors; she also held an extra overcoat under her arm. Maggie couldn't stay silent and whispered, "How'd you find me? How'd you unlock the door?"

"I've been here long enough to know where they keep the keys to almost anything," Kate whispered back. Then she pulled away from Maggie, holding up the small lantern so that the warm, yellow light cast dancing shadows across the room. "We have to be fast."

"What do you mean?"

"I'm getting you out of here. You can't stay." She handed the extra coat to Maggie.

"Thank God. These nuns are off their trolley."

"You're telling me. Look, I think I figured out where Eileen is hiding." Kate lowered the lantern as Maggie put the coat on. "Somehow the nuns found out about the German and the baby, but I don't think it was from her. Maybe his body didn't get washed away after all, or maybe there was some other evidence. Who knows, but they still haven't found Eileen or the baby, although everyone's searching. They know she's disappeared. We're going to have to rescue Eileen and then get away from this place ourselves." She paused, staring around the room. "I'm leaving too. I can't stand it here anymore, not after what I saw today. Things are only going to get much worse from now on. They know I'm your friend."

"Where will we go?"

"I don't know. Out of Wales and all the way back to England, if we can. I have a cousin outside Manchester. He's a veterinarian and lives on a farm. We could stay with him and hide out."

It sounded very scary to Maggie, and she suddenly thought of her mom. "We'll get in trouble for leaving."

"It'll be harder if we stay." Kate's voice was low and insistent. "Mother Superior has been telling everyone that you and the German pilot were having a sexual relationship—"

"What?!" Maggie was beyond shocked.

"Like you said yourself, she's insane, and because she's so paranoid, she sees evil everywhere she looks. I think she and her cabal have split from the church—they're no more Roman Catholic than the devil is. If you stay here, you'll be punished. Do you really want to spend months locked in a hole? I definitely don't, and that's where I'll be headed too after getting these keys and breaking you out. I stood with you in that chapel today, when everyone else ran. Don't let me down."

Maggie nodded, although she still didn't think that fleeing the school was a wise decision. Then, despite herself, she pictured the Reverend Mother's deformed face and fanatical eyes, and realized that maybe it was better to face Nazi bombs, her fear of the unknown, and her mother's inevitable wrath than deal with a madwoman. Besides, they still had to try to rescue the baby. "So where is Eileen?"

"Follow me and I'll show you," Kate said, heading for the doorway, her confidence inspiring Maggie. "We can get out through a back way that the servants use, or at least I think we can. And listen, if we get caught, just start running for the trees. Most of the nuns are too old to catch up."

With a flourish, Kate extinguished the lantern and slipped over to the door. She opened it and stepped over the threshold. Maggie took a deep breath and went after her. *Dear Lord, what am I doing?* She shut the door quietly behind her, and Kate locked it again. Hopefully the nuns would still believe she was trapped inside.

Maggie shadowed Kate as they walked silently and swiftly through the maze-like corridors of the school. Maggie had no idea where they were going, so she followed blindly, hoping that Kate would get them to safety. When they reached the intersection of two particularly wide corridors, Kate stopped abruptly, as did Maggie. The two girls could hear adult voices coming their way.

Kate grabbed Maggie's sleeve and pulled at her, indicating that they should head left. They moved as quickly as they could without making any noise, except for the occasional creaking of floorboards beneath their feet, and when they reached one of the many staircases, they descended it. Maggie's heart was in her mouth the whole time, because she thought that surely they'd encounter one of the nuns along the way, and get recaptured and then tortured. Every time she thought of Mother Superior burning the Welsh cook's face, she felt like she was going to throw up. She still couldn't believe that it had come to this—sneaking out of the very place that was supposed to protect her during wartime.

Maggie and Kate finally reached the ground level of the school, and came to a solid oak door. "This leads outside, to the gardens in the back," Kate whispered.

"What if it's locked?"

"Only one way to find out . . ." Kate grabbed the handle, turned it hard, and the door sprung open with a squeal of rusty hinges, letting in the darkness and the cold night air. "We made it!" Kate said, sounding triumphant and excited, like this was an adventure for her despite the gravity of the situation. Maggie wasn't as enthusiastic; she realized she was leaving with none of her possessions or clothes, or her suitcase.

"Is this really a good idea?" she whispered to Kate.

"We can always turn ourselves back in. Let's get outside first, okay?"

Maggie nodded.

The two girls moved rapidly through the doorway, both of them keeping low to the ground. The darkness of the

Welsh countryside was extreme, although it was still relatively early in the evening. Maggie kept looking around in every direction, afraid they were going to get spotted from one of the windows. She felt like a fugitive, even though she knew she hadn't done anything wrong.

"Where are we going?" she whispered, as she and Kate moved away from the school and farther into the unknown darkness.

Kate didn't stop moving, but said, "See those trees? I thought about it for a long time, and I finally realized Eileen must have gone into the forest. She's hiding out there somewhere, I just know it. I remembered that there's an empty mausoleum where girls used to go sometimes, to sneak altar wine and cigarettes, and do other things they shouldn't. That's where I think she is."

"But it's just a guess. You don't know for sure."

"I don't, but I thought about where I'd hide with a baby, and the answer finally popped into my head. The baby's probably crying, so she can't hide with him in the school anywhere. The nuns don't know that girls go into the mausoleum, because it's supposed to be a sacred place, but I'm betting Eileen knows all about it. She's smart."

"How can the nuns not know?" Maggie wanted to stay totally silent, but whispering made her feel safer, and not so alone. Besides, she had so many questions.

"It's just too sacrilegious for them to conceive of," Kate told her.

Abandoned mausoleums at night sounded frightening, but it was far better than being locked up in a room awaiting a cruel punishment. *And we can always go back if things don't work out*, Maggie thought. *Just like Kate said.*

Maggie's eyes were getting used to the darkness, so she was able to see better. Above her stretched a sky pinpricked with stars, the sliver of a moon hanging delicately in it. Ahead was the dark forest filled with old, barely visible tombstones.

"Could this get any spookier?" she muttered glumly.

Kate laughed softly and said, "We're almost there."

Finally, once they were well inside the edge of the forest, Kate stopped, crouching down in the foliage and underbrush. "Eileen!" she called out softly but insistently. "Eileen, where are you? It's me, Kate, and I've got the new girl Maggie with me. I know you're out here." There was no answer, other than the unsettling noises of a forest at night, and Maggie rubbed her arms for warmth. "Eileen, come on, you silly fat cow!" Kate snapped.

"Maybe we should be nicer about it," Maggie pointed out.

"Eileen barely ever listens to reason." Kate started moving forward with Maggie in tow. "Try to hear the baby if you can. The baby will give her away."

As Maggie moved, she felt brambles tear at her hands and legs, but she ignored their stinging barbs. It was difficult to avoid them, so she put up with them as best she could and kept heading forward. She soon found herself crouching next to Kate at one side of the cemetery, surrounded by the large gray tombstones. She wondered who was buried out here—*Was it only dead nuns from the convent?*—and she shuddered. She glanced back at the school in the distance, lights gleaming in its windows, and she wondered if the nuns had figured out that she and Kate were gone yet. *Probably not.* She guessed all hell would break loose if they knew.

"Eileen!" Kate called again. Then she turned to Maggie and pointed at a gray, bunker-like mausoleum ahead of them to the right. It was large, with jagged fallen stones around the base of it, barely visible in the shards of moonlight. "Let's go look."

"Are you sure this is safe?" Maggie asked. She didn't want to act cowardly, but the memory of Eileen killing the Nazi was suddenly fresh in her mind again. "She might be as dangerous as the nuns."

"She's not dangerous, she's just barmy. There's a big difference." Kate crawled forward purposefully, and Maggie followed in her wake, her hands and feet slipping on the wet, dirty leaves. Kate paused for a moment, and Maggie nearly ran into her.

"Hear that?" Kate whispered back, almost triumphantly. And indeed, Maggie did hear something: the unmistakable muffled cry of a baby. "Eileen's in the mausoleum, like I said," Kate continued. "I should be a detective." With a burst of energy, she scrabbled forward and up to the marble structure. Maggie reached her only a few seconds later, moving over the rocks to get to the opening of the mausoleum.

Maggie peered into its depths over Kate's shoulder and saw Eileen illuminated by a shaft of moonlight. She was clutching the baby tightly, and sitting on the marble floor, which was littered with illicit cigarette butts. The top of Eileen's uniform was lowered at a shoulder and her blouse was open, so that one of her nipples was exposed. She hadn't really developed breasts yet, Maggie noticed, but that wasn't stopping her from repeatedly mushing the baby's face against her chest, like she was trying to get it to suckle her.

Eileen looked up at Maggie and Kate with a serene gaze on her face. "I was hoping you wouldn't find me," she burbled cheerfully. "I've been here for days, camping out."

"Have you lost your bloody mind!" Kate screeched, as Maggie continued to stare in grim fascination and shock at the grotesque scene. *Kate sure wasn't kidding when she said Eileen was barmy*, Maggie thought.

"What are you doing here?" Eileen asked innocently, over the cries of the infant. "I've got everything under control."

"Pull your shirt back up! What do you think you're playing at with that baby?" Kate's tone sounded outraged; Maggie just felt queasy.

"I'm trying to feed him, of course. He's been crying an awful lot. I figure he's hungry, and thirsty too. I sneaked him more water and milk but he sicked them up. I thought he might want breast milk."

Kate lurched forward and into the mausoleum as Maggie lingered at the opening, wondering how Eileen could be so confused. "You can't feed a baby that way," Kate explained to her. "Only a mother can. Besides, you're not even old enough."

"Yes, I am," Eileen said, pushing the squalling baby's mouth harder against her naked chest. "He doesn't have anyone else but me." The baby was flailing angrily, hammering his tiny, exhausted fists against her flesh.

"You're going to suffocate him if you keep doing that," Maggie said.

Kate leaned forward menacingly over Eileen. She was much bigger than the younger girl and used her size to her advantage. "Get dressed and stop doing that right now, or I'm going to take the baby away from you, understand? And then I'm going to slap you."

"You don't have to be so mean," Eileen retorted, but Kate's attitude had the required effect and Eileen pulled the baby away from her chest, letting his head fall back precariously. "I'm only trying to do right by the child."

"You've lost your marbles, Eileen," Kate told her. "Not that you had too many of them to begin with." The baby's screams weren't muffled anymore and had become dangerously loud. Kate looked back at Maggie. "Jesus, why couldn't we have got a quiet baby? This one sounds like it's got colic or something."

"See, I told you I was helping," Eileen pointed out with a pout as she got her top back on. "He's crying 'cause he wants more milk."

"He's crying because he's cold and hungry, and you're hurting him," Kate told her.

"Look, we've got to get away from here if we're going to do it," Maggie said to Kate, worried. "Someone will hear us if they come near this cemetery." Now that they'd made it this far, she realized they had to commit to their plan. Any unnecessary delay or fooling around would mean that they'd be recaptured by the nuns.

"You're leaving?" Eileen asked. "You and Kate? I'm leaving too. Did you know that?"

"I figured as much," Maggie said, suddenly annoyed at the girl. "I know you lied to me. You made up that bollocks about Sister Hatton, and you hung me out to dry."

Eileen gazed past Kate at her. "I knew you'd be all right. The baby is what's important. Who would look after him without me?"

"Enough nonsense," Kate murmured. "Maggie, you're right. We better start moving."

But Eileen wasn't done talking. "I've named the baby already, did you know that? We've bonded, like a mother and child does. His name is Brett."

It took Maggie a moment to remember that Brett was the name of Eileen's deceased younger brother.

"Brett is six feet under with a cherry on top," Kate pointed out tactlessly. "This is someone else's baby—and he's not part of your family."

"No, he's Brett. He's come back to me in spirit. And now he's mine." Eileen spoke with an odd mixture of precociousness and immaturity that gave Maggie goose bumps, although she wasn't entirely sure why. The baby had stopped crying for a moment and was looking off into the distance blearily, like he was having trouble focusing his eyes. Maggie knew he had to be freezing and starving by now, and probably sick from continuous exposure to the elements. His cute little face was scrunched up in pain. "His name is Brett!" Eileen reiterated firmly, as though warding off a future contradiction.

"Okay, whatever floats your boat," Kate sighed, "but

we've got to hurry. Maggie and I are headed for my cousin's farm outside Manchester." She brushed back her hair. "You're going to come with us."

"I'm not going to Manchester," Eileen said.

"What are you going to do, then? Stay out here in a mausoleum for the rest of your life? That's not very healthy."

"No, I'm going to Liverpool."

"Why would you go there?" Maggie asked, thinking that they were wasting time indulging Eileen's craziness. She kept looking around, half expecting to see nuns with torches headed in their direction. "What's in Liverpool for you?"

"An address . . ." Eileen looked like she didn't want to say any more. *Maybe she's about to go mute again*, Maggie thought. The baby was crying, and even Kate was starting to look worried, like she was afraid they might be discovered soon too.

"Listen, what does it matter? Liverpool's on the way. We can drop you off there," Maggie said to Eileen, thinking quickly. "That way we can travel together for most of the journey, and help you with the baby." She couldn't bring herself to call him Brett. "But what about Samantha? Won't she be worried if you leave?"

"No," Eileen said, snuggling the infant to her chest again. "We do our own thing."

Kate was eyeing her closely, as though something had unexpectedly occurred to her. "Who do you know in Liverpool, Eileen? What address are you talking about?"

"That's my business, not yours." But she looked unsure of herself, glancing down at the cap covering the baby's head. Maggie noticed that at some point, Eileen must have turned it inside out so the swastika no longer showed. Maggie was thankful for that, at least.

"Don't make me thrash the truth out of you," Kate was threatening the girl.

"Look, we better get a move on," Maggie broke in. "We can fight later, okay? We just need to get away from the school and find someplace to hide until we gather our wits. If we argue now, we'll get caught, and then we won't get to Liverpool, or Manchester, or anywhere at all."

Kate glanced at her. "Agreed." She looked back at Eileen. "Stand up. We're leaving, and you're coming with us. Bring the baby."

"You mean *Brett*?" Eileen piped up. She stood up slowly, clutching the crying infant to her now clothed chest. Maggie wanted to take the baby away from Eileen, because she knew the girl was really unstable, but it would probably provoke a scene if she tried.

"So how do we get anywhere?" Maggie asked Kate softly. "I'm lost already."

"Follow me," Kate said. "There's a path back here that'll take us to the roadway. The cooks and scullery maids use it as a shortcut—I've seen them do it in the mornings. We can find it, get to the road, and hitch a ride."

"With who?" Maggie asked, doubting the quality of the plan. "It's so late. Won't people be suspicious? Won't they know where we've come from because of our uniforms?"

"That's why we've got to think up a good story," Kate retorted. "It's wartime. Everyone has a story during war. We can make up something good while we walk."

The baby emitted a sharp cat-like cry and made Maggie jump.

"It's going to be okay, Brett," Eileen murmured in the baby's ear. "I've got you, chickadee. You're safe."

"For now," Kate added ominously. "Let's try to keep him that way." She looked at Maggie and said, "C'mon." Then she stepped out of the mausoleum, plunging back into the cold Welsh wind. Eileen and Maggie emerged after her. Maggie knew that their plan—if it could even be called that—was woefully inadequate, but she couldn't think of anything better. She hoped that Kate had some really good ideas hidden up her sleeve, or else she knew they were probably going to get caught and returned to the convent. *And I bet our punishment will be even worse than before.* Kate seemed so confident that they'd be okay, but Maggie knew that confidence could sometimes be completely misguided.

"Are you sure you know where you're going?" she asked Kate as the three girls crunched through the leaves, accompanied by the muffled sound of the crying baby.

"Positive. But if I'm wrong, no one can say we didn't try."

"Fantastic," Maggie muttered. She wondered what Kate's mother was like and assumed she was far more permissive than her own. She was scared about what would happen when the convent told her mom that she'd run away. It would be tough for her to explain things; she guessed her mom would probably take the school's side. Still, it would be worth it as long as she never had to go back to Wales.

The girls continued walking through the forest, Maggie trying to bundle up against the cold. Eileen was next to her, holding the baby against her shoulder and patting his back. Maggie glanced up ahead, looking for the road, but suddenly stopped walking when she thought she saw something move.

"Wait!" she hissed. Kate and Eileen turned to look at her.

"What is it?" Kate asked.

"Up ahead." Maggie was still watching. "I think something's there." What she'd seen was a temporary flash of white against the dark foliage.

"It's probably just an animal," Eileen said, trying to sound dismissive but failing, because Maggie could sense the fear coming through in her voice. "If Daddy was here, he'd take it down with a round to the temple."

Kate ignored her. "Could it be a nun? Or someone else from the convent?" She was now scanning the forest in front of them too.

"I don't know. I didn't get a good enough look."

Maggie continued to watch, but she didn't see the movement come again. *Maybe it was a deer.* Maggie didn't know what sorts of animals existed in the Welsh countryside, and she didn't like the idea of coming across a surprise.

"I don't see anything," Eileen said finally. Maggie noticed that she wasn't even looking ahead anymore, but was occupied with the baby, who thankfully wasn't making noise at that moment except for some gentle cooing sounds.

"I think we're okay," Kate said, glancing at Maggie.

Maggie nodded. She knew she hadn't been imagining things, but perhaps it was nothing to worry about. There were probably all kinds of benign creatures out in the woods; in fact, it was probably safer here than in London after dark. As long as whatever Maggie had seen wasn't a nun or a Nazi, she knew they would be all right. Maggie took a step forward. "Let's just keep going."

But as soon as those words left her mouth, she saw the movement again, and this time it wasn't just a fleeting glimpse of some nebulous form in the trees. This time, it was very real. From a hundred paces ahead of them, a white figure slowly emerged from a wall of foliage. To Maggie's surprise, she realized it was a girl about her age, and the girl was clutching two beige suitcases, one in either hand.

Maggie, Kate, and Eileen were all so startled by this apparition that they stopped moving almost on cue. The girl with the luggage kept walking forward. She lifted one of the suitcases with her right hand, like she was trying to wave, but it was too heavy for her to complete the gesture. She didn't call out to them, perhaps because she didn't want to make noise and attract attention. She just kept moving forward until she was about fifteen paces away, and then she stopped and stared, with an air of impatient expectancy. She was tall, with blonde hair pulled back tightly from her dainty face, and she was wearing a St. Garan's school uniform. Maggie couldn't tell if she was also wearing lipstick and rouge, or if her lips and cheeks were just bright red from the cold. She sported a gold necklace, and a dangling bracelet on her left wrist.

Eileen had lapsed into silence, and Maggie didn't know what to say either, so it was up to Kate to speak. "What the bloody hell are you doing here?" she called out softly, but with venom in her voice. "Are you following us?"

"No!" the girl whispered loudly, looking surprised by Kate's hostility. "I mean, yes."

"I thought so. Why?"

"Because you're leaving St. Garan's, aren't you?" From the girl's plummy accent, with its round vowels and crisp intonation, Maggie could tell she was from a finer part of London than the rest of them. "Is that—" The girl broke off. She was looking at the writhing bundle in Eileen's arms. Her voice rose a little in volume and pitch as she said, "Is that a baby you've got there?"

"None of your business," Kate told the girl. "You're one of the rich slags from upstairs. I've seen you around, with your hair slides and your slippers, haven't I? You've never said one word to me, only to your friends."

"They're not friends, they're just acquaintances. My parents sent me here, like yours did. I'm no different from you," the girl insisted, standing there awkwardly, not far away, still holding her luggage. She kept eyeing Eileen and the baby, her knitted brows arranged into a questioning look that received no answer. "I need your help."

"No. You're spoiled and horrible," Kate continued. "If you're so much like us, then why do you have two suitcases, and we have nothing?"

"Poor planning on your part?" the girl unexpectedly snapped back, as though she'd finally tired of getting insulted. "Look, these are my things. I had to take them with me. I didn't want those vile nuns to get their hands on them. They're monstrous."

"Your things or the nuns?" Kate jabbed back.

The girl turned away from Kate, tilted her head in Eileen's direction, and then asked Maggie, "Whose child is that?" It was clear she was unable to keep her curiosity in check. "I've heard all kinds of stories about you and some German soldier, but nothing about a baby."

"Eileen and I found the baby with the German," Maggie replied, finally finding her own voice. "He was a pilot who was trying to defect to Britain. We think the baby is his son. The German died, so we're taking the baby with us, basically."

"Oh." The girl sounded either disbelieving or just plain confused.

"Look, why would you want to come anywhere with us?" Maggie asked the girl. "We're leaving because we have to."

"Yes, you should just stay here. Exactly," Kate added. "You girls with money have a pretty good life here."

"But I want to leave too," the girl replied. She put her two suitcases down on the forest floor and walked the rest of the way over to the group. She reached Maggie and stuck out her hand, still deliberately ignoring Kate and Eileen. "You look like the most sensible one of the lot, despite the rumors. My name's Alison Prescott. Pleasure to make your acquaintance."

Maggie took her limp hand and shook it, not knowing what else to do, and then introduced herself. She could tell that Alison wasn't much older than she was, but the girl was definitely putting on airs and trying to act like an adult.

Yet, the question remained, what was she doing out here in the woods with them?

Grudgingly, Kate and Eileen also shook Alison's pale extended hand. "So, what's the story?" Kate asked her mockingly. "Why'd you want to leave with us ragtags?"

Alison fiddled with her necklace. "I have a boyfriend. In Wrenley. We've been writing letters back and forth, in secret code like out of a book. I'm running away to be with him. His name's Robert, and he's a lieutenant, and he just got a month's leave because he injured his leg in a training routine. I'm going to be with him."

Maggie and the other girls digested this information. It wasn't what Maggie had expected.

"So why do you need us for all that?" Kate asked. "We're not your matchmaking service."

"I can't very well travel alone, can I?" Alison asked, as though the answer to Kate's question was self-evident. "It's dangerous. We're at war. I need to go along with a group. It's not a good time for a girl to be traveling on her own. I saw what was happening—" She paused. "Kate, I did follow you, and I figured out that you were going to help Maggie escape. I went and packed my stuff in advance and planned to meet you out here, on the way to the road. I knew you'd take this path."

"So our misfortune provided you with a golden opportunity. Right. Got it."

"It's not like that," Alison said to Kate, a note of pleading creeping into her voice. "I'd be too scared to do it alone. Wouldn't you? It's miles and miles to Wrenley."

Either Kate wasn't buying the story or she just wanted

to give Alison a hard time, because she said, "You want someone to carry your suitcases, no doubt. That's why you need me and Maggie."

"No, I can handle them. And I have some money on me too, that my dad sent on my birthday. Together we can make it out of here. We all hate St. Garan's and the nuns. Let that be the tie that binds us."

The baby started to cry again, and Maggie took that as a sign to intervene. There was way too much talking going on and not enough walking. "Listen, I really don't want to get caught by Mother Superior, or any of her minions either, so we need to go. Alison, we're headed all the way to Manchester, to where one of Kate's cousins lives—"

Kate cut her off brusquely. "Don't tell her that!"

"Why not?"

"She doesn't need to know. Besides, the upper classes are untrustworthy. Everyone knows that." The words reminded Maggie of what Eileen had said about the Germans. *It's no wonder the world has gone mad*, she thought, *with everyone at one another's throats*. The baby was starting to cry louder, despite Eileen's ministrations.

"Wrenley is on our way, I think," Maggie said to Kate, even though she didn't really know—she just wanted to begin their journey. "We can take Alison along. Why not?"

"Only if she pays us, and we don't have to carry any of her luggage," Kate retorted.

"Fine," Alison agreed at once. "I don't want you touching my things anyway. You might break them—or infect them with lice. And I'll pay you when we get there." She threw Eileen an imperious glance. "Can she even talk?"

Eileen looked back at her with guileless eyes, still remaining silent.

"Only when she wants to," Kate said. "Obviously she doesn't think you're worth talking to."

"Shall we?" Maggie asked pointedly, starting to move forward again. She could tell that Kate and Alison obviously loathed each other, but to her, class warfare didn't matter much here. All she cared about was putting more distance between her and the nuns. In a way, she was even glad to have another girl traveling with them. Alison was pretty stuck up, but she also seemed relatively normal, much more so than Eileen.

As Maggie began to walk, Kate and Alison finally stopped squabbling for a moment and followed suit. Soon the four of them were making good pace through the forest. Branches snapped under their feet as they moved in a cold, silent procession for many minutes. The trees here were thinner, Maggie noted, and the light of the moon penetrated their leaves, allowing them to see where they were going, albeit barely. But it also meant they'd be easier to spot if any nuns were around. Eileen was managing to keep the baby fairly quiet by holding him tightly, swaddling him. Maggie thought it was curious that the infant wasn't crying more, and she hoped there wasn't anything wrong with him. In a way, she was afraid to get too attached to him, in case he didn't make it. *Aren't babies supposed to be fragile?* Alison was making far more noise than the baby, struggling for breath as she carried her heavy suitcases along, bumping them on the ground.

"Alison's slowing us down," Kate whispered to Maggie.

The two of them were walking almost side by side, with Eileen and Alison behind them. "I think we should ditch her."

"I heard that!" Alison called out.

"You want us to get caught?" Kate rebuked her, turning around. "Why don't you just leave all your junk so you can catch up?"

Alison blurted out her answer between gasps for air: "All I have are my things . . . I don't want anyone else to have them . . . My clothes are in here . . . I want to look nice for Robert . . . He's as handsome as a picture star." She paused, straining to lift her bags up and over the swollen root of a tree. "You don't have a boyfriend, I bet . . . You wouldn't understand." Her tone was too petulant to invoke anything but mild annoyance.

"Where's Eileen's gun when you need it?" Kate muttered under her breath for Maggie's benefit.

The group finally paused for a minute to rest, Maggie and her companions looking around in all directions. There was no sign that any of the nuns had followed them, and it looked like they'd gotten away with their escape for the time being. The only problem was, there was also no trace of a road or any indication that civilization was nearby.

"Where's the road?" Maggie asked Kate.

"I don't know." Kate shivered, wrapping her scarf around the lower portion of her face. "Maybe a mile from here? It's just taking longer than I thought because it's dark, and because of the cold." She turned to glare at Alison and said, "And because of your bloody suitcases, eh?"

Maggie expected Alison to say something like "Piss off!" But Alison was now inexplicably trying to sound refined and classy, despite the circumstances, and she primly said, "You're not being very nice to me."

"I guess I'm not a nice girl," Kate sneered in response. "Shove that up your bum!"

Tired of listening to the banter, Maggie walked over to Eileen and asked, "How's the baby doing?" She was half afraid he'd get really sick, or maybe even die, while they were walking with him. *Would we even notice?* She continued to worry that they should have left him at the convent with the nuns, although there wasn't any proof he would have been safer there.

Eileen had apparently decided to start speaking again, because she said, "Brett is just fine." Maggie wondered if there was some sort of loose connection in her head, like a rusted phone line that only transmitted signals from her brain to her mouth every now and then. "He's been sleeping, I think."

"Just don't try breast-feeding him again," Kate called out.

Alison was staring at Eileen, seemingly startled that the girl had finally spoken.

"See," Kate said to Alison. "We told you she could talk."

Alison nodded. "That you did."

"Ready to get moving again?" Maggie asked the group tiredly. Kate and Eileen were, but Alison looked like she was about to cry at the prospect of carrying her suitcases any farther. Maggie thought about offering to help, but she knew it would aggravate Kate, and to be honest, she thought it was pretty foolish of Alison to insist on lugging so much stuff with her. Fortunately, it seemed like Alison was starting to come to that conclusion on her own.

"I guess if it's another mile, I'm going to have to leave some things behind," she finally admitted. She wiped her brow and Maggie saw that despite the cold air, she'd been sweating from exertion.

"Good thinking," Kate pointed out. "Stash the suitcases somewhere, and maybe there'll be a chance to send someone back for them later." Maggie knew that Kate was lying, but at least she was acting better than before. They couldn't afford to argue so much—unity was what they'd need to help them get to Wrenley, Liverpool, and to the farm outside Manchester.

At first, it seemed like Alison was acquiescing to Kate, because she laid her suitcases down flat on the ground. But then she popped one of them open, the latch making an unexpectedly loud snapping sound. The baby immediately began to cry, taking big, sobbing gulps of air.

"You woke Brett!" Eileen said, pointing out the obvious. She started rocking the baby back and forth gently, in imitation of a mother with her child.

"I have to get a few items," Alison replied as she began poring through the contents of the suitcase.

"We don't have all night!" Maggie told her. The baby's cries and the delays were making her increasingly nervous. She and Kate exchanged a glance.

"Just leave everything," Kate told Alison. "If we get caught, it'll all get taken away from you anyway."

"Hold on, hold on," Alison whispered. Maggie realized that she was taking articles of clothing and jewelry—earrings, necklaces, and several gold bracelets—out of the suitcase and stuffing them into all the pockets of her jacket. Maggie gaped. *It's like she has a whole jewelry store in there!* She'd never seen a girl her age who owned this much jewelry, costume or otherwise. Kate looked equally surprised, and more than a little envious.

Alison turned to the other suitcase and opened it, more softly this time, and extracted a large, plush object that she tucked under her arm. "Okay, now I'm ready to go," she said in a sad voice, as though it pained her to leave anything at all behind.

Kate gazed at her with a look of frank disgust, eyeing what was under Alison's arm. "A teddy bear?" Her tone indicated that she thought owning a stuffed animal was incredibly childish. "Are you serious? You're going to carry it with you like that?" Indeed, Maggie observed that Alison was tightly clutching a large brown teddy bear, with shiny plastic eyes that glinted in the moonlight.

"Everyone has something they love irrationally," Alison pointed out, as though daring the others to disagree. "My parents gave it to me. I always sleep with it no matter where I am. The bear's name is Rupert, of course."

"Look, okay, fine," Maggie said, thinking it didn't matter, as long as it meant they could get moving again. "I understand."

Eileen looked at the bear longingly, even as she pressed the baby to her chest. His cries were now much lower in volume, deadened by her clothes and her body. "That bear is bigger than Brett. Did you know that my daddy shot a bear once? He was in Africa then. I always wanted to shoot a bear and stuff it, just like Daddy did."

Alison looked horrified, but Kate said, "Better a bear than another human being."

Eileen smiled shyly as she rocked the baby. "Maybe."

Maggie and the group began walking through the woods again. The meager leaves on the skeletal branches were fluttering in the night breeze, the thin tree limbs waving like arms. Maggie was looking forward to the moment when they'd stumble onto gravel or pavement and make their way back to the real world.

She wasn't expecting that they would come across anybody else out here in the forest, not after Alison. She'd assumed that the entire landscape all around them was deserted. But after another twenty minutes of lurching along in the semidarkness, Maggie realized that they weren't completely alone. Way in the distance, she saw a pair of electric white lights that grew from hazy pinpoints into something much larger as the girls traveled closer.

Maggie and the others stopped moving, puzzled and scared, turning to one another for some kind of answer as to why lights would be on so far out in the countryside.

"I think it's a parked car," Maggie said at last.

After a beat of silence, Kate turned to her and said, "Me too. I guess we'll have to go and suss it out."

"Or not," Alison added, sounding frightened.

Eileen just clutched the mewling baby tighter.

Maggie looked directly toward the lights again, even though they hurt her eyes. Their glow was unusually bright and cast strange shadows through the trees like a second moon. They had the unusual quality of blanching all the color from everything, so the green leaves seemed black, and their faces very pale, making Maggie feel like she was in a movie. *It has to be a really large car, maybe a lorry, to have such piercing lights*, she realized.

"It's probably run off the side of the road," Kate pointed out. "Standing here won't do us any good."

"Neither will rushing forward and getting caught by someone," Alison said, her voice getting louder.

"Brett wants to sleep," Eileen snapped at her in a guttural whisper that took everyone by surprise. "Stop scaring him."

"Okay, we just need to think," Maggie said, trying to figure out what her aunt would do in the same situation, as she braced herself against the wind. "Let's put our heads together and we can figure out some sort of plan." Her words hung in the air as the girls looked at her blankly. "Just give me a second." She was starting to get a bad feeling that they were in over their heads, and had no clue what kinds of nasty things were waiting for them on the journey ahead.

8

Carnival

After much debate, Maggie and her fellow travelers agreed to go forward and find out what was producing the light. They decided to sneak around the perimeter of the brightness, try to covertly see what it was, and ascertain if there was any way to get around it. It could be a constable's vehicle sent by the nuns to capture them, Maggie knew, or it could be part of some secret military installation. Of course Maggie also held out hope, however doubtful, that it was just a normal person who could help them.

As Maggie approached, leading the pack through the trees alongside Kate, she finally saw that the illumination was indeed coming from a pair of headlamps. A massive lorry was pulled off onto a roadside strip of grass.

At least we found the road! Maggie thought to herself, suddenly realizing that this meant they were closer to freedom. As she and the others moved through the forest, keeping to one side of the lights, she saw more details of the vehicle: it was a giant transport truck, with a large canvas back and canvas sides. There were paintings on the canvas, but she couldn't make them out in the darkness. It looked, oddly, almost like the kind of truck that belonged to a performing circus or carnival, but she knew there were definitely no carnivals out here in this wasteland.

The whole scene was both surreal and creepy at once. As they moved nearer still, Maggie saw that the truck seemed to be abandoned, even though its lights were turned on.

"Any thoughts?" Kate whispered to Maggie. "Because I could really use some clever ideas right now."

"We keep moving," Maggie replied, motioning with one hand to indicate that they should cut behind the truck and intersect with the road farther down. None of the girls disagreed. Her intuition told her it was obviously too risky to go and investigate the truck. So with a final glance at the bizarre vehicle, Maggie and the others began hiking away over the rough terrain.

It was at that unfortunate moment that the baby decided to unleash his loudest squall yet. The sound pealed out into the night, and Alison let out a surprised yelp of her own.

"Christ!" Kate swore.

"Brett, Brett," Eileen was beseeching the baby, trying to calm him down as he continued to wail.

"That isn't even his name!" Kate hissed. "Maybe that's why he's mad! He's not your brother, for pete's sake, so get a grip!"

"Shut up," Maggie implored, because Kate's sudden lack of volume control wasn't helping their situation either. But it was too late: Maggie heard a noise come from within the vehicle, and she knew that someone was in there, and that he or she had heard them.

"Oh no," Alison murmured, clutching her teddy bear so tightly Maggie thought her fingernails might pierce its fuzzy skin. Maggie guessed that Alison was probably regretting coming with them right about now.

Paralyzed by inertia and fear, Maggie and the three girls crouched down in the damp foliage, looking into one another's wide eyes. She knew if they started running, the noise would give their position away. They might be able to hide in the darkness, but if the person inside had a flashlight, or was a constable, he'd be able to find and corral them pretty fast. Maggie also wasn't sure if Eileen would be able to run while clutching the baby. Most of all, she didn't want the baby to get hurt, not after all he had been through already.

"I see a man," Kate said flatly, looking past them back at the truck. Maggie tried to follow her gaze.

In the dim light, with the headlamps facing mostly away from them, it was hard to discern precisely what she was seeing. The painted canvas truck seemed to be shaking slightly, and two long things were sticking out from the back of it. It took Maggie a second to realize the two things were white legs, and that an extremely large man was wriggling his way out of the vehicle.

"Don't worry, Brett," Maggie heard Eileen whisper softly next to her. "I love you, and I'll protect you no matter what."

Maggie ignored Eileen and focused on the man, who was now pushing himself upward onto his legs. He was very tall, but it was hard to see more than that in the faint moonlight. Maggie saw him gaze in their general direction. It was clear that he couldn't see them, but it was equally clear that he knew someone was in the forest with him, and he didn't seem too happy about it.

"Who's there?" he called out in a thick Northern accent. Maggie was relieved he wasn't Welsh, because it probably meant he wasn't associated with St. Garan's.

He reached back into the truck and pulled out an electric torch, which he switched on and started shining all around him. Fortunately, the light was too dim to reach Maggie and the others where they hid in the underbrush, watching in tense silence. Maggie prayed that Eileen could keep the baby quiet, and that Kate and Alison wouldn't do anything foolish.

Unexpectedly, the man turned the flashlight on his own face, holding it outward and under his chin to show himself. His features resolved to display a soot-covered face and large eyes, beneath a balding dome. He was shirtless, wearing only a pair of trousers. "Come on out, wherever you are!" he cried. The light glinted on his teeth and Maggie saw that he was missing quite a few, while others had been replaced with gold. "Show yourself now. I don't want trouble." He sounded almost scared, a revelation that came as another relief to Maggie. *If he's scared himself, then it probably means he's not dangerous.* The man started swinging his torch around again, illuminating patches of forest close to him.

"There's four of us and one of him," Maggie whispered. "Looks harmless, maybe a gypsy."

"Is that . . . a carnival wagon?" Alison asked all of a

sudden, as the man's torch lit up the side of the vehicle momentarily, showing what looked like a poorly painted image of a tiger jumping through a burning hoop. Next to that, Maggie thought she saw a clown juggling a pair of bowling pins. Then the flash of light was gone.

"I always did like the circus," Eileen piped up, as though totally oblivious to the potential danger of their situation. "I bet Brett would enjoy it, wouldn't you, Brett?" Maggie knew that out of all of them, crazy Eileen was probably the least equipped to handle a baby, but that was how things had worked out, and it was too late now to try to change the dynamic.

Kate was sighing with relief. "Circus. I was afraid he was military. You never know these days."

Maggie wasn't so sure. "Will he help us, or should we keep walking?"

Kate didn't have an answer, and neither did anyone else. They were cold, tired, and hungry—and the baby had it worse.

"We could always call out to him, and then run away if he tries anything funny," Maggie proposed, still somewhat wary of this strange man.

Kate seemed to like the idea. "He's big, which means he's probably slow. Let's just do it before we change our minds. He can give us a ride into town, or at least help us out with provisions. If he's circus folk, then he's probably as much of an outcast in this part of Wales as we are."

"Don't they like the circus here?" Eileen asked.

"No, they don't. The nuns think it's blasphemy and sinning. Don't ask why."

"If there's any weirdness, we start running for the road, and we keep running," Maggie reiterated. The last thing she wanted was to have another drawn-out conversation here in the cold. She hadn't forgotten that the nuns could already be coming after them, to lock her back up.

"Fine. We'll go closer, and I'll yell something at him."

"What are you going to yell?" Alison asked Kate nervously.

"I'll figure something out, teddy-bear girl."

"You better hide the baby," Maggie instructed Eileen. "Put him under your jacket or something, just in case." Eileen frowned but obeyed, unbuttoning her jacket and secreting the baby inside. It made her look like she was pregnant with a writhing mass, but at least the baby was completely hidden. Maggie worried that their uniforms might give them away, but there were no other options at this point.

The man was still swinging his torch around as Maggie and the girls crept closer to him in the foliage. When they got about ten yards away, Kate motioned for all of them to pause. "Wish me luck, Maggie," she whispered. Taking a deep breath, she got up unsteadily and called out to the man standing by the truck.

"Hullo there!" Kate yelled. "You, sir! Yes, you. Do you think you could help us?"

The man spun around, holding the flashlight out in front of him like a weapon. They were now close enough—*too close*, thought Maggie—that the wide beam illuminated all of them.

The man clearly hadn't been anticipating any visitors at this hour of the night, let alone a group of four exhausted, bedraggled girls. "Blimey!" he said in surprise when he saw them crouching there like ghosts. "Where'd you lot come from?" He wiped his grease-covered hands on his dirty pants. Maggie and the girls just kept staring at him nervously, so he said, "Spit it out, lasses. What are you doing here? Where are you from?"

"London," Kate said, speaking for the group.

"Really? You're a long way from home, then," the man retorted. For some reason, he looked like he was trying not to laugh. He squinted at them. "You know that, don't you?"

"We need to get to Manchester by way of Wrenley and Liverpool," Kate continued, ignoring his question. Maggie heard some confused murmuring from Alison and Eileen behind her, but she understood what Kate was doing. If they could convince this man to drive them out of here in his lorry, then they'd be able to put enough distance between themselves and the convent that they wouldn't have to worry about the nuns anymore.

"Manchester! That's a hop of two hundred miles or so. What are you doing way out here in the country?" The man seemed to be slowly recovering from the surprise of seeing them.

Kate glanced back at Maggie quickly, as if seeking support.

"We got lost," Maggie called out into the night, standing up as Eileen and Alison shifted nervously behind her, concealing the baby. "We've been staying at my aunt and uncle's place because of the blitz. We were walking back to a friend's house after school, and we were playing a game—a stupid game—and we lost our way . . . We were supposed to meet our parents outside Manchester tonight, but we can't find our uncle—he was the one who was going to drive us all the way back there. We've been walking all day . . ."

The story didn't sound plausible at all; in fact, it sounded quite pathetic. But it was better than saying nothing. The man just kept looking at them, rubbing his jaw in apparent contemplation. "Why are you going back to Manchester? Doesn't sound safe. The war's still on, or haven't you heard?"

"My dad's sick," Kate improvised. "We have to get home right away, just for a short visit. He might not make it. That's why we need your help—"

"We're sisters," Alison suddenly added in her prim voice. "All four of us."

"Really." The man sounded extremely skeptical, like maybe he didn't believe her, and he had good reason not to. The four of them didn't look alike at all—even their accents were totally different—and Maggie was sure the man had noticed. She just hoped that Alison wouldn't say anything else and make their story even more difficult to believe. The man finally sighed. "Won't your parents be worried? They've probably called the police."

"We're real independent," Kate told him. "We're almost full grown."

"You don't half look it." The man frowned. "But what's in it for me, then?"

"What do you mean?" Maggie asked, sensing their opportunity slipping away.

"I've stopped here for the night already. I'm about to

grab a nap till sunup. I don't plan to drive to Manchester anytime soon, unless it's worth my time."

"Listen, we need to see our dad . . . before it's too late and he's dead," Kate said, trying to inject a note of pleading desperation into her voice. It sounded forced to Maggie, like a bad stage actress, but it seemed to pass muster with the man. Perhaps during war, all kinds of peculiar events became normal and even mundane to people like him.

He sighed again. "Manchester. Blimey. Your parents got money?"

Kate nodded the affirmative. "If you get us there in one piece, they do. They're rich. Our dad is a barrister."

This lie seemed to please the man very much. He pushed the greasy remnants of his hair back from his high forehead, grinning. Maggie saw that his lips were slightly swollen and pockmarked with cold sores. "I guess we can work something out." His eyes found Alison's necklace, which was glinting in the glow of his torch. "Of course, a nice down payment would sweeten the deal, if you get my drift. I've always got room for the gold and shiny."

He kept staring at Alison's necklace, but Alison didn't understand what he meant. Maggie turned back to her and said gently but firmly, "I think we have to give him something of value."

Kate added, "Your necklace, pea-brain. Cough it up."

"Oh," Alison said, surprised. She looked like she didn't want to part with her gold, but she knew she didn't have any choice. With a face that looked both resigned and distraught, she unlatched the necklace with one hand and held it outstretched, dangling it like a fishing lure in the light. The man walked forward and took it from her, putting it in the pocket of his pants in one smooth gesture. Maggie was glad he didn't know about all the other jewelry hidden in Alison's pockets.

"Real gold, right?" he asked, now standing so close to them that Maggie could smell the stink of his sweat and tobacco.

"Of course," Kate affirmed. "But we need to—"

"Mister, do you have animals in your lorry?" Eileen asked, interrupting Kate. *Not now, Eileen!* Maggie thought. *Don't draw attention to yourself!* Eileen's hands were pressed to her chest and belly, where the baby was still hidden under the folds of her jacket, hopefully out of view in the darkness. Maggie didn't know what the man would do if he saw the baby move, or if the baby started crying. That would complicate their little story for sure. Fortunately, Eileen was still standing several paces behind Maggie and Kate, so the flashlight's glow didn't reach her as fully.

The man looked confused at Eileen's strange question, until she added, "You're from the circus, aren't you? My daddy always takes me to the circus, every year."

The man suddenly laughed, shaking his head. "Circus? Cor, not anymore." He jerked his head behind him, in the direction of his truck. "I used to be, until they requisitioned me and my rig for other purposes. There's not much use for the circus right now, and I'm too long in the tooth to serve in the army. But it turns out they still had use for an old git like me. Know what's inside my lorry, girls?"

"Animals?" Eileen asked again cluelessly, but with a note of pathetic hope in her voice.

"Not likely. It's bodies I've got now. Corpses."

The words took a few seconds to sink in. "Corpses?" Maggie asked, hoping she'd misheard him.

"Aye, dead bodies. Human beings. That's what I have, a whole payload. The truck's full to choking with 'em."

Maggie felt goose bumps crawl all over her skin, like tiny burrowing insects. She wondered if the man was fooling with them, but it didn't seem that way. His face looked very serious as he elaborated.

"Cemeteries are getting hit by bombs in London. I'm on official duty—I scrape up the corpses and coffins and take them out here to Wales and rebury them in peace. I got a load from Highsmith, forty wretched souls in all, and they need new plots of land to call home. Some say the whole thing's sacrilegious, but I say let God worry about that. We can't have bodies floating down the Thames."

Maggie felt sadness, revulsion, and fear at the same time. *Of all the things to encounter late at night in the wilderness, could anything be much worse than a truckful of corpses?* She wished the man had shared this information before he'd swiped Alison's necklace.

"Ew," she heard Alison say behind her. "I'm really scared!"

The man heard her and laughed. "There's no need to fear the dead! Only the living. A dead body can't hurt you, unless it's wracked by disease."

Maggie shuddered again and thought, *Thanks for sharing that.*

"So will you take us along or what?" Kate pressed. "Time's on fire here."

The man laughed again. "Time *is* on fire. I like that." He lowered the torch and clicked it off, plunging them into the semi-blackness. "Sure. I'll take you. But your parents better make it worth my while, do you understand? The necklace is just a down payment for petrol."

"How does two hundred pounds sound?" Kate asked without missing a beat. "Is that enough money for you?"

The man cackled greedily. "Lass, I'd drive to Dublin and back again for two hundred pounds, and I hate the goddamn Irish." He turned away brusquely but gestured for them to follow. Maggie was still nervous, but the man seemed decent enough, if very strange.

"Where are we going to ride?" Alison called out hopefully. "Up front with you?"

The man turned around, and even in the dark, Maggie could see his gold-toothed grin. "Where do you think I'll put you? The only place there's space, that's where—and it's not up front."

"Oh God, no, I—" Alison began twittering, but Kate shut her down.

"Wherever you want us to ride is fine," she told the man firmly. "We're not choosy. We're not spoiled."

The idea of riding in back with the coffins terrified Maggie, of course, but at the same time, she realized it was the only possible place all four of them could fit.

"I'm not riding with any dead bodies," Alison muttered in a tearful voice, but no one was really listening to her, except maybe her teddy bear. Maggie and Kate were following the man, and Eileen was covertly checking on the blissfully silent baby underneath her jacket. Maggie prayed he hadn't been suffocated by accident.

"Please, no, please," Alison continued to whimper as the man opened up the canvas tarp at the back of the vehicle for them, providing an entryway.

"I'm no happier than you about this," Maggie told Alison, "but we don't have a choice. Just focus on Robert and tough it out."

"Watch your step," the man said to them mock-solicitously. He'd turned his torch on again and was illuminating the interior of his truck. At first, it didn't look as bad as Maggie had imagined; there were merely rows of stacked coffins, with some space near the back where she and the others could fit. Then all at once, a nasty, earthy smell assaulted her nostrils and she gagged.

The man laughed. "Smells like roses, eh? It gets better if you hold your nose."

"Whatever you say," Kate told him, brushing past Maggie to board the vehicle, like she was impatient for the journey to begin. Maggie was still trying to stifle her disgust, as well as her urge to vomit.

"There's no way I'm getting in there," Alison whined, clutching her bear for comfort. There was something about her tone that grated on Maggie's nerves, even though she understood where Alison was coming from. Or maybe it was Alison's teddy bear that annoyed her; its dead eyes and vapid grin seemed to poke fun at their bleak situation. Either way, it gave Maggie the impetus to clamber on board herself. Kate extended a hand and helped her up and inside. Maggie tried to take shallow breaths once she was in the truck, so that the smell didn't totally overwhelm her.

"Breathe through your mouth," Kate said, sounding glad that Maggie had joined her. "I've smelled worse cooking at St. Garan's."

The two girls peered back out to see that Eileen was following them too, delicately negotiating the metal step while still secretly holding the baby. Maggie wasn't sure how she was managing it all. She heard the baby make sleepy whimpering noises, but luckily, the man didn't seem to notice.

Eileen eventually got inside and sat cross-legged on the wooden floor between Maggie and Kate, pulling her jacket lower to swaddle the infant. Only Alison remained outside, hesitating, as the man continued to hold the torch, pinning her in its warm circle.

"I'm too frightened," Alison said. "I can't do this. Not with all those bodies. I can smell them from here."

Maggie wanted to coach her and say, *You've made it this far. In a couple hours we'll be home free, if you just stay calm.* Yet she knew the man was listening, and she couldn't say anything that would jeopardize their fiction. So instead, she pointedly said, "Dad might not survive much longer, Alison. We have to see him one last time. We need to stick together . . ."

Alison looked confused, like she'd forgotten their story. "What?"

"Get in the bloody truck!" Kate snapped at her. "Or I'm going to climb back out and tear that teddy bear of yours into a hundred and one pieces! And then I'll make you eat them!"

"You wouldn't!" Alison gasped.

"I sure as hell would."

Maggie heard a sudden gurgle, followed by a soft cry, and realized that the baby had finally woken up. If the man heard, things would certainly become much harder to explain. "Eileen, do something!" she whispered.

Kate heard the noise and stood up to create a distraction. "Alison, get in here, or you'll wish you never got born. After I'm done with your stuffed animal, I'll get started on your face. You won't look so pretty with your nose broken, you spoiled little tart. Stop wasting our time and start helping us!"

There was something very convincing about Kate's no-nonsense tone and her violent threats, and her attitude worked magic on Alison. Wiping away tears, Alison grabbed hold of the truck's iron railing firmly, as though she wanted to prove Kate wrong. She hauled herself up, with no help from the others, and finally managed to stagger inside with the rest of them. When she retched at the odor, Maggie couldn't help but feel bad for her. She took hold of the girl's shoulders and steered her into a sitting position next to them.

"Bon voyage, sisters," the man called out, like he was enjoying their bickering, as he headed up to the cab. They could see the flickering light of his flashlight through the painted canvas sides as he moved up front. Maggie heaved a sigh of relief, because somehow he miraculously still hadn't heard the infant.

Maggie knew they were taking a big gamble by placing their fate in the hands of a random stranger they didn't know. Yet it felt like a worthwhile risk because they needed to get away from Briarley and the convent, and this was their best chance so far. *Our only chance, in fact*, Maggie thought.

The engine started, making a deep clattering racket as it turned over, and the truck slowly began to move. A dim lightbulb hanging above their heads flickered on. Maggie tried not to think about all the corpses on board with them. It wasn't as hard as she thought it might be—it was still dark enough inside that the coffins were just shadowy boxes. Maggie was jostled into Eileen as the vehicle picked up speed, pulling onto the gravel road.

"We made it!" Kate said to Maggie, the elation evident in her voice. "That's the last of St. Garan's for us. Manchester, here I come!"

"I hope so." Maggie knew she couldn't completely relax because they were still too close to the school. She thought it was possible that the nuns had reported their absence, and the police would just flag down the truck farther along the deserted road. *I guess we'll find out soon enough.*

"Ow!" Eileen yelped, as the vehicle went over a large, noisy bump. The man was driving even faster now. It was loud and uncomfortable in the back, and Maggie's nose still hadn't gotten used to the smell of the corpses. She pulled back a small, loose flap of canvas to peer outside at the trees rushing past. Then she let the flap fall back into place because she didn't want to risk having a car from the school pass them and see that they were inside.

The baby had started crying again, and the noise was now unbelievably loud in the close confines of the lorry. Thankfully the sound of the engine and the road was even louder, so that there was no way for their driver to hear.

"How's he doing?" Kate asked Eileen, nodding at the baby. Eileen was holding his head out of her jacket, so that his red, screaming face was barely visible in the gloom. "He sure is crying a lot."

"That's what babies do," Eileen retorted. "He's wet himself too."

"He's probably hungry," Maggie pointed out, wondering how long babies could go without food and water. "I know I am." She was suddenly distracted by a loud whimpering sound, and realized it was coming from Alison. Kate heard the noise as well and looked annoyed.

"What are *you* crying about? You're worse than the baby," she told Alison. "Pull yourself together."

"I'm just scared," Alison managed to say, trying to hold back a sob, and failing. She was still holding her teddy bear tightly. "I just want to see Robert, and I don't like being around all these dead bodies."

"Oh, grow a spine," Kate said. "Or if you can't, maybe you should buy one with all your gold when you get to Wrenley."

"Hey, look, it's okay," Maggie said, trying to keep the peace. "We're all in the same position now—we've all got the same goals. If it wasn't for Alison's necklace, we probably wouldn't even be on this truck."

"Don't be too sure, and don't start taking her side," Kate snapped back. "I rescued you from that room upstairs, or have you already forgotten? Believe me, Alison's like every other upper-class swot you'll ever meet, the kind of girl who wouldn't spit on someone like you or me if we were on fire."

"I'm not like that," Alison protested. "Honest, I'm not. And how can you talk about me like I'm not even here! Just because my parents have money doesn't mean I'm a bad person. You don't know me at all." The baby was crying louder and louder, despite Eileen's attention, and Kate seemed to be getting increasingly aggravated at Alison, almost like she was suddenly looking for a fight. Maggie leaned back against the wooden edge of the caravan, listening to the sound of the gravel beneath the wheels and longing to be somewhere—anywhere—else.

"I know your type, and that's enough for me," Kate was saying in a vaguely threatening way to Alison. Maggie was just about to try to muster the energy to intervene again, but Alison spoke up instead.

"You're just so ignorant, Kate—" she began, her voice shaking with a new bout of angry tears. "You're an ignorant, low-class bully with nothing to offer the world. You're common, Kate! A common nobody!" Suddenly, Kate had had enough, and she leaned over and snatched the teddy bear out of Alison's arms.

"No!" Alison gasped, with such outrage and vehemence that even the baby was startled into silence for an instant.

Kate gripped the stuffed animal, her fingers clasped around its neck like she was strangling it. Maggie just hoped Kate wasn't going to start acting as crazy as Eileen or then they'd really be in trouble.

"Give him back!" Alison yelled.

"Be quiet," Eileen advised. "You don't need to scream. Think about Brett."

"Give Rupert back to me, or else," Alison told Kate firmly.

Maggie could see that in the dim light, Kate was smiling. "Or what? Or nothing. Look at my hands, Alison. I'm strangling Rupert. Do you see? He can't breathe. Urgh, he's choking!" She made fake choking sounds. "I'm killing him, Alison. He's almost dead!" Kate's voice was light and teasing, but her tone was deceptive, because Maggie heard real, hard malice beneath it.

"No, don't," Alison whispered, tears running down her crinkled-up face. "Don't hurt him like that."

"You can't choke a teddy bear," Eileen told Alison as she patted the squalling baby on his head. And then, as though confiding a secret: "Teddy bears aren't really alive . . ."

Maggie was pretty much revolted by the whole scene. Here they were in a caravan filled with coffins, and they were fighting and squabbling over a stuffed animal, like a group of spoiled five-year-olds, or patients from a lunatic asylum. *It's like these girls don't understand how serious our predicament really is*, Maggie thought. They should be trying to figure out how to get Alison off at Wrenley, and Eileen at Liverpool, without making their driver suspicious—given they were supposed to be sisters. "Just give the stupid bear back," she said to Kate. "I can't stand to see Alison cry anymore."

"Fine," Kate relented. She released her grip around the bear's neck. "I'll give it back, all right." But instead of holding it out to Alison, who was waiting expectantly, Kate abruptly got up onto her knees and then her feet, gripping the coffin stack behind her for balance as the truck swayed.

"What are you doing?" Alison asked.

"Giving you what you deserve."

Maggie had an awful feeling she knew exactly what Kate was about to do, but it was all happening too fast, and she felt powerless to stop it. She tried to get onto her feet and block Kate's actions, but she couldn't move quickly enough because of the erratic movements of the vehicle.

"You want your toy bear?" Kate asked, her voice now dripping with naked hatred. "Then go fetch, you ugly, spoiled bitch! Fetch like a dog!"

"Don't you dare!" screamed Alison, but before anyone could stop her, Kate lunged to the rear of the truck and tossed the stuffed animal out the back flap and onto the road.

"Rupert!" Alison cried, as she scrabbled forward across the wood floor. As she reached the edge, Kate moved back, so that Alison almost fell out of the vehicle. Instead, Alison managed to keep her balance, as she pushed back the canvas to reveal the bear tumbling head over heels down the gravel road, growing smaller and smaller as the truck sped away from it. Alison collapsed to the floor of the lorry, her head in her hands, shaking.

"Why'd you have to do that?" Maggie asked Kate, annoyed at her friend's mean actions.

"I didn't have to. I wanted to. There's a big difference."

Kate was breathing hard, a look of victory on her face. "This isn't a teddy-bear world, Maggie. This is the real world. I thought you understood that. The real world is harsh as fuck. I never got a teddy bear growing up. I never got a gold necklace. I was just lucky if my dad didn't beat me when he got home from the bookmaker's, or do worse. Alison is spoiled. I wanted to teach her a lesson for her own good, so that's what I did."

"All you did was make her have a nervous breakdown," Maggie pointed out truthfully, because now Alison was sobbing harder than before, curled up near the edge of the truck.

"She'll be okay. Maybe this'll teach her not to flaunt her wealth so much."

"She wasn't flaunting anything. This will probably just make her hate you more, and the rest of us too. Did you think about that? You shouldn't push people so far."

"Why not? It's fun."

Maggie looked around. She hated this new side to her friend, and there was no one to appeal to for a rational, impartial judgment. Eileen was dealing with the baby, and Alison was still weeping and moaning.

"You're like me," Kate continued. "That's why I helped you to begin with. I can tell that you're a kindred spirit. You and me, our families are the soul of Britain. I've got no affection for snobs like Alison. Besides, Alison has her Lieutenant Robert, at least supposedly. Who cares if she has a teddy bear? You and me, I'm betting that all we've got right now is each other."

"But we're strongest if we all stick together," Maggie

pointed out, although what Kate had said was depressingly true. "You don't have to make people feel bad about themselves."

"Maggie? Kate?" Eileen suddenly piped up, over the noises of the baby and the engine. Maggie prayed that the girl wasn't going to say something deranged, because she felt like she just couldn't take any more weirdness or hostility in one day.

"Yeah?" Kate replied warily.

"I don't know if we're going the right way."

Maggie didn't understand. "What do you mean?"

"I've got a good sense of direction. I always have, according to Daddy. I don't think we're headed to Manchester. I think we're headed back up the road, back to where we came from, in the direction of St. Garan's."

Eileen's words froze the blood in Maggie's veins. *Surely there's no way the girl can be right,* Maggie tried to tell herself.

Kate looked equally shocked. "How can you tell?"

"Just the way we're moving," Eileen said calmly. The baby had burped up thin liquid at some point, and it had run all over the front of her uniform. "Manchester is north. We're headed south." Although Eileen was mentally disturbed on some level, Maggie thought that her words now held the unmistakable ring of truth.

"Why would the man lie to us?" Maggie asked. "He wants to get two hundred pounds. He doesn't have a motive for lying."

"What if . . . What if he plans to do things to us, like hurt us or something?" Eileen asked.

"I doubt it," Maggie said, but the words sounded a little unsure even to her.

"Look, you could be wrong about this, Eileen. Why should we trust you?"

Eileen shrugged, shifting the baby from one side to the other under her jacket. "You don't have to, Kate. I'm telling the truth, though. Daddy taught me all kinds of things. Look where the moon is. I'm just saying."

Maggie scrutinized Kate and saw her own confusion and fear reflected back at her. Eileen's words had clearly unnerved Kate, because she said, "Maybe we should make the driver stop for a moment. Make sure that everything's okay."

Maggie suddenly heard a loud noise, and she spun around. "Jesus!" She'd been so distracted by what Eileen had told them, she hadn't noticed that Alison had crawled silently past her, on her hands and knees across the floor. Alison had now reached the pile of coffins, and seemed to be grappling with one of them.

"What are you doing?!" Kate asked.

For a moment, Maggie thought that Alison had gone totally insane and was trying to climb into an occupied coffin, and her stomach lurched. Then she realized that Alison was no longer crying, or looking as distraught. Instead, the girl wore a resolute look on her face as she took hold of one of the coffin's pinewood lids and shoved it backward brutally, making a loud clattering sound. The wooden lid almost rammed into Kate's head, and she leapt backward to avoid getting hit. Maggie did the same, unsure what Alison was up to, and terrified of seeing a dead body. She didn't understand why Alison—who'd been the most afraid of the coffins—was now the one who'd suddenly opened one up.

"What the hell—" Kate began, totally shocked.

"Look at this," Alison cut her off. Her voice was now calm and cold, as though she'd reached some sort of emotional catharsis after her breakdown. Tears still stained her cheeks, and she hadn't bothered to wipe them away, even though she held a silk monogrammed hanky in one hand. Maggie fought the urge to cover her eyes; she still couldn't bring herself to peer down into the coffin and see the decaying corpse she assumed was inside.

"Oh my God," she heard Kate breathe. Then there was a long silence. "How did you know?" Kate finally asked.

Maggie looked at Kate and then back at Alison, uncomprehending. The two girls were staring each other down.

"You think I'm useless, but I'm not," Alison said, her voice now quavering slightly. "Just because I loved my teddy bear, and because I like nice things, you think I'm stupid and empty inside. That's not how it is. I hear things, I listen. When Eileen said all that about going in the wrong direction, I realized why none of this felt right to me from the start." She paused, her hands on her hips. "I've seen this truck before. This man isn't just working for the army. He's also working for the nuns."

"What are you talking about?!" Maggie asked.

"Look inside the coffin," Kate muttered. "Then you'll get the picture."

Maggie slowly swiveled her eyes toward the interior of the coffin. When she saw what was in there, she gasped in surprise. Instead of a body, she saw a coffin filled with all sorts of enticing items—all the items that were currently on the list of rationed products in Britain. There was cheese, fruit, chocolate, and bottles of wine, all packed tightly between wads of crumpled-up old newspapers.

"Contraband," was all Maggie said.

"I remembered I once saw a truck like this one pulling into the convent at night," Allison said. "I was up late, sick, and Sister Gifford was taking me from my bed to the infirmary. We passed a window and I saw this lorry back then, with nuns loading bales of goods out of it. Sister Gifford told me not to look, that I was just having a fever dream. But I wasn't—it was real."

"So the nuns are corrupt, like everyone else," Kate said. "I'm guessing this bloke is a smuggler. He's probably been bringing parcels of food here for the nuns to eat, and probably hoard, while everyone else goes without."

Maggie wouldn't have believed such a thing was possible if not for the cruel treatment she'd received at the hands of Mother Superior. And the proof was right in front of her, literally staring her in the face.

"If this man works with the convent, then he probably knows where we're from." The pieces were slowly coming together in Maggie's mind, and she didn't like the picture they were forming. "I doubt he's stupid enough to believe our story."

Kate nodded slowly. "I bet he was waiting to make his delivery until it was late and everyone was asleep, just hiding out here in the forest, biding his time. Who knows if all the nuns are even in on it? Maybe it's just a few of them."

"If he knows who we are, then he's taking us back there," Maggie added. "We're just another piece of merchandise for him to smuggle in. He probably pegged us as runaways from the start."

Eileen was now standing with them, holding the baby openly in her arms.

"We have to get off this ride and make a run for it," Kate said. No one disagreed with her.

"We could go back into the forest," Alison said, "and start walking again. Maybe hide for a while."

Still holding the baby, Eileen stepped forward and reached into the coffin, extracting a chocolate bar. She stuffed it into her pocket, and then reached in and took out another piece of chocolate.

"Good idea," Kate said, diving in for an orange, as Maggie quickly did the same. "No sense thinking on an empty stomach." Soon their pockets were bulging with sweets. It was then that Eileen moved over to another coffin, still holding the baby, and with effort shoved the lid partially off.

"I think we have enough—" Maggie began, but then she stopped speaking as the overwhelming stench of decaying flesh reached her nostrils.

"Oh God!" Alison said, choking. Eileen was making gagging noises too, and trying to protect the baby from the smell. Maggie felt burning bile rise in her throat, but she forced it back down. The smell of death was strong and elemental. She didn't even have to look at that coffin to know that unlike the other one, it did indeed carry a corpse.

194

"Cover him back up," Kate instructed, pinching her nose.

"You heard what he said, the bodies might carry diseases." Eileen fumbled with the lid, the baby screaming in her arms, so Kate stepped over to help with a frustrated sigh, hauling the pinewood lid back over the body. "He should have nailed these lids down," Kate grumbled.

"I wish that hadn't just happened," Alison muttered, and Maggie silently agreed.

"Don't open any more coffins," Kate admonished Eileen.

"I was only trying to help," Eileen said, but even she looked dismayed, like the blood had been drained out of her, and Maggie knew she wasn't likely to go digging in more of those awful wooden containers anytime soon.

Trying to breathe through her mouth so she didn't have to smell the stench of the corpse, Maggie said, "How are we going to escape?"

Kate returned her gaze. "There's only one way. I doubt the man's going to stop driving until he reaches St. Garan's, if that's where he's headed. We're going to have to jump."

"What if we get hurt?" Alison asked. She sounded nervous, but no longer pathetic and whining like before. Maybe in some weird, sick way, Kate's brutality had actually helped her find a core of inner strength, Maggie thought. Or maybe her previous attitude had been some kind of act for sympathy; it was hard to tell, and Maggie was just relieved the two girls had stopped fighting.

"I don't want Brett to get hurt," Eileen said.

"Me neither. We'll all go to the back, and then whenever the lorry slows down, we'll jump," Maggie said, trying to think quickly. If the man really was taking them to the school, then there couldn't be that much time left. "I think I remember going up a bit of a hill before getting to the convent. That'll slow the lorry. We can jump then."

"Okay," Kate said quickly, shaking her head in frustration. "So the one guy who says he'll help us turns out to be working with the enemy. Can you believe it?!" She paused, as if swallowing her anger. "Alison, you in?" Maggie noticed that she'd tempered her hostile attitude toward the rich girl, as though Alison's discovery of the contraband had made her a legitimate member of the group.

"I'm in," Alison replied. "Chivvy up."

Maggie felt fear in her gut, but she told herself this was their only chance. They had to get off the truck and back into the woods if they wanted to reach civilization with their freedom, and lives, intact.

9

The Rhystone Express

When the right moment finally arrived, Maggie took a deep breath and prepared to leap from the rear of the truck with her companions, onto the dusty road. She felt the blood churning through her veins and could hear it beating fast in her ears. She pushed the canvas back and saw that the ground beneath them was rushing by very rapidly. It looked like it was going to hurt a lot to jump out of the lorry and onto the gravel, resulting in skinned knees and elbows, and maybe much worse.

"I'm ready," she said, glancing at Eileen, worried about the baby. The girl had swaddled the infant in her jacket again and pressed the bundle into her chest, protecting him as best she could. *We're probably traumatizing this child for life*, Maggie thought. *That is, if we can even keep him alive*.

"I'm ready too," Eileen said over the noise of the vehicle.

Kate looked back and forth at the girls. "Then let's do it when he slows. Count of four."

"I'm scared," Alison said, matter-of-factly.

"I've been scared since I got to Wales," Maggie confessed to her. "But once we do this, we can get back into the forest and run for it. We have to face our fear, okay?" Even as Maggie said the words, she knew she didn't fully believe them herself. She just wanted to help Alison find the necessary motivation to leap out of the moving vehicle.

"All right," Kate said, with a crooked smile, as the truck shifted gears. "It's time." Maggie knew that Kate had to be scared too, but Kate was better at masking it than everyone else, perhaps because she was the eldest. Maggie guessed that Kate was a more complicated character than she'd seemed at first. "Eileen, keep hold of that baby."

Eileen nodded.

Maggie felt Kate reach over and squeeze her hand. "We'll be fine," Kate said. "It won't hurt worse than getting beaten by a nun—and it'll be over much faster." With those faintly comforting words, Kate began the countdown, starting with the number four and moving backward. Maggie mouthed the numbers along with her friend, staring at the gravel moving past. It was disorienting, and it made her feel dizzy. She wished they'd never been gullible enough to board the lorry in the first place. *Too late now.*

"One!" Kate finally yelled, and together, the girls jumped out the back of the truck and tumbled onto the desolate road.

The impact was much harder than Maggie had expected, because she landed awkwardly and slipped. One second she'd been holding Kate's hand, and the next, she was wrenched violently away from her and skidding across the painful gravel. She had no idea how quickly the man had been driving, but it was obviously fast enough that her body still had momentum, and she tumbled down the road, the breath knocked from her lungs. Maggie was too much in shock to feel the pain of the tiny pebbles and stones shredding and tearing at her skin. Instead, she just felt the multiple impacts in a numb sort of way, registering the damage being done to her body without really feeling it.

When she finally came to a stop, she lay on her side gasping like a fish out of water, trying to force air into her lungs. For a moment, it felt like she really was drowning, and she struggled and coughed for breath. Finally she managed to take in a lungful of cold air and started to calm down. *I'm still alive*, she told herself, testing her arms and legs to see if they worked. They did, and she managed to push herself upright so that she was sitting on the gravel road. Only then did she look down at her legs and see that they were all bloody with scratches.

A more pressing problem was that she didn't see any of her three companions on the road. *Did they wimp out on me?* she thought. *Are they still in the lorry?* She could see the taillights of the truck in the distance, already part-way up the road. Fortunately, it didn't look like the driver was stopping, at least not yet. Maggie started to get to her feet, on shaky legs. She didn't want to yell for anyone in case it attracted unwanted attention, and also because her nerves were so shot, she didn't know if she could formulate actual words.

"Kate—" she finally managed to gasp, brushing dirt out of her hair and from her eyes. "Eileen?!"

She turned around, suddenly afraid that she really was all alone on this stretch of forbidding road, but then she saw Kate in the darkness, crouched down on her hands and knees.

"Kate, are you okay?" she asked, moving toward the girl.

"That was . . . painful," Kate managed to say between gritted teeth. "He was supposed to be going slower."

Maggie had the urge to laugh, out of relief that they were still alive, and out of mania and fear. She felt like she was nearing some sort of breaking point, but she knew she couldn't afford to let herself go crazy. She had to stay focused.

Kate stood all the way up, her face contorted in agony. "I hurt my sodding back," she gasped, as Maggie helped support her weight.

Maggie was starting to feel the sting and throb of her own injuries. "Just take deep breaths," she told Kate.

"Deep breaths hurt," Kate replied. She was now rubbing the small of her back with one hand, trying to massage away some of the pain. Maggie saw there were tiny lacerations peppering her face and arms. "I landed on my tailbone," she muttered. "That was *not* part of the plan!"

Just then, as Maggie was helping Kate take a tentative step forward, Eileen emerged from the darkness.

"Is the baby all right?" Maggie called urgently, worried about their precious cargo.

"Sure," Eileen said, almost cheerfully. As she got closer,

from the light of the moon Maggie could see that Eileen was remarkably unscathed. Whereas Maggie and Kate were covered in cuts and abrasions, Eileen's skin appeared almost totally unbroken. *She sure is lucky*, Maggie thought. Even more impressive was that the baby seemed fine too. He was crying in Eileen's arms, but as far as Maggie could tell, it looked like she'd managed to protect him.

"I rolled when I hit the ground," Eileen explained. "I should have told you to do the same, but I forgot. I learned it from Daddy. He's always in fights, and he just curls into a ball. Then the people's feet don't hurt his face when he gets kicked, at least that's what he says. So I did the same thing, and I think he's right, because I feel fine."

"Bully for you," Kate muttered as she swiped blood away from a cut above her right eye.

The swaddled infant unleashed a wail, and Maggie said, "You better check the baby and see if he's hurt." She couldn't believe he had survived for this long.

"Oh, he's dandy, like I knew he'd be," Eileen replied. "I protected him how I was meant to, with my body. Jumping off that lorry was no big thing."

"I'm glad you're both doing so well," Kate said, sounding a bit annoyed, "but just keep him quiet, okay? I don't want him jeopardizing our escape."

"I'll try my—"

"Wait, where's Alison?" Maggie suddenly interrupted, realizing there was still no sign of the final girl. She was afraid that perhaps Alison had fallen and got knocked unconscious, or broken her neck.

"Alison!" Kate called, looking up and down the road,

squinting to see in the darkness. The lights of the truck had long since disappeared. "Eileen, did you see where she went?"

Eileen shook her head, unexpectedly mute again, or perhaps she was just occupied with the baby, who was burbling away, stunningly oblivious to the trauma.

"Alison!" Maggie yelled, as loudly as she dared, and Kate followed suit again. When they got no response after a few tries, an ominous silence fell, broken only by the sounds of the Welsh countryside at night.

"I bet that coward didn't even jump," Kate said finally, shaking her head. "Can you believe it? What a wally. She's probably still on the truck, wetting her knickers and pining after dear old teddy."

But just as the words left Kate's mouth, Maggie heard a rustling noise from the shrubs and heather at the side of the road, under the thin canopy of trees. For a moment, her heart raced again in panic, until she heard a furious voice declare, "I did too jump!"

Alison emerged from the brush, covered in dirt and leaves, swiping at herself furiously as if trying to get clean again. "I got thrown into the bushes. I almost died!"

Kate looked surprised. "Sorry," she offered, trying to recover. "I just figured that you chickened out."

"Well, you figured wrong," Alison snapped. "I told you not to underestimate me. You're not the only girl who's hard enough to survive out here, or do difficult things. I'll do anything to get back to Robert."

"Fair enough," Kate said, wincing. Maggie could tell she was still in pain from her back, but was trying to hide it from

Alison. "So you jumped. Good on yer, like they say. Would you like a medal?"

"No, even though I did save our skins by figuring out the truth about the truck." Alison coughed, pulling leaves out of her hair. "And I still won't forgive you for what you did to Rupert."

"Maybe we'll find your bear on our way back," Kate replied. Maggie couldn't tell whether Kate was trying to appease Alison or just starting to mock her again. Either way, Alison didn't bother to respond.

"I think the truck's really gone," Maggie pointed out, trying to bring everyone's attention back to their dire situation. "We're lost, but I think we're safe."

Kate looked at her. "Maybe, but that man transports things for a living. I'll bet he noticed the weight change when we leapt off the back. He might be turning around for us right now. Or going to the convent to tell the nuns what he saw."

Maggie realized Kate could be right. "Then we need to get out of sight. We have to get off the road."

"How do we know which way to go?" Alison asked. "We don't even know how far we are from St. Garan's. If we blunder around in the dark like nutters, we might end up right back there. I *need* to get to Wrenley."

"Hell, we all need something," Kate murmured. "Let's just move to the edge of the road so we can strategize. We'll be able to hear if the truck comes back, and if it does, we'll head deeper into the woods where he won't be able to find us."

Kate's plan sounded like a good one to Maggie, so

she and the other girls walked carefully over to the gully at the edge of the road and stood there, partially concealed by the trees. They waited for a moment in near silence, shivering, watching the road for any sign of the vehicle.

"At least we've got food," Maggie said, suddenly remembering their haul from the coffin. She thought that maybe something to eat would help revive her and keep her warm. She took out a chocolate bar, which had been obliterated into tiny pieces by her leap from the truck, and popped a morsel into her mouth.

"Yeah, I'm famished," Kate said, taking the remnants of a scone out of her pocket and munching it thoughtfully as she rubbed her back again.

"My orange got smushed," Eileen said, as she pulled out a wet, pulpy thing and started sucking at its juice. Then she held a piece against the baby's lips, trying to get the juice to run inside his mouth. The baby just started crying and spitting.

Alison looked at them like they'd lost their minds. "I can't believe you're just standing here eating like a bunch of pigs, especially food that came out of a coffin."

"You don't understand," Kate explained, through a mouthful of scone. "I haven't had one piece of fresh fruit or a single vegetable in over a fortnight. You get oranges and candy every day, I bet."

"Cod-liver oil," Eileen spoke out suddenly. "That's what the nuns make us have, to fortify us. It tastes like poop. I hate it."

"That's right," Kate agreed, glancing at Maggie. "Alison

gets fresh produce, and we get cod-liver oil. Doesn't seem fair, does it?"

"It's not my fault your family's poor," Alison retorted. "Maybe they're not ambitious enough to get nice things for themselves."

Kate snorted. "Out here your money and class mean nothing. I'd put odds on Eileen getting back home safe and sound before I would on you."

Maggie ignored the ongoing argument, feeling some sanity and peace returning to her as the chocolate reached her stomach and created a sensation of warmth. She rubbed her arms and legs vigorously, accidentally making her scratches sting worse. Thankfully it wasn't colder outside, and there wasn't a wind, or it would be nearly unbearable. She knew that the cold weather in Wales often gave people chilblains, which were extremely painful swellings of the feet and hands. She was in enough pain already.

Maggie, Kate, and Eileen finished eating as Alison watched. Maggie actually felt sorry for Alison, because Kate had been riding her pretty hard again and showed few signs of letting up. But Maggie didn't feel too bad—her main goal was to get to the farm near Manchester and hopefully find help for the baby along the way, not broker the peace between a bunch of squabbling girls. Kate and Alison could feud as much as they wanted, as long as it didn't get in the way of their return to safety. And although Eileen was very odd, she seemed to be doing a good job of taking care of the baby, probably still thinking he was the spirit of her departed brother.

"We need a better plan," Maggie said finally, speaking

over Alison, who was responding to yet another of Kate's barbs. "I don't know why the driver hasn't come back for us—maybe we weren't worth the trouble. But if we stay out here too long, we're going to get exposed to the elements and run out of food, and eventually someone's going to see us. We look suspicious. I don't want to get sent back."

"Me neither," Kate agreed. "We should start walking again, on the edge of the road so no one can see. Another car will probably come along at some point and we can try our story all over again."

"And that worked so well for us the first time," Alison said sarcastically.

"You have a better idea?" Kate asked.

Alison didn't respond.

Kate spat on the side of the road, like a boy. "I didn't think so."

The baby let out a spectacularly loud squeal, and Maggie flinched. "Time to walk," she said, jamming her hands in her pockets for warmth. She took a few steps down the road, her feet crunching on the gravel, trying to lead through her actions.

"She's right," Maggie heard Kate say. "We walk or we'll get caught. It's that simple. Maggie, wait up." Maggie heard footsteps behind her and felt Kate's hand on her shoulder. Maggie turned to look at her. "Keep going," Kate encouraged. "Walking's better than standing around like a bunch of tossers."

As Maggie walked with Kate next to her, she heard Alison sigh and mutter epithets under her breath as she struggled to catch up. She glanced back and saw that

Eileen and the baby were also following a pace behind. Maggie was relieved; it felt good to be doing something proactive rather than arguing.

Maggie and her companions settled into a steady rhythm of walking as they moved as quickly and quietly as they could down the deserted road. Maggie felt exhausted; she hadn't got any rest for the last several days, and she felt like she'd fallen into some horrible nightmare. Ever since her aunt had got injured, and her mom had sprung the awful surprise of going to Wales on her, life had seemed barely tolerable. It was becoming more difficult to keep any sort of positive attitude, and she understood why Kate and Alison were being so petty and mean to each other. In general, the girls didn't talk much anymore as they walked, mainly because they were all so fatigued and frightened. For better or worse, there was no sign of any vehicles at all. The gravel path just stretched out in front of them between the trees, as though it went on forever.

Maggie noticed that the only sounds were those of their feet, and the noises of the baby. She'd never known that babies could produce such wide and disturbing arrays of sound. Sometimes the baby emitted cute little burbling chirps, as though everything was just peachy, and then at other points he shrieked and wailed so much that it hurt Maggie's ears. Eileen was trying to feed him another orange, but Maggie knew the baby needed more help than any of them could provide, or at least more rest and warmth. It would be a tragedy if the infant made it through a plane crash and a leap off a truck, only to die of neglect because none of them knew how to care for him.

Maggie thought about the German and wondered what spirit could have possessed him to put his own child's life in danger like this. *He must have been really desperate.* She still couldn't believe that Eileen had shot him, even if he was a Nazi. But on the other hand, Eileen was taking remarkably good care of his baby, so perhaps in a strange way, everything evened out. Maggie wondered if German babies were different from British ones, if there was something inside them that made them grow up and become evil. She hoped not, or else it meant they really were helping the enemy.

Maggie and the three other girls walked for nearly two hours in the miserable damp climate. Maggie's feet were aching from being confined in her school shoes. None of them had been prepared for a long journey on foot, except Alison, who was wearing a new pair of Wellington boots that kept her feet nice and dry. Maggie was thirsty, freezing, and just wanted to curl up in a patch of heather and go to sleep. She was starting to wonder how much more of this journey her body and mind could take, when Kate suddenly stopped walking.

"Listen!" she hissed, holding out her arm to bring Maggie to a halt too. Maggie stopped moving, but she'd already heard the sound herself. "Eileen, keep that baby quiet!" Kate instructed, trying to listen, but neither Eileen nor the baby paid Kate any attention. Yet the noise was still quite audible: the distant yet unmistakable sound of an approaching train.

Eileen and Alison realized what it was at the same time, a few beats behind Maggie and Kate, and Alison started babbling excitedly.

"We found the train station! We made it!" Alison said. "We got away from the nuns."

"Don't be a fool!" Kate snapped. "We couldn't have walked that far. The nearest station is miles and miles from St. Garan's."

"It's another train," Eileen said suddenly, her thin, silvery voice pealing out into the night air, surprising them.

"What do you mean, another train?" Maggie asked.

Eileen looked up at her, as she rocked the baby in her arms. "I know all about trains from Daddy. It's a hobby of his, like hunting. He memorizes their timetables. This is another train, the Rhystone Express. It's not the same one that goes from London to Carmarthen."

"You and your bloody dad," Kate muttered. "Is there anything he didn't teach you?"

Maggie was confused. "How come none of us knew about this train before?"

Eileen grinned. "This line doesn't stop here. It's express, and it only stops a few times. It goes from Rhystone to Ranmael direct. You used to have to be really posh to afford the fare. Now soldiers get to use it, so they run the trains all the time. They've got red leather seats and dining cars. I've always wanted to ride the Rhystone Express." Eileen's eyes went all misty and distant, like she was lost in a private reverie. "They serve duck à l'orange," she murmured, apropos of nothing. "And all the fancy rolls you can eat."

"Brilliant," Kate said mockingly. "Fancy rolls and roast duck will solve all our problems, I'm sure. I'll make you up a buffet."

But Maggie was listening even more closely to the train, and felt like she could hear the pounding of the engine, and the clacking of wheels on the tracks. "It's not that far away."

"But this train won't help us," Alison said glumly. She'd gone from the picture of enthusiasm to total despair in the frame of a few seconds. "If Eileen's right—"

"Which I am," Eileen interrupted as she patted the baby's back.

Alison glared at her. "If you're right, then the train doesn't even stop here, so there's no way for us to get on board, or to get help. Even if we go down to the tracks, trains will just keep passing us by. We'll be stranded like we are now!"

"Except we won't be stuck on this road anymore, like easy targets," Maggie pointed out. She liked the idea of finding the tracks, because she thought perhaps they could follow them until they reached some kind of town or settlement. *Assuming this part of Wales actually has any towns.*

The noise of the train reached them again, and Kate pointed to their left. "It's close. I say we head into the woods, before it's too late."

"Why should we do what you say?" Alison asked, sounding huffy. "Who died and made you the Queen of England?"

"Rupert did," Kate retorted, and then cackled wildly at her witticism.

Eileen shifted the baby in her arms. Maggie realized that Eileen's arms were probably sore from carrying him all this time, but she hadn't uttered a single word of complaint.

The baby smelled horrible too, and needed changing, but it didn't seem to bother Eileen. The girl looked down lovingly at the bundle in her arms. "Brett, what do you think we should do?" she asked him, sounding quite serious.

"Oh, for God's sake," Alison said, rolling her eyes. "Now she's asking the baby?"

"He probably has better ideas than you do," Kate told her.

Once again, Maggie found herself in the position of reluctant peacekeeper. "Let's go down to the tracks," she said. "It won't take long, and we can always come back up here."

Kate nodded, and Eileen murmured words of agreement: "Brett thinks that's a top idea." Outnumbered again, Alison just sighed.

Maggie and Kate led the charge through the trees and down the gentle embankment. It was difficult going at first, even though the continuing noise of the train made it easy for them to travel roughly in the right direction. The damp ground sucked at Maggie's shoes, making her feel like she was walking in quicksand, and her ankles were getting cut by brambles in the underbrush. At one point, a branch snapped back and nearly smacked Kate in the face, but Kate just kept on plowing forward, as did everyone else, even Alison.

The sounds of the train grew louder as Maggie and the girls moved through the foliage. Finally, the trees started to thin, and Maggie stumbled out the other side of the woods, into a wide clearing. About twenty yards ahead of her, a large black train trundled slowly past, creating gusts of wind that rippled Maggie's hair. She crouched to the ground, unsure what to do next and nervous about being spotted. The noise of the train was deafening, and each time the metal joiners connecting the cars clanked, they sounded like medieval knights doing battle with swords.

To Maggie, the train looked massive and imposing. Large windows, lit from within with that spooky blue light, revealed a surprisingly sparse population of passengers. Maggie didn't know if the occupants of the train could see her or not. Her companions staggered out of the forest next to her, with Alison cursing and the baby squawking.

"Jesus!" Kate yelled. "That's one impressive train . . ."

"I told you the Rhystone was a beauty," Eileen cried over the rushing noise of the engines and the screams of the baby, who'd decided to get increasingly agitated by all the noise. "I can't wait to tell Daddy that I saw it."

Maggie realized the train had to be incredibly long if it was still going past since they'd first heard it so many minutes ago. Yet it couldn't go on forever, and soon they'd be left all alone on the desolate tracks. "Why's it going so slowly?" she asked Eileen, thinking that the girl might know.

"Beats me," Eileen replied loudly. She was covering the baby's ears with her palms to protect him from the racket. "Maybe there's a coal stop ahead. Maybe it's not level ground. I'll ask Daddy about it."

"In order to do that, you have to get back to your daddy," Kate pointed out. "Which means we need to think sharp, and act sharper."

Maggie watched the train continue to move. An idea

was forming in her mind. It wasn't a pleasant idea, but the speed of the train—or rather, its lack of speed—had suggested the notion. "What if—" she began, but then stopped. She didn't know if she had the courage to actually carry through with her plan, so perhaps it wasn't worth suggesting.

"Tell me quick," Kate said.

"We could—" Maggie began again, feeling like her chest was going to burst from all the stress. "We could . . . try to get on board somehow."

"The train doesn't stop here, remember?" Alison pointed out. Eileen was silent, stroking the baby's forehead.

"I know," Maggie said, "but that doesn't mean they don't have room for four more passengers, and a baby."

Kate understood at once what she was proposing. "You mean get on it while it's moving, don't you?" Her face broke into a grin of manic excitement. "I was about to say the very same thing. Let's do it!"

"No way," Alison retorted, her skin blanching from fear. "That's too dangerous."

On the one hand, Maggie wholeheartedly agreed with Alison, but on the other, she knew it was better to take action than just wander around in the dark and cold. When morning came, unless they hid themselves well, they'd undoubtedly get discovered. She stared at the train, trying to gauge whether they could make it. For whatever reason, it seemed to be moving even more leisurely than before. *Maybe it's a sign*, she mused. *Something's finally going our way at last.* "I think we should do it," Maggie said, speaking before raw terror could silence her.

"Me too," Kate agreed at once. "But not this train—it's almost gone. The next one. We hide here and wait until then."

"Will there be a next one?" Maggie asked.

Eileen nodded. "They're running the Express every two hours, because of the soldiers. We can get the next one, like Kate said. It's probably the eleven fifteen."

Thank God Eileen knows so much about train schedules, Maggie thought. Lunatic or not, she was definitely quite helpful.

"I refuse to jump on a moving train," Alison said steadfastly.

"Fine, you're a coward, so that's no problem—stay here and look after yourself."

"I'm not just thinking about me!" Alison yelled at Kate. "I'm thinking about the baby too, for God's sake. He could get killed if we try to get on that train. All of us could."

"And what will those nuns do to us? Read us a bedtime story and put us down for a nap? It's war. We could die any moment from a German bomb anyway. Death is always just one breath away."

"I want to go," Eileen spoke up. "Brett's going to be fine. I just know it. He's never leaving me again, not like the first Brett. I'll see to that. Brett and I will be together for all eternity."

The train finally passed them by, churning and hissing and clattering its way along the tracks like a living animal, receding into the distance.

"We're going to do it," Kate told Alison pointedly in the silence. "With or without you. Hopefully without." She sank down in the brush. "We can run alongside the train and jump up between the cars. They won't even know we got on board if we do it right."

Maggie stared out at the barren tracks. *Will I really be able to do that when the time comes?* she wondered. She guessed she would soon find out.

The two hours passed remarkably quickly, with much of the time spent in silence. Eileen was busy with the baby, Alison was sulking, and even Kate seemed too tired to talk very much. They were all well hidden in the brush, and Maggie wasn't as worried about being discovered by the nuns, or the lorry driver, anymore. *I think our plan's going to work*, she told herself, trying to build up her confidence. *As long as we actually have the strength and courage to go through with it.*

Eventually she heard the rumble of another train coming down the tracks from a distance, and gazed wildly at the other girls. "I think it's here," she said. The girls all listened as the sound grew louder with each passing moment. Soon the train emerged from the darkness, looking exactly like the first one.

"There's no more time to think!" Kate said, lurching forward. "Only time to run. Come with us if you want, Alison. If not, good riddance!"

Maggie rose up too, with Eileen right next to her. There was no need for a count of four this time, only need for mindless, sudden action. Maggie found herself hurtling away from the forest edge, across the flat terrain and toward the train, along with Kate and Eileen. She wasn't sure if Alison was coming with them, but there wasn't time to worry about her now.

It only took a few seconds for Maggie and the others to reach the tracks, and they began running along parallel to them. The train seemed impossibly huge now, the metal wheels as large as Maggie's entire body, and she realized that if she slipped and fell in her attempt to get on board, she'd easily get sucked underneath and eviscerated by them.

Maggie tried to keep her panic at bay. *If I run fast enough, I can grab on to the side of the train where the cars are coupled together*, she told herself. The train was going slowly, and she saw metal handles there designed for the porters to use. She thought that if she could get hold of one as she ran, she could haul herself onto the shaky metal platform between the two cars. It was risky, but she guessed she could make it, and then try to help the others on board.

Maggie's heart hammered as she raced forward and managed to get her left hand up against the side of the train. The metal surface was freezing cold, and it startled her, because she thought it would be hot. She kept her hand against it as she ran. She could hear and feel Kate right on her heels, but she didn't have a chance to look back to see if Eileen and Alison were running too.

I'm going to make it, she told herself. *I'm not going back to those crazy nuns, not ever!* With a massive surge of energy she clasped onto the metal handle with both hands and pulled herself upward, her muscles straining. For a sickening moment she thought she might not have enough strength in her body, and that she was going to fall backward. But then her right foot managed to find purchase on part of the train's carapace, and she lunged forward onto the corrugated metal sheet between the cars, banging her head and elbows in the process. She was on the train.

Dazed, Maggie swung around as rapidly as she could, and poked her head out to see where the others were, the wind making her eyes sting. As she blinked away the dirt and dust, she saw that to her surprise, Kate wasn't right behind her like she'd thought; instead, Eileen was there, holding the squalling baby tightly under one arm like a smoked ham. She hadn't thought Eileen could move so quickly, because the girl's legs were short and stubby, but clearly her size was deceptive. Surprisingly, Kate and Alison were lingering several steps behind. They seemed to be screaming at each other, wasting their breath on yet another meaningless, irrational argument.

"Help me, Maggie!" Eileen gasped, her legs pumping up and down like pistons. "I'm almost there!"

Maggie brought herself into a kneeling position, first making sure her balance was stabilized because she felt so precarious. Then she reached out both hands and grabbed hold of the shoulders of Eileen's jacket. It occurred to her that Eileen might drop the baby accidentally, and that the smartest thing was to have Eileen hand her the infant first. But Maggie knew that Eileen would never let go of her prized possession, which meant the only option was to help Eileen on board and hope that the baby would be okay. He'd been through so much already that

Maggie knew he was tough, perhaps tougher than all of them put together.

"Push up with your feet!" Maggie yelled at Eileen over the unearthly din, afraid their lives could end at any point. "Come on!"

"I'm trying!"

"Try harder!" Maggie grabbed at Eileen's coat again and with all the strength she could muster, she pulled the girl up and onto the sheet of metal. Maggie collapsed backward and Eileen sprawled on top of her, still holding the baby.

"I knew I could do it," Eileen cried, flailing to keep her equilibrium on the rickety platform. She glanced down at the screaming bundle under her arm and screeched, "I did it for you, Brett!"

Relieved that Eileen and the baby seemed to be all right, Maggie extracted herself from underneath the girl and peered back out, ready to help Kate and Alison on board next. But to her horror, the girls were much farther back than she'd imagined possible. For a moment, she didn't understand why, until she realized that the train seemed to be picking up speed again, and that Kate's injured back was slowing her down.

"Kate!" she screamed. "Alison! You have to run faster! You're going to get left behind . . ."

She saw Kate trying to grab on to the train at the end of the next car, but her hands kept slipping, and she had to back away so she didn't fall under the carriage and get crushed. Alison was having even worse luck, several paces behind.

"Run!" Maggie screamed.

Kate looked up and saw Maggie's head sticking out, and she yelled something at her, but Maggie couldn't hear the words.

The train moved faster and faster, the noise of the wheels intensifying. Maggie realized that Kate and Alison were going to get stranded on the tracks. She was about to call out some more words of encouragement, although her heart knew they'd be useless, but then she saw Kate finally give up and stop running. The girl veered away from the train, flinging her arms in the air out of despair, and screaming violent curses.

"No!" Maggie cried. "Don't quit!" But it was too late. Kate and Alison were already receding into the distance. Maggie saw Alison catch up to Kate and tumble into her, clutching at her chest. The two girls fell to the ground, and to Maggie's surprise, it suddenly looked like Kate was attacking Alison, pummeling her with clenched fists. In the final instant that the scene was still visible, Maggie saw Kate climb to her feet and start kicking Alison violently, seemingly out of frustration and anger. It made Maggie feel sick.

"Those two, they're bonkers," Eileen yelled into Maggie's ear, as though she herself hadn't shot and killed a man. "Daddy always said it was hard to find a girl with a good head on her shoulders, like me and Mum. I think he was right."

"Just belt up, okay?" Maggie said, too tired, scared, and depressed to bear any more babbling from Eileen. "It's just us now. We have to be careful and low-key, or we're going to get discovered and tossed off this train. Hopefully no one heard us already." She pulled her head back and got to her feet, helping Eileen up. *I can't believe Kate and Alison are really gone*, she thought. *What are we going to do now?* In a matter of minutes, their group had been cut in half. Maggie felt like Kate had been ripped away from her, and she had no clue how to deal with Eileen and the baby by herself.

Maggie grabbed on to the door that led to one of the train's passenger cars. "We need to get inside this carriage. If it's almost empty, we'll find vacant seats and sit there. The conductor's probably passed through already—we'll be safe, understand? If this car is full, then we'll have to keep walking through it until we find an empty one." Her tone was firm.

"Sure." Eileen was letting the baby clutch at her fingers, barely listening.

"We have to pretend that we're sisters, traveling with our mum. If anyone asks, she's somewhere on the train. We can't let anyone know we're on our own, or they'll get suspicious because of the baby."

Eileen nodded. "Brett is our brother. That's what we'll say."

"Exactly. But the less *you* say, the better. Let me do the talking." Maggie pushed down on the latch, and forced the door open with a loud, hissing sound. She stepped into the back of the car, trailed by Eileen with the baby. She knew this train would either be their salvation, or bring a quick, unpleasant end to their journey.

10

Runaways

Maggie and Eileen paused in the open doorway of the train car. Without the other two girls, the journey seemed much more frightening to Maggie, and she felt very alone. She'd been certain they were all going to reach freedom together, but now she wasn't sure of anything, and didn't know if she'd get to see Kate or Alison ever again. She didn't even really know where this train was going, although she supposed she could rely on Eileen for information. But without Kate, Maggie no longer had any clear destination. *We're really, truly lost.*

"The Rhystone Express," Eileen breathed, and Maggie could hear the naked excitement in her voice as the girl looked around. It was like Eileen didn't understand the severity of their predicament. "It's even plusher than I imagined."

"Better than that, it's empty," Maggie whispered back as she shut the door behind them. She smoothed down her hair and wiped her face, trying to look presentable instead of dirty, grubby, and scared. Indeed, the train was nearly deserted, except for a handful of passengers, all facing forward, away from them. None paid Maggie or Eileen any mind. Maggie hoped they would all assume the girls had wandered in from another car and were merely switching their seats. She was still afraid their school uniforms might give them away, but guessed that no one would notice and put it all together.

Maggie guided Eileen to a seat by the window in the middle of the car and then sat down next to her and the baby. In the blue light, she saw their ghostly reflections floating in the pane of glass. It was hard to believe that she'd been on a train similar to this one just a few days ago. So many things had changed since then, and she felt like a different person. The baby was quiet as Eileen cooed and clucked at it like a chicken. Maggie kept looking around nervously, afraid that a constable would burst in at any moment and arrest them.

Maggie checked out the other passengers. There was an old couple near the back, and a young man up front, slouched in his aisle seat, seemingly asleep. He sported the tatty overcoat of a tramp, and unkempt hair, and he kept one leg stretched out in front of him as though it was injured. Maggie didn't want to stare at him too much, in case he sensed it and turned back to look at her, so she scrunched down in her seat. She felt so sad about Kate and Alison. *Where are we going, and what are we going to do when we get there?* She didn't even know when the train would stop or where they should get off.

She and Eileen sat there for a long time, over an hour and a half, as the train hurtled along its northern journey up the coast of Wales. She knew that now they were quite far from the school, although she'd never feel far enough from that place. She wondered what life would have been like there if the German had never shown up. Perhaps it would have been tolerable, but probably not. She also worried obsessively about Kate and Alison, and what would happen to the two of them now. Would they get captured? Would they board the next train? Or would they head back to St. Garan's in defeat? Maggie couldn't imagine Kate giving up too easily. She didn't even know if Kate and Alison would manage to stick together, given how much Kate seemed to hate the upper class girl.

Eileen talked to the baby as Maggie sat in her seat, trying to recover her senses and calm herself so that she could think up a decent plan. Occasionally, she leaned over Eileen and cupped her hands to the window, trying to see past the reflections and out into the darkness, but there was nothing but black.

Maggie was just starting to let herself relax a little when suddenly it felt like the train was slowing again. At first, she thought it was like before, just a momentary lessening of speed, but the train began to slow so much that Maggie realized it was preparing to stop.

"Are we at a station?" she asked Eileen anxiously.

The girl just looked at her. "I told you, there aren't any stations out here. Not yet."

Maggie craned forward to look through the window again, but she saw no signs of life. She felt incredibly uneasy about their situation; she couldn't think of any reason why the train would come to a full stop way out here. She prayed it wasn't because the police had somehow found out that she and Eileen had sneaked on board. *Did Kate or Alison snitch on us?* It didn't seem possible, but what if the nuns had found them already and tortured them? Maggie tried to put the thought out of her mind. She also hoped that the slowdown wasn't due to some sort of engine trouble. If the train broke down, they'd probably have to spend the rest of the night in the cold, barren countryside. And the longer they were out here, the greater their chances of getting caught.

Maggie kept her hands pressed to the glass, scanning the landscape as the train came to a halt. To her surprise, she thought she saw a flicker of light outside off to the right, like a flashlight or an oil lamp. She tracked it with her eyes and realized it was steadily approaching the train.

Eileen saw it too and whispered, "What's that?" But before Maggie could make out what, or who, it was, the door to their car opened with a clank.

"Bloody hell," she heard the old woman behind them mutter, in a very unladylike way, as her husband tried to calm her.

Maggie then heard footsteps shuffling around just outside the door, and she became filled with true fear. *They've found us!* she thought. "We're with our mum," she hissed at Eileen, afraid that the girl would give them away. "Remember that. Don't do anything weird. Just hold the baby."

For once Eileen looked frightened too. *Maybe she realizes if we get discovered, "Brett" will get taken away from her.*

When the footsteps stopped, it was the conductor's face

that poked through the doorway at the front of the car. He must be moving down the length of the train, she thought. He scanned the car, his eyes grazing Maggie and Eileen, and he cried, "All out! All out!" For a second, she thought that surely the conductor had to know about them, but his eyes moved onward like he was seeking something—or someone—else.

Keeping their heads down, Maggie and Eileen shuffled to the open door with the baby. The old couple was following them, muttering under their breath. Only the young man at the front of the car didn't move. As Maggie passed him, she saw that his skin was very white and his eyes were glassy. She looked away, not even wanting to know what was wrong with him, because she and Eileen had enough troubles of their own.

Maggie stepped down precariously onto the metal steps, helping Eileen with the baby, and then onto the sand and gravel that lined this section of the track. To either side of them were little clumps of fellow dislodged travelers, all standing puzzled in the cold of the night. Some were wearing nightgowns and rubbing their eyes from sleep. Maggie had once been envious of these passengers from the Pullman cars, which had compartments with beds. She'd once thought there was something exotic and vaguely romantic about sleeping on a train. Now, after all that had happened, and the loss of Kate and Alison, she never wanted to see a train again.

Maggie looked out into the darkness that lay in all directions, omnipresent and smothering. The train had stirred up whorls of dust near the edge of the tracks, and the particles were backlit by the blue light streaming from the train's windows, so it looked like the air was full of tiny shimmering sprites. The cold night breeze and the heat from the train caused them to dance and sparkle in the air, like miniature stars. Maggie stood among them with Eileen and the baby, feeling very small, as she watched the dust clouds rise toward the heavens.

"If they come after us, do we run?" Eileen whispered over the sound of the train and the baby.

Maggie nodded, although she felt so tired that even the thought of running made her want to collapse on the ground and wail from exhaustion. "It depends how many there are. Don't do anything yet."

"What's going on 'ere?" she heard a heavy man from the next car querulously ask a woman, presumably his daughter. The woman's reply was too soft for Maggie to hear. "I'm not making a scene!" the man ranted drunkenly, as his daughter tried to quiet him down. Maggie was glad he was yelling, because that meant he'd distract attention from her and Eileen.

Maggie looked up and saw a cadre of uniformed men approaching with flashlights from the darkness. She looked around in her confusion, but noticed that no one else knew what was happening either.

"They're here for us!" Eileen yelped. "The coppers! They're going to steal Brett . . ."

"We don't know that yet," Maggie said, although she felt like she was going to throw up. "Stay calm." She longed for those times when Eileen went mute.

Behind the men, she saw and heard a military jeep

emerge from the darkness, its tires nearly skidding on the grass and gravel as it traversed its way toward the train tracks. Behind that jeep was another one. Maggie felt the crushing weight of defeat. *Looks like we're done for,* she thought numbly. *It's back to St. Garan's and the nuns for sure.*

One of the men finally came into view, stepping into the light from the train's windows. He was in full dress as an army captain, the royal insignia visible on his starched sleeve.

The train conductor, and someone who appeared to be his assistant, rushed away from the train and up to the captain, as other military men congregated behind them.

"We should run now, while we still can," Eileen whispered.

Maggie felt like her spirit was close to being broken. "We won't get far. And if we start running, they'll know for sure."

"But—" Eileen broke off, looking around desperately. "I think they already know."

Maggie tried to listen to what the conductor and the captain were saying, but she only caught scattered phrases. "Yes, he's on board," she heard the captain say in a clipped Northern accent. *Are they talking about the baby?* Maggie wondered. The captain sounded serious, no-nonsense, how Maggie would expect someone dressed like that to sound. The conductor was nodding and gesticulating wildly, like he wanted to both impress and please the captain.

Maggie didn't know why it suddenly occurred to her, but for some reason she thought to look back at the train, through the very window of the car that she and Eileen had been riding in. The car was empty, save for the young man who still held his seat, staring out into the darkness with ferociously blank eyes. She didn't know why he hadn't disembarked with everyone else.

"Maybe they're not here for us," Maggie murmured to herself, feeling a sudden jolt of hope. "Maybe something else is going on."

When Maggie looked back at Eileen, she was startled to see that the captain and his men were only a few feet away from her and her companion. The captain peered down at the two of them, and the wriggling baby in Eileen's arms. With his thin nose and thinner lips, the captain looked as severe as a cruel priest. "Names?" he demanded.

"Sarah Jones," Maggie lied in response, trying to think quickly as her eyes shied away from the man's questioning gaze.

"Eileen Jones," Eileen managed, at least remembering to lie about her last name. But her eyes moved back and forth shiftily, like she was about to confess her guilt.

The captain noticed her nervousness, and he glanced down at the baby in her arms, his face twisting into a sneer.

"We're sisters traveling with our mum," Maggie blurted out. "She's right over there." She pointed nebulously at the thin crowd. For a moment, Maggie thought the man would see through their ruse, but he obviously had other things on his mind. He brushed past them without a word, followed by his companions. They strode up the metal steps and into the body of the train, heading toward the young man sitting in the seat. Maggie watched through the window, wondering what was going on. *It doesn't look like they're chasing me and Eileen after all*, she thought. Indeed, they were calling out to the man in the train as they walked down the aisle in his direction, but he still seemed to be in a daze.

"I think we're going to be okay," Maggie said softly to Eileen. "They're not here because of us. They're after someone else—whoever that man is, I guess. We're fine." She was just letting her anxious, tense muscles loosen for a moment when everything changed in a blur of motion and noise.

The young man exploded up and out of his seat, screaming in a high-pitched voice of terror and rage that carried through the open door of the train and into the outside air. Maggie stumbled back in surprise, clutching Eileen's arm. She noticed that even the captain seemed startled, but only for an instant. Maggie and Eileen watched along with the other displaced passengers as the captain and his men lurched toward the young man. Yet he was faster than they were, and he scrabbled out the back end of the car and into the car behind it, evading his pursuers. The whole time, he continued screaming like a madman as the army men followed a few steps behind.

Maggie felt terrified, but to her shock, she heard the crazy fat man laughing nearby. "Go get 'im, boys!" the man was yelling to the soldiers. "Send him to the brig!" The man started coughing and hacking from the exertion of his jeers. Maggie wondered for a moment if he was prematurely senile, but then she heard other passengers chattering, and a word caught her ear: "Deserter."

In a flash she realized exactly why the train had been stopped and why the soldiers were here. The scruffy young man had left the army, absent without leave, and the captain and his men were here to take him back. Now it all made sense, and she tried to relax again, although the cold air was still slicing through her clothes, and her heart was racing much faster than normal. The fat man continued his coughing and cackling, and it began to irritate one of the soldiers in the jeep.

"Control yourself, sir," the soldier called out brusquely. "This will be over soon."

"My arse!" the man spat back, as his desperate daughter tried to appease him and keep him quiet.

Maggie stepped away from him with Eileen, heading toward another cluster of people, a big family with thick, ruddy faces. She and Eileen walked over and stood near them, huddled together with their crying baby. The family scanned Maggie and Eileen up and down like the strangers they were, but no one said anything to them. Maggie realized it was best for her and Eileen if it looked like they were attached to a group of people, instead of on their own.

She heard the deserter scream again, and she turned to look, unable to stop herself. The man had reappeared, and he was now out of the train, stumbling toward the crowd of passengers. He was greasy, and his filthy hair was matted with dirt. Maggie realized he must have exited the other side of the train and somehow slipped underneath it in an attempt to avoid his captors. But his efforts were in vain: Maggie saw and heard the soldiers right behind him. He continued to shamble toward the waiting crowd, as though he was going to seek refuge with them, just like Maggie and Eileen had done.

Maggie and Eileen shrank back from the deserter as he approached, as did the rest of the people. The way he moved unnerved Maggie. His gait was desperate and uneven, like a wounded fox being hunted by hounds. People in the crowd were yelling curses and taunts at him.

It was only as he drew even nearer that Maggie realized he was holding something pressed up tight to his own neck. As it glinted in the blue light from the windows of the train, Maggie realized it was a six-inch carving knife. She and Eileen stumbled backward with the murmuring crowd, trying to put even more space between themselves and the armed man.

Two soldiers burst from the door of the train car next to them and saw the man's knife. They paused several yards away, uncertain what to do without their commanding officer there to give them orders.

"Devon Palmer," Maggie heard one of the soldiers call to the deserter. "That's you, innit?"

The man did not respond. He just tilted his head back, giving them full view of the knife at his neck. Maggie wanted to look away, but she couldn't make her eyes close and shut out the horror. She managed to glance down at Eileen and saw that the girl was covering the baby's eyes with her hands.

"No peeking, Brett," Eileen said softly.

"By order of the war resolution, we're here to take you back," the soldier said to the man with the knife. "You've been gone a long time, but your service to His Majesty isn't over yet." The soldier was speaking with remarkable calm, although Maggie noticed he was slowly advancing on the deserter. "You can't take leave whenever you want. You know that."

"I'm never going back," the deserter yelled. His voice sounded young and scared, and Maggie wondered how old he was. Perhaps not much older than she was. But there was real conviction to his voice, and he continued to hold the knife firmly.

Maggie glanced back at the small groups of her fellow travelers. Some of them were looking away, as though they didn't want to witness the unsavory scene, but the fat man was taking delight in the situation. A shaft of light caught his watery eyes and Maggie could see the vicious glee in them.

"He's weak!" the man called out. "Send him to the Huns, I tell you. He's weak just like they are!"

The soldier and the deserter both ignored him.

"Come with us, son," the soldier told the deserter softly. "It's easier for everyone this way." He paused for a moment, now only six or seven paces away from the other man. "We're in this war together."

For a moment, Maggie thought the deserter might be vacillating, because he called out, "What happens if I go back?"

"You'll face justice for being absent without leave, you'll pay your penalty to the king, and you'll be returned to the war effort—where you belong."

"I refuse!" the deserter yelled, shutting down again, his

eyes going far away. "You can't make me go anywhere that I don't want to!"

At that precise moment, the captain stepped out from the shadows between two of the train's cars, his cap shadowing his features. Maggie was afraid of this man, afraid that after he'd dealt with the deserter, he would question her and Eileen. It was an irrational fear, perhaps, but she didn't want to take any chances. She tried to pull on Eileen's arm and merge with the crowd, but Eileen was now transfixed by the scene and wouldn't move. The baby was crying in earnest.

"Stop acting like a nancy boy and put down that bloody kitchen knife," snapped the captain. He walked right up to the young man with his hand outstretched, reaching to take the knife away. "Come to your senses."

Maggie saw the deserter's eyes swivel in her direction for some unknown reason, and thought, *Please don't look at us!*

"This war is an abomination," he said, boldly staring at her and Eileen, his voice rising on a tide of hysterical madness. "I won't grow up. I'm going to stay young and innocent like those girls and that baby, sir! See them? They are innocents! I won't do what you tell me to do anymore. I hate being alive." The night air blew his tangled hair back in a halo of dust and light, as Maggie tried to hide from his words. "God bless this country, and God bless the king!" the man raved. "You can have my life for free, but not my innocence."

Then he shut his eyes and stuck the knife right into the front of his neck. The majority of the six-inch blade just disappeared cleanly into his flesh, like a steak knife through gelatin. Then he yanked the blade sideways as hard as he could, partially decapitating himself. A stream of blood jetted out and sprayed all over the captain's face, dappling his eyes and mouth.

"Jesus!" the captain swore, rushing forward to catch the man's convulsing body as it fell into his arms. In a paralytic haze, Maggie saw other army officers rush toward the scene. One of them turned back to the crowd and said furiously, "The show's over! Did you get your shilling's worth?"

Most of the crowd still stood there in disbelief. There was nowhere for them to go except back on the train, and no one quite knew if it was safe to do that yet. Maggie heard some voices muttering, and she couldn't tell if they were murmuring prayers or condemning the act of self-violence they'd just witnessed. *Why had the man singled her and Eileen out?* She didn't understand, but it wasn't a good omen.

Maggie was too numb to move, the blood thick in her veins, making her limbs feel lethargic. The officers were now blocking the deserter's body so that Maggie couldn't see him anymore. And she didn't want to see. She'd witnessed enough blood in the past few weeks to last a lifetime.

"He'll be all right, if his mind holds steady," one of the women was saying to her daughter, improbably. "That's the important thing. His mind. We'll win the war through courage and our resolute nature. They can fix a body easier than a mind. The mind is the key to it all."

Good luck getting his head reattached to his neck, Maggie thought grimly. His body was way beyond fixing, and she knew the man would die.

The soldiers were now gathering up his body; it was spasming and his arms were flailing, as though he was entering his death throes. One of the soldiers had pressed a wadded towel against the pulsing wound, and they hustled him toward the waiting jeep, his body writhing in their arms like some kind of grotesque biblical tableau. The captain walked a pace behind, his head down.

It's going to be okay, Maggie told herself, exhaling into the night air. She also tried to tell herself that what the man had done didn't have any meaning for her and Eileen. She had to believe that. The man's apparent suicide was just another violent act in a life that was increasingly becoming a parade of meaningless, violent incidents strung together without logic or reason. Maggie was just about to turn to Eileen, when she heard a man's sharp voice cut through the air.

"You two!" the voice snapped, and she realized with cold shock that the voice belonged to the army captain, and that he was calling to her and Eileen. He'd turned back around, away from his men, and was now heading directly toward them.

Maggie fought the urge to run as she tightened her grip on Eileen's arm. She knew the best course of action was to stay put, because if they ran, it would immediately raise his suspicions.

"Yes, sir?" she asked.

"You say you're here with your mother?" the captain

asked. He'd wiped the blood off his face, but had missed a few spots on his neck. Maggie tried not to stare at them.

"That's right," Maggie said, praying that Eileen wouldn't speak. "Our mum's right over there."

The captain gazed at her long and hard. "Take me to her."

"Sir?" Maggie felt like she could barely breathe, and under her hand she sensed Eileen's muscles tensing in fear.

"You and your sister have a young infant in your care. That child should be under closer supervision." He paused. "That man called you 'innocents.' Do you know him?"

"No, sir," Maggie said. "I've never seen him before in my life . . ."

The captain was openly glaring at Maggie and Eileen now. "Something's not right here," he said. "Something's going on, isn't it?"

How could this happen? Maggie wondered in despair. She felt like all her nightmares were coming true at once. *It's like we have the worst luck in the world!*

"No, sir—nothing's going on," Maggie said, but she knew the captain saw the fear in her eyes. She knew he could sense it radiating off her and Eileen in waves, because that's what he was trained to do. From the corner of her eye, Maggie noticed that the sparse groups of people from the train were now all watching her and Eileen get interrogated—the new sideshow attraction.

"I need to speak to your mother at once," the captain said, reaching out to grab Maggie by the collar. "I'm starting to think you're unsupervised out here, that you're running wild—"

Suddenly, a lady stepped out from the crowd of people, loudly pushing her way toward Maggie and Eileen, and making the captain pause. "There you are!" she crowed in a harsh Cockney accent.

Confused, Maggie turned around to look directly at this stranger. The woman was wearing a white fur coat, stockings, and a stylish purple hat. These were all difficult items to acquire during wartime, so Maggie knew she was either rich or well connected. She was in late middle-age but trying to look younger, with heavy lipstick and rouged cheeks. What little hair Maggie could see sticking out from under her hat was an odd, fake golden color.

"Are you the mother of these children?" the captain asked stiffly, relinquishing his hold on Maggie's coat.

"Why, of course I am," the woman declared sweetly. She rushed up to Maggie and Eileen, tottering on high heels, and draped her arms around them. "Hello, dearies. Mummy's here now." Maggie could smell the pungent scent of her heavy perfume. "They got away from me, the little devils," the woman continued. She ruffled Maggie's hair playfully. Maggie was totally confounded as to why this woman would lie and want to help them, but she wasn't about to look a gift horse in the mouth. This woman could be their unexpected escape route from an awful predicament.

"Mum, we just got frightened— By all the chaos—" Maggie managed to stutter, playing along.

"Yes, I bet you did, luv," the strange lady continued. "That poor boy—I hope he makes it to fight another day." She looked up at the captain and batted her kohl-rimmed eyes playfully. "Thank you for finding my children for me.

They get up to terrible mischief, you know. Do you have any wee ones at home?"

The captain looked like he had quite a few choice words for the woman, but before he could even say anything, the conductor interrupted him.

"All aboard!" Maggie heard the officious voice blare out over the noise of the crowd and the thrumming of the train. The conductor had reappeared and was using a megaphone to call out to the scattered passengers. "The train shall be departing in two minutes. We have a schedule to keep, ladies and gentlemen. Find your seats, please."

"If you don't mind," the woman said to the captain, giving him a wide, toothy smile. "My children and I must board at once. The little one is cold as an ice lolly, no doubt. We mustn't get stranded out here, and catch the pneumonia. We wouldn't want that at all."

The captain hesitated for a moment and then said, "Yes, okay, fine," in disgust. Maggie could sense his lingering suspicions, but there wasn't much he could do. She knew he had to get back to his men and the remains of the deserter. Maggie, Eileen, and the baby had been saved by the apparent kindness of a stranger. *But how had the woman known that we needed her help?* Maggie wondered.

The captain turned to leave without so much as a goodbye or an apology, and the lady called out, "Safe travels to you and yours, sir!" Maggie could hear the smile in her voice. The captain raised one hand dismissively as a response, and he disappeared into the darkness.

"Shall we, girls?" the lady said, and she grasped Maggie and Eileen firmly by their shoulders. Unlike her sweet voice, her grip was like an iron vise.

"You're not really our mum," Eileen said rudely, surprising Maggie by speaking up in front of a stranger.

"I'm your fairy godmother, you ungrateful little hussy. Now hush up and get on board."

"Why'd you help us?" Maggie whispered, filled with burning curiosity, but almost afraid to learn the reason.

"I know runaways when I see 'em," the woman said, guiding them up the stairs and back onto the train. "You're lucky I was here, or that dreadful man would have taken you back to whatever pit you escaped from. And with a baby, no less! Which one of yours is it? No wait, don't answer. I don't even want to know. What's happened to this nation's morals?"

"I want—" Eileen began again, but the lady shoved her forward down the aisle.

"Hush up means no talking! From either of you. Or I'll turn right back around and tell those officers the truth. You'll do as I say from now on, if you want to get where you're going and keep your liberty." The woman pushed them toward a row of empty seats and made them sit down. She sat across the aisle from them. "This is your lucky day, runaways. I'm going to help you. I believe we can come to a mutually beneficial arrangement." Maggie had no idea what the woman was talking about, but was afraid to question her too much. "Just keep quiet, and I'll take you with me when I disembark at Bristonwyn. You'll understand then."

Maggie sat back in her seat, grateful but still confused

and nervous, huddling up against the chill that now permeated the train. The doors had been left open during the incident with the deserter, and the carriage now smelled like the night: dusky, with a hint of damp earth. It was an ancient, vaguely menacing smell. Maggie was looking forward to daylight, when the sun's rays would banish the memories of this journey from her troubled mind.

She glanced over at Eileen and the baby, and saw that they both looked quite sleepy. The woman was leaning over and giving the baby something to drink from a flask, and Eileen wasn't stopping her. *Maybe this woman will turn out to be the best thing that's happened to us so far*, Maggie thought. *Our savior.*

The train began to move again, heading up the tracks through the barren Welsh countryside. Outside was only darkness, and Maggie hoped it would end very soon.

11

The House on Wyncote Road

everal hours later, Maggie and Eileen—who was still clutching the baby—disembarked the train at Bristonwyn Station with their new patron leading the way. The woman had essentially refused to talk to them for the duration of the journey, and any attempt at asking her questions had resulted only in rebukes.

Now that they were off the train, Maggie felt lost, and in more ways than one. She missed Kate and Alison dreadfully, especially Kate, and still found it hard to deal with their absence. Only a few other passengers had gotten off along with them at Bristonwyn, but they'd already disappeared into the dark, deserted streets of the Welsh mining town, and Maggie felt isolated.

She and Eileen were guided by the lady away from the station and onto a wide street lined with low homes and businesses, most of them decrepit-looking pubs and thrift stores, all of them shuttered at this late hour. The freezing air smelled of foul, industrial smoke, and the town looked downtrodden and forgotten, like some of the worst parts of London.

"Where are you taking us?" Maggie asked the woman, hoping that now they were off the train, she'd be more forthcoming.

"I'm tired and cold," Eileen moaned, "and so's Brett. He's awfully sleepy."

"Aye, is Brett the little creature's name?" the lady asked, and then she laughed. "You're so young to have a baby."

"He's my brother," Eileen said. Maggie didn't know whether Eileen was still deliberately lying, or whether her mind had got mixed up and she really believed that the infant was related to her.

Maggie sighed and said to the woman, "Look, I need to know where we're going, and what your name is. And where you came from . . ."

"Too many questions, dearie," the woman replied, still plunging forward, her high heels slapping down unsteadily on the cobblestones. "I'm not asking where you're from, am I? Or *your* names? It's curiosity that killed the cat, or haven't you heard?" She paused for a moment, hiking up her skirt, and then she continued walking. "I know you're running from something, and that's enough for me. I was your age once—it wasn't an easy age, and I didn't even have a war going on. I'm here to help you, dearies. I'm going to take you in for the night at my lodging house."

"You have a lodging house?" Maggie asked, her voice tinged with both suspicion and optimism.

"Of course I do, on Wyncote Road. Bristonwyn is a lay-over for soldiers, and other travelers too. I provide a place for the night . . . for a decent fee, of course."

"We don't have any money," Maggie said, suddenly afraid that the lady would expect them to pay her.

She just cackled. "Of course you don't. Runaways never do." She started picking up her pace. "Now come along. I don't like being out here at nighttime. You never know what rough elements you might run into."

Maggie and Eileen hustled after her. The silence on the street was eerie, and Maggie consoled herself with the thought that at least she was free of the convent, even if Kate and Alison had been lost. Eileen didn't seem to care, or even really notice, that the other two girls were gone. It was clear that all she cared about was the baby.

"You still didn't tell us your name," Maggie pointed out to the woman. "What are we supposed to call you?"

"I'm known as Miss Gravenor, but you can call me Colleen."

"I'm Maggie—"

"I don't need to know your name!" Colleen interrupted quickly. "Please. It won't do me a lick of good. It's best if you just keep it to yourself. Now look, we're almost home. My boarding house is close to the station. I've got beds for you, and a nice cup of hot cocoa to boot."

Thank God, Maggie thought to herself. *I think we really lucked out for once.* She'd been warding off fatigue and cold so long, she felt she might collapse at the very mention of a bed. It almost sounded too good to be true.

"Brett will be sleeping in my bed," Eileen announced loudly, and Colleen laughed.

"Is that so? Yes, well, I suppose you can take care of

the baby if you wish, although I'll make sure we heat some milk for him."

"Milk would be acceptable," Eileen said, and the woman laughed again.

"What a strange girl you are," she said to Eileen, "but I suppose the normal ones never end up here with me. Only the desperate ones."

"You said your house is close?" Maggie asked, still dreaming about the bed and the hot cocoa.

"Right here," Colleen said, pointing to a row of three-story, crumbling brick homes coming up on their left. When she pointed, Maggie noticed that her fingernails were very long, and lacquered with gleaming red polish that reflected the light of the few stray streetlamps.

The boarding house looked in complete disrepair, but Maggie thought that it couldn't be any worse than her lodgings at St. Garan's. "And we can stay the whole night?" Maggie asked, for reassurance. She still didn't exactly trust this woman, but fatigue and hunger had taken over her senses and dulled them slightly.

"You can stay the night, and longer if you wish. Now lower your voices, I don't want you to wake any of my other lodgers."

Maggie fell silent, and Eileen tried to keep the baby from making too much noise as they approached Colleen's house. The woman led them through an iron gate and up a flight of four sagging wooden steps to the thick front door, which was peeling long strips of blue paint. She produced a bronze key from her pocket and unlocked it, and then she turned to the two girls.

"Remember to be quiet," she whispered. "Put the blanket over that little creature's head if he starts to wail."

Eileen nodded.

Slowly, Colleen opened the door, and Maggie and Eileen stepped over the threshold and into her home. It was surprisingly spacious inside, with the entrance opening up into a large foyer, but it smelled like mildew and some other indefinable dank stench. It was very dark, with dim electric lanterns flickering on the walls like candles, and black floors strewn with patterned rugs. It didn't resemble any kind of hotel or boarding house that Maggie had seen before, and it had an uncanny air of decayed opulence. *Who could live in a place like this?* Colleen shut the door behind them and locked it, as Maggie and Eileen peered around their new surroundings. Maggie saw a small wooden table by the door with a pot of dead flowers in it.

"This way, dearies," Colleen said, as she headed off down a hallway. There was a vague oriental feel to the place, Maggie noted: the swirling designs on the rugs matched the strange gold paintings hanging on the walls. She looked up and saw that above her, the high ceiling was marred with yellow water stains.

Maggie repressed her nervousness and continued to follow Colleen down the hall. They passed a closed door, and Maggie thought she heard thumping sounds from within. She glanced over at Eileen to see if her companion heard them too. But Eileen, as usual, was occupied with the baby and didn't even look up.

"Eileen!" Maggie whispered twice, trying to get the girl's

attention, before she gave up. *Clearly, I'm on my own here*, she thought glumly.

"So we'll put you in this room," Colleen said to Maggie when they reached another door, this one at the top of a flight of stairs. The dim light outside the room was buzzing loudly, like a trapped fly. "You're dog tired—I can see the sandman in your pretty eyes. It's well past the witching hour, you know."

"Wait, you're putting us in separate rooms?" Maggie asked, feeling even more concerned. She didn't want to get separated from Eileen and the baby in this spooky, foreign place. Colleen seemed harmless enough, but her tenants might not be; Maggie thought it was best if she and Eileen stuck together.

"Yes, separate rooms," Colleen said blithely, opening the door. "Go inside and freshen up. There's a sink in there, and a loo as well. I just had plumbing installed last winter, and it cost a pretty penny. I'll be in soon with the cocoa."

"Eileen?" Maggie asked yet again, but Eileen was in her own mental zone, tickling the baby's chin.

"Go on," Colleen encouraged Maggie, sensing her uncertainty. "The bedbugs won't bite. I'll be right back."

Maggie stepped inside tentatively, wondering if it was the right decision to stay. There was one tiny lamp sitting on the nightstand, illuminating the peeling floral wallpaper. The room had a small window on the wall opposite the door, but shutters covered it, and it looked like they'd been nailed shut for some reason. She turned back to look at Colleen, but the woman was already closing the door behind her.

Maggie stood in the dusty room, trying to make sense of her situation. She walked over to a small closet, and indeed, discovered a toilet and sink hidden inside. She went to the bathroom and washed her hands. There was no towel to dry them on, so she used the hem of her dirty uniform. Then she took her jacket off and went over and sat on the narrow bed. It was soft and lumpy, but she didn't feel in the mood to complain. She lay down, scrunching the pillow underneath her head, and stared up at the ceiling. She felt a sensation of movement in her body, as though she were still on the train. *What a night*, she thought as she shut her eyes. *Am I ever going to get back to familiar ground?*

Just as she started to drift away from fatigue, the door opened again, startling her. She sat up on the bed as Colleen entered the room, holding a ceramic mug.

"I see you've made yourself at home," Colleen said, smiling. "Here, drink this. It'll warm your bones." Colleen came over and sat on the bed next to Maggie, handing her the mug.

"Thank you for taking us in," Maggie told her as she took a tentative sip of the warm cocoa. It tasted delicious, and she could feel it running down her throat and into her starving stomach.

Colleen nodded graciously. "I've always been disposed to helping runaways. I know how tough it can be out there in the world, especially with a young child. You and your friend must have been through a lot."

"We have," Maggie said, taking another sip of the liquid. "We were trying to get to a farm outside Manchester. We didn't make it, obviously."

Colleen looked thoughtful. "Manchester's far, and the Germans have made it quite inhospitable these days. Bristonwyn has much of its own to offer."

Maggie just nodded, even though the town had looked pretty grim to her. She drank more of her cocoa, leaning back and pulling up the thin woolen bedspread.

"I was a runaway once myself," Colleen continued. "That's how I can spot girls like you and little Eileen. I was in your very position, with no money and no friends or family in the world."

Maggie was about to respond when she suddenly felt a wave of nausea and dizziness pass over her. *What the hell was that?* she wondered. The feeling surprised her, because it had come out of nowhere. "I don't feel so good," she murmured. It was like her equilibrium had suddenly been altered, and she tried not to move her head, waiting for the feeling to subside.

"Probably just tiredness," Colleen said sympathetically. "It'll pass of its own accord."

But the sensation was growing stronger with every second, and it felt much more than simple tiredness to Maggie. Each time she moved even a tiny bit, the whole world became unfocused and blurry. She felt very heavy, and she let her body fall back down onto the mattress. She also felt sick to her stomach, and she struggled not to throw up all over the bedspread because she didn't want to make a mess. *I don't think I can make it to the toilet*, she realized in a cold sweat.

"Have more cocoa," Colleen said, helpfully bringing the mug over to her side. "It'll settle your tummy, luv."

"No more cocoa," Maggie whispered as saliva flooded her mouth from nausea. Her stomach was staging a revolt against the liquid.

Colleen placed the mug on the nightstand. "Well, it's here if you want it."

"I'm sorry," Maggie said suddenly, choking vomit back down.

Colleen laughed. "For what, dearie?"

"For feeling sick." Maggie knew it was a stupid thing to apologize for, because she couldn't help it, but she felt bad nonetheless. She tried to sit up but was hit with another round of dizziness so severe it felt like she'd pass out. She didn't know what disease had hit her, but it had come on with great suddenness and severity.

"You don't need to apologize for anything," Colleen said, with unexpected force. "I bet you've had to apologize for many things over the years, but that part of your existence is over. Today is the start of your new life, here in Bristonwyn."

Maggie didn't quite understand, but she felt too tired and queasy to talk any more, so she laid back on the bed again, resting her head against the pillow.

"That's right, make yourself comfy," Colleen said. "You'll feel right as rain in the morning, I'm sure. Just remember to have more cocoa whenever the mood strikes you." Colleen stood up and walked over to the door. "I'll be seeing you soon. Don't worry your pretty little head about anything."

Maggie wanted to call out to her to stay, because she didn't want to be left alone in this weird, sickly state. Yet she found that she barely had the strength to mouth any words, let alone speak. She just lay there curled up on her side, trying to think straight, although her head felt fuzzy. All the people she missed flooded into her mind: her mom, her aunt, all her school friends from London, and most of all Kate and Alison. She shut her eyes.

Maybe if I sleep, I'll feel better, like Colleen said, Maggie told herself. It didn't take much effort for her body to obey this command. She felt herself drifting into a strange, uneasy slumber almost despite herself, and before she knew it, darkness had closed in all around her.

Sometime later, Maggie woke up. She wasn't sure what had woken her, perhaps some sort of noise, and she struggled to get her sticky eyelids open. She no longer felt quite as sick as before, but her arms and legs were still heavy as lead. For a moment, she didn't know where she was, and panic welled up inside her, but then she remembered Colleen and the boarding house, and she started to calm down.

She'd got on her back somehow, so she managed to roll over and face the doorway. It was then that her mind almost shut down again, because she saw that the door was open, and she wasn't alone in the room.

Standing in the doorway was the most terrifying apparition that Maggie had seen in her life. It was a large, pale man with a gas mask strapped onto his sweaty, balding face, so that she couldn't see any of his features. He was wearing a white undershirt speckled with stains, and a pair of crisp military slacks; in one hand, he held a leather belt with a large metal buckle dangling from it. Maggie was so stunned that she assumed she was dreaming.

She just lay there staring at this monstrous figure, silhouetted by the light of the hall, as she tried to force herself to wake up.

"Take off your clothes," the man finally said, his gruff London accent muffled by the gas mask. He swung the door shut behind him, and the loud sound startled Maggie into action. She knew at once that she was indeed awake, and in terrible trouble—awful things were about to happen to her unless she did something about it.

Maggie tried to leap up and out of the bed, but she was still so dizzy and dazed that she only succeeded in falling forward and getting tangled in the covers. In a heap, she toppled over and fell onto the wooden floor, cracking the back of her head against the wall. She writhed in the covers, struggling desperately to free her arms and legs and get on her feet. *God help me!* she thought in a panic. She had no idea who this interloper was, but it was pretty clear even to her stunned mind that he planned on doing her harm.

"Colleen! Colleen!" Maggie tried to scream for help as she curled up in the corner of the room, kicking at the covers, but the words only came out as a faint whisper. She felt drugged, narcotized, and she didn't understand why. The world was fading in and out with every heartbeat, and she was terrified that she'd pass out and this man would be on her in an instant, doing whatever he wanted.

"Miss Gravenor can't hear nothing," the man said through the gas mask, still standing by the door. "Miss Gravenor only hears what she wants to hear." He took a step closer. "Don't play no more games, lass." He raised the belt. "You'll get a lashing right quick. Miss Gravenor said you were good to go."

"Please . . . don't hurt me," Maggie whispered. She knew she was losing the battle to stay awake, and that fact was as scary as the man himself. *How can I keep him away from me?!*

The man whipped the belt onto the bed, where it made an explosive concussion and knocked up a cloud of dust from the sheets. "I bet you like to get hurt, don't you?"

"No . . ." Maggie moaned, uncomprehending. "Stop it! Are you crazy?"

The man gasped for air through his mask, the muscles in his neck rippling. He took a step closer so that now only the narrow bed separated the two of them. He snapped the belt again, this time just a few feet from Maggie's face, and then he laughed, a wretched, convulsive sound that echoed off the walls of the dismal room. "I haven't had a girl in four months. Do you know how that feels to a man?"

Does he think I'm someone else? Maggie wondered. She tried to press herself as tightly as she could against the wall, as a survival instinct. "Don't," she said. The man just kept laughing.

In those last instants, Maggie was seized with the conviction that someone was going to come in and rescue her from this violent, apparently insane man. It was just some inner belief that suddenly sprang to the surface of her mind in her darkest time of need. So far, despite all the traumas she'd endured, she had made it through mostly unscathed, and she prayed that now someone would intervene and stop this lunatic from attacking her. But the man moved closer, around the edge of the bed, his progress unimpeded. Through the mask, his breathing continued to be distorted and grotesque.

"I'll take your clothes off for you," he breathed wetly. His voice grew fainter as Maggie finally started to pass out, unable to continue the fight. *I tried*, she thought, *I tried.* "You better be a virgin, like Miss Gravenor said," she heard him mutter, "because that's what I paid for . . ." Then the world condensed to a small circle of black, like the contracting aperture of a camera, and Maggie knew no more.

When she woke up again, hours later, she was back on the bed, with the bedspread pulled up and over her, to keep her warm. It was morning, and tiny rays of daylight poked in through the slats of the boarded-up window. Maggie's mouth was dry as a cotton ball and she coughed, trying to get her breath.

"Morning, dearie," she heard a chipper voice say, and she realized that Colleen was sitting on a wooden stool at the foot of the bed, staring at her. The woman's makeup was even heavier than before, her rouge so thick that she looked like a clown.

"It's you," Maggie said, feeling revulsion like she'd never known.

Colleen smiled. In the light of day, Maggie could see that her teeth were yellowed and pitted with decay. "You gave my customer quite a fright last night. He thought you were dead, you see." Colleen leaned closer. "You can't go scaring my johns like that. I had to give him credit with another girl, just to keep the lug quiet. He's a sensitive soul, because most of his face got blown off in the war. That's why he wears the mask." She patted her gold hair into place where it sat on her head like a muffin top. "Don't worry, though. He didn't touch you, luv. You got lucky. He wasn't interested in a corpse—he wanted a girl who'd fight back and give him what for. But you won't stay lucky forever, not here you won't."

"Where is *here*?" Maggie asked, her voice cracking. She'd been taking a silent inventory of her body to see if she'd been violated or not. Everything felt okay.

"You're in a brothel," Colleen replied breezily. "Don't you know what that is? Runaways always do." Maggie felt like throwing up again. "A brothel is a place where men come to have sex with girls," Colleen continued in her perky voice, but her blue eyes were cold and lifeless, like her soul had curled up and died long ago. "You are now one of those girls, one of my girls. What you did last night is understandable, and even forgivable, but it can't happen again. You have a job to do now, because you're a working girl."

Maggie tried to think straight. "You put something in my cocoa last night, didn't you? You poisoned me."

Colleen smiled a little sheepishly. "It was just to relax you, dearie. The first time's always the hardest. Many of our clientele are soldiers, like that chap last night, and they can get a bit rough and ready. I had no idea you'd crash out like that. It was just a couple of sleeping pills to make you loosey goosey."

Exhausted and sickened, Maggie closed her eyes. She didn't know how it was possible that her life had come to this horrendous juncture, but she was about to learn.

"You've been sent here to me, to become part of my stable," Colleen continued. "It's not a bad life—men pay me for their pleasure, and in return, I take care of you. I'll feed you, buy you nice clothes, and give you a place to stay that's safe from the law, and the government remand homes. I've got eighteen other girls in the house at the moment, and another full house three hours from here in Cornweth, and one in Liverpool too. We're like a big family."

Maggie opened her eyes and raised her head to look at Colleen. There was something she didn't understand pulsing away at the back of her mind. "You said I was sent to you?" she asked slowly. "What do you mean?"

"Well, surely you didn't think this was all a coincidence, dearie? That you ended up here with me in Bristonwyn?" Colleen emitted a tinkling laugh. "I knew you were coming. Everything was set up in advance. That's why I met you on the train, of course."

"What are you talking about?" Maggie asked. She had a very bad feeling about where this conversation was heading.

Colleen leaned closer, her perfume a palpable presence hovering around her like a cloud. She looked vaguely amused. "I thought you would have figured it out by now."

"All I know is that you're evil, and you're keeping me prisoner against my will."

"Please, Maggie Leigh. All of us are prisoners of one sort or another."

How does she know my last name? Maggie wondered, startled. *Did Eileen tell her?*

"Now, let me clear things up for you," Colleen continued. "You were brought to Bristonwyn deliberately, by the girl you know as Eileen. Her friend Kate was supposed to be with you—but Eileen said you ran into another girl on the way, and that the girl slowed you down, so Kate missed the train. You see, the Mother Superior of St. Garan's is my elder sister, Valerie Watson, although the resemblance isn't clear anymore because of her face, poor thing . . . We have an arrangement: girls who possess a certain look—but lack money and social standing—arrive at the school and are shipped onward to me, if their personalities are deemed placid and amiable enough."

She saw the stricken, disbelieving look on Maggie's face and added, "I poach a handful a year, and we tell the parents they've run off. Most of the nuns don't even know the truth about what we do—they're sheep and will do whatever Valerie instructs them." She paused to let this sink in. "Kate befriends new girls, tests them, and then lets my sister know if they fit the bill. Eileen helps too—but this trip will be her last. Now that she's found a baby, we've decided to let her raise it here. A young child will be quite useful to me, for many different reasons, and Eileen's almost old enough to be put to work too."

Maggie was speechless. She thought that Colleen had to be lying, but the woman's expression remained guileless. *Can it really be true? That St. Garan's funnels girls to a depraved whorehouse?* It sounded like the ravings of a psychopath, but so many of the details seemed correct. Maggie felt her cheeks burn like she'd been slapped across the face.

Colleen appeared to sense her doubts. "Eileen and Kate are very clever girls—my sister only works with the best and brightest. They had their eyes on you from the first night you showed up at the school. They lured you on the journey—they knew where everything was from the start. The lorry driver was in on it too, although from what I hear, that wealthy girl almost gave the game away when she recognized that he worked with the school. I'm sure Kate's dealt with her by now."

"You're a monster . . ." Maggie breathed, interrupting the litany. "How could you and Eileen do this to me? And Kate . . ." Her words trailed away; it still seemed impossible to believe that her friend had been in on everything, and had used her like this, like she was nothing but a piece of garbage. "Why would anyone help you?"

"For money, for food, and for protection," Colleen replied, smiling. "Some girls will do almost anything for chocolate and a few extra pence. Wrong and right don't matter much when there's a war going on. Supply and demand, now that's what counts. I helped you, and now you're going to help me. Simple as cake."

Maggie's head was swimming. She didn't know what was real anymore and what was an illusion. "The German," she muttered. "Alison . . . The deserter . . . Were they part of it too?"

Colleen laughed. "How could they be? They were random acts of chance. Alison and that wretched young man on the train interfered with everything. I had to intervene much sooner than I normally would have. If the captain hadn't come along I would have watched you closer, to see if Eileen and Kate's assessment was correct. I was waiting for you the whole time, in the next car back."

"I won't stay here," Maggie managed to say through her narrowed throat. "I'll go straight to the police. I'll ring my mum."

"Really." Colleen's voice turned as flat and cold as her eyes, although the smile remained. "A girl like you doesn't have too many options. How are you going to leave this house if I don't let you? It's hard to break free if you're never left alone. And you don't have access to a telephone, now do you?"

"What about the baby?" Maggie asked, suddenly remembering that she wasn't alone in this plight.

"Brett, or whatever Eileen's calling it, will find a good home here. Who else would take in Nazi spawn?" Colleen paused. "Kate is going to help raise it too—I believe she and Eileen are more than friends, at least when the lights go down." She pursed her lips. "Look, I'm not a bad person, dearie. I'm just trying to survive during a war—I'm trying to do right for our boys too, and give them what they need. There's no harm in any of this."

Maggie knew she wouldn't get too far with a ruined creature like Colleen. "Just don't give me any more drugs," Maggie said. "And no more lies and games." She wanted to reach out and grab Colleen by the throat and throttle the life out of her, and then go after Eileen, but she repressed the urge. *For now.*

Colleen looked at her and nodded. "Okay. But you can't act like you did last night."

"I won't," Maggie said, thinking to herself, *I have to get out of this place as soon as I can. I have to get to the police.*

It was like Colleen had read her mind, because she suddenly stood up. "One more thing. I've had experience dealing with girls like you in the past. Girls who are hellions, who believe they don't have to abide by my rules." Colleen smoothed down her pink silk blouse. "Girls like you have to be broken. I don't mean physically, but mentally, like stallions. I'm not prepared to put you with a man after your show last night, and from the feral look in your eyes right now, that's a wise decision on my part." She licked her red lips. "I'm going to lock you down in the cellar for a few days, maybe longer, until you see things my way. No food, no light, a little water. It won't be long until you're begging to service a customer in exchange for a stale crumpet and spoilt milk. I've seen it go that way before."

Maggie felt terrified, but she supposed that being locked in a cellar was actually preferable to being assaulted and raped. She found it hard to look at Colleen because the woman disgusted her so much. "Do whatever you want," Maggie said.

"Oh, I will, dearie." She walked over to the door and opened it. "You can count on that." Lounging outside in the hallway were two rough-looking girls in their late teens, dressed in tattered lingerie and high heels. One of them had bruises all over her face and neck, and the other held a knife in her right hand; they both had thin cigarettes sticking out of their mouths like lollipop stems. "Eva and Penelope will escort you to the cellar, won't you, dearies." The two girls entered the room, and Maggie saw that there was no point struggling against them, not when one had a knife.

The girls grabbed Maggie and got her up off the bed under the watchful gaze of Colleen. They led her through the doorway and down another hallway and flight of stairs, one on either side of her, dragging her body along farther into the catacombs of the house. Maggie wondered if they'd once been unwitting pupils at the school, like she had, but she wasn't going to ask, because they looked like they'd smack her if she said a word. Colleen followed a few steps behind them, barking instructions. "Take her down there and tie her to the chair! She'll be spending some little time in the cellar."

One of the girls—Maggie wasn't sure whether it was Eva or Penelope—opened a narrow door in the wall. A gust of cold air came up, and Maggie saw that a flight of wooden stairs led down into a small stone basement. A sturdy wooden chair was in the center, and the girls wordlessly pulled her down the stairs, making her skin her shins on the bottom steps. Maggie bit her lip to stop from crying out in pain, because she didn't want to give these debased girls the satisfaction of knowing that they were hurting her.

The two girls forced her into the chair and tied her wrists and ankles with rope. Maggie could see that the chair had been soiled by its previous occupants but never cleaned. *Disgusting.* The entire cellar stank of sweat and fear. Colleen stood at the top, silently watching her prostitutes tie Maggie up. When she was loosely bound into place, the two girls stepped back and gazed at her pitilessly.

"This will last as long as you want it to," the girl with the bruises sneered, taking a drag off her cigarette. "You might think you're better'n us, but you're nothing and nobody. You'll learn that here right sharp." She turned away contemptuously with her companion in stride, and they headed back up the stairs where their madam waited. Only the smoke from their cigarettes lingered below.

"See you in a few days, dearie," Colleen called down to Maggie cheerfully. Then, without another word, she swung the door shut, plunging Maggie into total and terrifying darkness. Maggie heard a key turning in the lock, and she knew that she was truly trapped.

For the next few minutes, Maggie intermittently sobbed and stared at the walls, trying to figure out a plan of escape. She still couldn't believe what Colleen had said about Eileen and Kate, and wondered if it could all be some giant lie to drive her insane and break her spirit. *Yet it explains so much,* she realized dismally. *The story is crazy and sick enough that it's probably true, at least partially.*

Maggie thought she might have a breakdown from the terror and the stress, but she struggled to hold on to her sanity. *I still have to keep it together,* she told herself through the tears. *I can't crack up.* Just then, when she wasn't expecting to see another human face for days, the door swung open again.

Maggie looked up at the top of the stairs and saw that Eileen was standing there. But it was a very different-looking version of Eileen than from the night before: the girl was now wearing mascara and her hair was combed out to make her look older. Wrapped around her neck was a sultry black feather boa, like a parody of a prostitute from an American noir. "Hullo there, Maggie," Eileen called down to her, waving lazily with one hand. In the other was a fork with a yellow hunk of fresh pineapple on it, dripping juices onto the landing.

Maggie didn't know what to believe anymore, or whether she could trust Eileen or not. "You have to help me!" Maggie called up to her urgently, praying that everything Colleen had told her was lies, but Eileen just stood there, looking down at her in the chair impassively. "You need to run and get help!"

"I'm sorry they locked you up," Eileen remarked finally.

"They're planning to do a lot worse! Listen—you have to get us out of here. Try to find a phone, and if you can't, run out of this house and get to the police!"

Eileen didn't respond at first, and her silence made Maggie furious and scared. Eileen raised the piece of pineapple to her lips and took a messy bite.

"Do you know this is a whorehouse? Men are going to pay to have sex with us!" Maggie yelled at Eileen bluntly, trying to shake the girl out of her torpor.

"I know that," Eileen said blandly, munching on the pineapple; flecks sprayed from her mouth when she spoke. "But I think it's nice here, and everyone's happy I brought you—they think you're really pretty, although they're sad Kate's not back yet. The other girls said they're going to help me raise Brett. All of them are so nice. I want to be just like them. Colleen said that I can be, one day really soon."

Maggie let her head fall down onto her chest. *So it was true.* Eileen had been crazy since the start, so there was no reason to think she'd be any different now. *How had I not seen it?* she wondered in frantic dismay. Eileen and Kate had duped her completely, because the complexity of their plan had masked a simple truth about their true natures: they were evil.

"I'll let you help me with Brett," Eileen continued shyly, like she was giving Maggie a present. "No one will ever hurt us. I think he likes you, and I know Colleen does."

Now Maggie was the one who couldn't find the words to respond. She finally managed to say, "Colleen's crazy. And so are you for helping her."

Eileen looked offended. "You're the one who's crazy. In here it's much safer than the real world, and less boring than all those nuns. I don't believe in Jesus anymore, not really."

"I could have guessed that, Eileen," Maggie told the girl, although she knew getting through to her now was hopeless. "I don't think you know anything about the real world, only about manipulating people. Kate said you were a genius, and maybe you are, but you're also a sociopath, and so is she. I guess I was an easy mark for you, but I know I'm a good person, that I'm not . . . corrupted inside like you and Kate."

Eileen shifted awkwardly, like she didn't know what to say, pulling the feather boa down so that it hung over her chest. "Don't say bad things about Kate. You're her friend."

Maggie saw an opportunity to try to get at Eileen, and shake her up. "Kate's gone. She and Alison were fighting by the tracks, remember? I bet the police have got Kate now. You'll never see her again!"

Eileen looked disturbed. "She'll be here soon."

"You two are a real team. She's your lover, isn't she? That's what Colleen told me. That you've slept with her—"

"Bye-bye, Maggie!" Eileen said angrily, cutting her off, like she was embarrassed. "That's a lie. Kate's my best mate in the whole world, and that's all she is. Stop telling fibs." She started swinging the door shut.

Maggie was through trying to reason with the very girl who'd put her in this hellish place. "Fuck you!" she screamed, slamming from side to side in the chair so hard that she nearly tipped over into the muck and filth on the floor. "Fuck you to hell!"

Eileen nodded somberly as she closed the door all the way, plunging the cellar into blackness. It was only then that Maggie started to cry again, great big gulping sobs. She cried out of fear and frustration, and also anger and sadness. She cried not only for herself, but for the baby, and for Alison, and for her aunt and her mom, and her lost friendship with Kate and Eileen. *How am I going to get out of this one?* she thought, feeling the tears run down her face and onto her chest. *Help me, someone,* she prayed. *I can't do this alone.* Yet no voice answered her prayers, and she remained down in the darkness, a prisoner of a scheme she was still struggling to comprehend.

Colleen kept Maggie in the cellar for nearly a week. On the afternoon of the third day, Eileen was sent down with a pitcher of cool water. She barely spoke to Maggie, and her makeup had become more extreme, so that she resembled a miniature version of Colleen. By that point, Maggie's spirits had collapsed under total despair, but she still refused to beg to be let out. She saw great irony in the fact that she was locked back up in a room again, just like she'd been at St. Garan's. In the end, the two places were just different manifestations of the same systems of control and repression. *My life is over,* she thought dismally. *I'll never be free again.*

The bindings on Maggie's body were loose enough that she could shift around with effort, but only just. Her arms and legs would frequently fall asleep, and there was no toilet other than the chair she sat on.

At night she had dreams that were so vivid they were inseparable from real life. One night she dreamed that she was escaping the house, and that she managed to find the baby and take him with her. But the baby wouldn't stop crying and making noise, and lights started to come on in the halls and she knew she was about to be discovered. Just as she stood there, trying to make the agonizing choice between leaving the baby behind and risking getting caught, she woke up gasping and coughing. Even the nightmare world of the dream was preferable to reality, because at least in her dreams she had a chance of escape.

At night and all during the day, she heard the heavy footsteps above her of both the prostitutes and the clients. Sometimes she heard other sounds too: screams of either pain or ecstasy, she couldn't tell which. It was like being trapped in a mirrored fun house, because her sense of space and time was starting to distort. *Where am I?* she would often wake up thinking. Night and day had become one, blurring into each other with nothing to mark the difference between the two. Maggie prayed for any kind of relief from her suffering. At some points she wished that she would just go insane, or lapse into a coma, so she wouldn't have to deal with the brutal physical and mental agony.

It was sometime on the sixth day that Eva and Penelope opened the door and came downstairs to finally cut away her bindings. By then, Maggie was so weak from lack of food that she could barely stand up, speak, or even think. She had been going in and out of consciousness, hallucinating, and hearing voices that weren't there. Sometimes she heard her mom lecturing her about the Bible, and sometimes she thought she heard Kate's voice—friendly but ultimately fraudulent. She guessed that she was finally losing her mind, just like Colleen wanted.

Eva and Penelope took her to the bathroom and made her bathe, scrubbing her body with harsh chemical soap that smelled like lye, and then drying her with a rough towel. After that, she was taken into one of the large front rooms, with its shabby decor, and seated in front of Colleen in a spongy gold chair that sagged beneath her. Another figure, wearing a bulky winter coat with a hood, stood facing away from them, looking out the window at the bleak landscape. *Is this a customer?* she wondered. *Is this meant to be my first?* She knew she'd fight him tooth and nail, no matter what; she also knew she would probably lose.

"How are you feeling, dearie?" Colleen asked solicitously, although Maggie knew Colleen probably felt no real emotions. "We're still looking for Kate, I'd like you to know, but there's someone else here who wants to see you."

Maggie thought that now was the moment of truth, that she'd be forced to go upstairs and sleep with a man. Her head lolled against the back of the gold seat. "I'll do whatever you want," she whispered. "I'll do what you said. I need food. I need to sleep." But despite her fatigue and the truth in her words, her mind was still churning and attempting to come up with a way to fight. She'd try to kick the man between the legs, she told herself, where it would hurt him the most. *I'll fight like Britain fights the Nazis,* she swore.

It was then that the figure at the window turned around, and her heart froze as she gazed at the terrifying, deformed face staring back at her. Maggie was too paralyzed to even move, afraid it was another hallucination. "You," she managed to murmur softly. It wasn't a customer: it was Mother Superior.

The figure was scowling. "You have caused me so much grief, little girl!" Mother Superior snapped. "You and that German. You and Alison Prescott. Why did you interfere with my plans?"

Maggie sat there, looking at the deformed nun, thinking that surely it was the ultimate injury to have to listen to Mother Superior—who she now knew was totally corrupted—insult her.

"I guessed you'd be trouble the moment I set eyes on you. Kate said different, and so did Eileen. And so did Sister Bramley." Mother Superior's features were even more distorted and grotesque in the daylight, with bleeding sores on her cheeks where the burned skin was cracking. "But I always knew the truth."

Maggie didn't know what to say. "Why are you here?" she finally whispered.

"I wish I wasn't, let me tell you," Mother Superior continued angrily, her words sibilant with compressed rage. "Yet an offer was made to me that I could not turn down." She paused, her tongue darting out all over the blackened edges of her mouth. *She looks like a gargoyle*, Maggie realized dully. *Like a demon.* "When we chose to send you here, we were not aware that you had an aunt . . . an aunt with money."

"Aunt Joan?" Maggie asked, startled.

Mother Superior grimaced. "Who else." She paused. "Your aunt and I have come to an understanding."

Maggie didn't know what she meant at first, but then Colleen broke in and said, "You aunt's purchased you from us. You were for sale, like everything else these days. Like food and sex, like life and death. She offered six hundred pounds, and I accepted after consulting with my sister."

"Get it over with," Mother Superior hissed at Colleen. "Before the next spate of customers arrive!" Then to Maggie she spat, "Your aunt's waiting outside, you wretched heathen!"

You're the heathen, Maggie thought, but she was still too terrified of Mother Superior to say anything back. Instead, she pushed herself up from the chair on wobbly legs. Colleen moved forward to help her, but Maggie shot her a look that warned the woman to stay away.

Maggie found her footing and took a tentative step toward the door. She thought one of the two women would stop her, but neither of them did.

"That's right, get a move on," Mother Superior snapped. "You're free now. Don't let us see you again, ever."

It was only when Maggie reached the door, turned the knob and opened it that she dared to imagine she might be allowed to go free. Too scared to glance back behind her, she stepped over the threshold and out of the nightmare world she'd been trapped inside for the past week.

To her surprise, her aunt was standing right there, waiting in the cold, crisp air. Maggie had a sudden thought that it was all another illusion or trick. *How can Aunt Joan be here? How can it be over so suddenly?* There had to be more to it.

"You don't need to worry anymore," Aunt Joan said softly, reaching out to touch Maggie with a hand that was undeniably warm and real. Her face was swollen with healing lacerations from the bombing, and she wore a black patch over one eye. "You're coming with me. Can you walk?"

Maggie didn't know, but her aunt's physical presence gave her new strength, and she struggled forward, clawing onto her aunt's jacket for balance, and to make certain her aunt wasn't some apparition. She knew they had to get away from the house as quickly as possible. She heard steps behind her and realized that Colleen and Mother Superior were following them out.

"I took good care of her," Colleen babbled from behind them in the doorway, as Mother Superior lurked silently under her cowl. "Remember your promise now. No police. No trouble. Nothing personal."

"Indeed," Aunt Joan said coolly, as she helped Maggie walk down the short path toward the sidewalk.

"Pleasure doing business with you," Colleen called out, but Aunt Joan ignored her, as though Colleen didn't even exist. Maggie glanced back and saw that Colleen and Mother Superior had linked hands, and were standing there, two monstrous sisters frozen in a surreal pose, watching them like vultures. But Maggie knew that vultures only went after carrion, and things that had already begun dying. If she was still alive, they couldn't touch her now.

"I thought you might be dead . . ." Maggie said, wrapping her arms around her aunt. "The doctors said . . ."

"Doctors know nothing." Aunt Joan continued to support Maggie as they slowly walked away from the house. Maggie was still afraid that Colleen, or one of the crazy prostitutes, would run after her like a screaming banshee with a knife, but that didn't happen. The house was silent as Maggie and Aunt Joan walked away, although Maggie could sense eyes on her back. "Science is as inaccurate as faith," Aunt Joan murmured.

"You saved me," Maggie said, burrowing her head into her aunt's jacket.

Her aunt nodded. "I know." Then she pointed to a big black vehicle waiting on the other side of the empty street, half a block down. "That's our cab."

"How did you find me?" Maggie asked. Her head was clearing a little with the fresh air, although her body felt strange and light.

"Your mother told me what she'd done, and where she had sent you. She thought she was doing something good, but the school's become a cult, and many of the nuns have begun to worship Mother Superior like a god. I believe they've gone insane from too many years alone and isolated—they're no more Catholic now than the Nazis are. I began to learn all this when I asked around, and ultimately when I journeyed to St. Garan's on my own."

"You went there?" Maggie asked in surprise.

"Of course, looking for you. I met with Mother Superior and realized at once that she'd lost her way. I burst in on her, and found her burning her own face with matches and heated pieces of shrapnel. That's most likely why she looks that way—she's done it all to herself."

"Jesus."

"We don't need to think about her anymore. She's in your past, like a bad dream. Like what happened in the underground station. Put her in a box in your mind, close it, and forget about her forever."

271

"What about Eileen's baby," Maggie said, suddenly worried for him. She didn't care about Eileen or Kate anymore. They deserved whatever was in store for them.

"Colleen told me about the infant, but we can't save everyone, Maggie. Only ourselves for now. We'll tell the police what's going on here, and about the baby too. Hopefully they'll raid the entire house and rescue him, most likely take him to an orphanage . . . unless Colleen hides him, or sells him, or packs up and moves on before the police have time to do anything. We're at war. Prostitution and loose morals aren't a high priority right now."

Maggie felt a deep sadness. "Why did they let me go? Why didn't they hide me?"

"They just wanted money," Aunt Joan replied, as the two of them grew closer to the taxi. "And I pledged not to tell the police about them: a lie, of course. It also helped that I showed them my gun and threatened to use it."

Maggie was shocked. "What?!" Guns were unheard-of in Britain, except for soldiers and hunters. No ordinary citizens possessed firearms, especially not a woman.

"I got it in India. A single girl who travels the world can't do so unprepared." As they walked, Aunt Joan produced something small and shiny from the pocket of her coat. "It's a twenty-two caliber, with a mother-of-pearl inlay. It's quite the party piece." She stuffed it back in her pocket. "I've never fired it, but it's come in handy more than once. Some people only respect threats and intimidation."

So that's what it took, Maggie thought. *Money and a gun.* "How can they treat people that way?" She was still too shell-shocked to be as angry as she wanted. "They acted like I was their slave, like property. I don't understand."

"I'm glad if you don't understand. The evil that humans do to each other isn't something a girl your age should have to know about. Later, things will make more sense. We'll have plenty of time to talk about it in the future."

Maggie nodded. Her head felt quite fuzzy again.

"I'm taking you to India with me, to Bombay," her aunt continued as they walked. "I've booked passage on a freighter, and we leave in two days. It's a risk because of Nazi boats and bombs, but it's better to go to Bombay than stay here. There's no life for a young girl on this wretched island anymore." Maggie didn't disagree after everything that had happened.

"What about my mum?"

"She thinks this is for the best too. I convinced her, in no uncertain terms." Maggie wondered if she'd used the gun to threaten her, and she realized that she didn't care that much. She still loved her mother, but her mom had basically thrown her to the wolves. Maggie knew her loyalty would be to her aunt from here on out.

"There was another girl too," Maggie said suddenly, thinking about Alison with a jolt. "She wasn't like Kate and Eileen—she was like me, just lost. She was running away to find her boyfriend Robert, and she got stranded with Kate before we got on the train. I hope Kate didn't hurt her."

"Me too. Maybe she'll find Robert, maybe not. Either way, you might well see her again one day." Aunt Joan had a faraway look in her eyes. "In India, they believe in the concept of samsara, that everything comes back around again, that souls are reborn endlessly into different bodies until they reach a state of nirvana, where they learn not to care, where they have no earthly desires. Then they're free. Until then, they have to face their karma through cycles of reincarnation—whatever they've done in this life comes back to haunt them in the next. At the same time, each hardship they encounter in this life, and manage to overcome through good deeds, strengthens them and builds them up, so that when they die, they're closer to nirvana."

Hauntings and death sounded too scary to Maggie after what she'd been through. "I don't want to die," she muttered. "And I definitely don't want to come back as someone else."

Aunt Joan twisted her swollen face into a simulacrum of a smile. "You won't, not for a very long time, not while I'm around. I'm going to keep you safe and give you shelter. Do you still have that little Ganesh statue I gave you?"

"I think I lost it . . ." Maggie stopped walking and hugged her aunt, leaning into her for a warm embrace. "Thank you for finding me," she said, shutting her eyes. She felt like crying, but she didn't. Her aunt hugged her back tightly. In the damp and the cold, they stood like that for a very long time before they began walking toward the car that would take them away from this terrible place.